I0452727

Murder on M.O.S.S.
- Medical Mayhem -

Space Detective - A Skip Brown Adventure

by Pj Belanger

Cover Art by RB

Murder on MOSS
- Medical Mayhem –

Space Detective

A Skip Brown Adventure

Copyright 2014
BRP Publishing

This book is distributed in the United States by BRP Publishing

First Edition 2014

Printed in the United State of America
ISBN 978-0-9916415-2-9

BRP PUBLISHING
Email: pj@pjbelanger.com
Web: http://www.pjbelanger.com

Dedicated to:
Mackenzie, Leah, Zoe, Macy,
Austin and Cody
Thank you, kids, for all
the summer fun at our house.

Table of Contents

PROLOG

I seemed surrounded by a thick white fog. I put my hand out and the dense mist seemed to swirl around me. My body also seemed to be floating. Then it hit my brain! Was I dead? Had the satellite's shuttle craft exploded? Was this heaven or hell? I looked behind me, but no wings. *Really, Skip!,* my thoughts came rushing forward. *Do you really believe you're on cloud nine with the pearly gates wide opened?* **You?** *Better to look for horns!* My hand went to my head. I took a relieved breath, nothing there.

I wondered about my parents. Were they here somewhere? Almost on cue, my mother appeared. The petite woman hadn't aged a day. Just like I remembered her - light golden brownish colored hair was swept up behind her with a hair clip, some of it escaping to frame her slim oval face. She had dark blue eyes that had the intensity of sheer intelligence. I noticed her favorite violet sweater. She had been wearing that sweater the day she'd left, the day she died. "Have you been good?" she asked me. "Is Uncle Jack taking good care of you?"

She thought I was the eleven year old boy, not the thirty two year old man I was now. "Uncle Jack is dead, mom." Shouldn't she know this? I tried to reach out to her but the fog just swirled around me and she became blurred, wavering in the fog. My father seemed to come into focus right behind her.

"I told you not to leave him with your brother, Helen. He's a bad influence on the kids."

"Nonsense Jim," my mother seemed to frown back at him. "Killa will make sure they are raised properly."

"Humph!" my father replied. "We'll see." His receding hairline somewhat mimicked mine own. He had been forty years old when he died. Would I look like that in eight years? If I'm dead, I thought, it doesn't matter. My thoughts were getting jumbled, I tried to focus.

"How is Ray?" Mom turned back to me, her eyes seemed to water. I thought she was going to cry.

"He's great mom!" I yelled back. "He just won the Nestor championship! Don't cry, you're a grandmother. Ray's married. His wife, Julie, just had a baby boy. They call him Jim, after Dad. She seemed to not hear. My mother was drifting away taking my father with her. "Come back mom, come back."

Out of the fog walked my Uncle Jack. "Where are mom and dad?" I cried. "Bring them back Uncle Jack, go get them!" my little boy's voice seemed even younger.

"How are you?" he replied to me, completely ignoring my pleadings. "I missed you," he simple said.

"I know," I replied. All of a sudden my mind seemed to clear, returning to being an adult. "I'm sorry I never came back to Nestor after the accident. I should have." I felt the tears rolling down my cheeks. I tried to explain why I hadn't come to Nestor. "I wanted to come home but I couldn't control my seizures. I couldn't face everyone. I couldn't race anymore, the doctors wouldn't let me and I felt subhuman." I was rambling rapidly, throwing the words out into the fog.

"I know son, but I still missed you. You were the greatest racer ever. Take good care of Killa and your brother Ray." He started to fade.

"Come back," I yelled, "come back!" I tried to run but the thick cloud just confused me. "I'm the Sector Police Chief," I yelled into the whiteness. "I went to law school after I couldn't race anymore." I wasn't sure anyone was listening but still I yelled. "Killa and Ray are good. Julie's good. Come back."

Suddenly my former racing crew chief, Monticutticu, appeared. The tall lean Tohegian Clansman held out his long arms, his big hands beckoned me. His dark tanned leathery face smiled, his deep black eyes sparkled, his thick pointed ears prominently sticking out of his braided hair. I tried, I really tried to go forward but I couldn't. He would drift in and out of my eyesight.

Once again I found myself apologizing, "Monty, I'm sorry I never came back to see you. I should have returned for Uncle Jack's funeral but my epilepsy wasn't in control yet. I'm sorry…"

"Do not apologize to me, Bobmista." He used his favorite nickname for me; it meant little one in his Tohegian tongue. "My spirit roams the Tohegian fields of Casey in honor now. It is you I must thank. How is my brother? I feel him close to me."

"Your brother is with your family, he went back home." I replied. "Tony returned home, he's with the tribe now on Casey. He brought your body back."

"Ah, it is so…" He drifted out of sight with one last "Be at peace mi mioga."

"No, don't leave!" I screamed into the fog but I knew I was alone again. "Someone help me. Someone, anyone!" I hollered, cupping my hands around my mouth.

I heard flapping of wings. I was surrounded by a golden glow. Stepping out of the fog came a woman, an angel. Her golden hair reached down her white gown. Her blue eyes sparkled. Her hand reached for me and suddenly I felt my feet, they touched the ground, I felt steady and in control. "Is that better?" she sang.

"Yes, yes, thank you." I felt how inadequate the words were but I could not think of anything more profound, more meaningful. "Thank you," was the best I could do.

"Oh, you're welcome." She took my hand again, "I think it is time."

"Time?" I croaked. "Am I going to heaven?" I somehow managed to get out. My mouth felt dry.

She laughed, "No, silly. Time to wake up!"

My head began to throb and my eyes tried to focus. Unfortunately I was waking up and my sore body reminded me I was alive…

MAPS

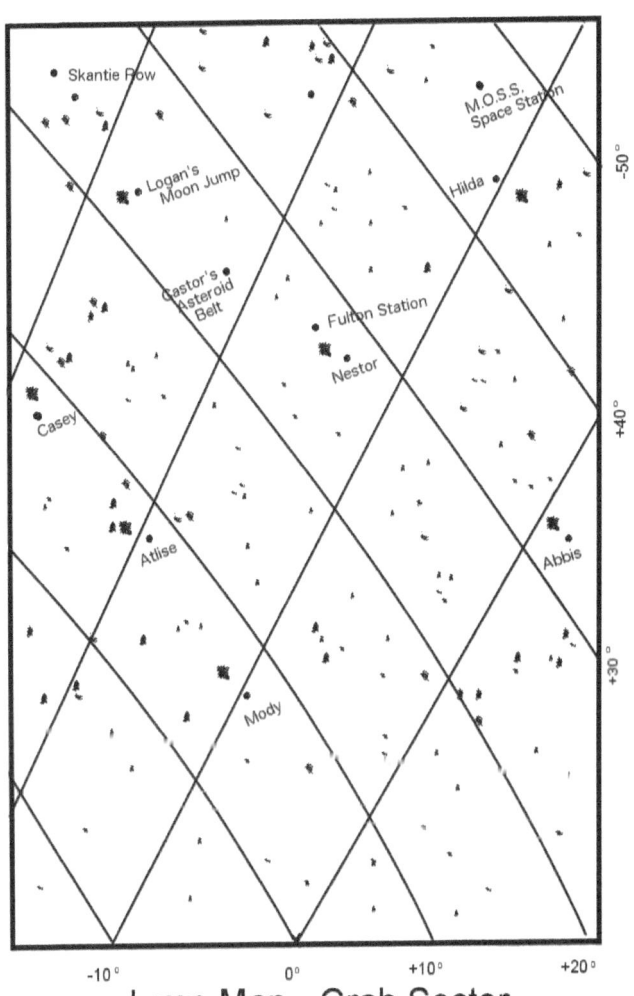

Jump Map - Crab Sector

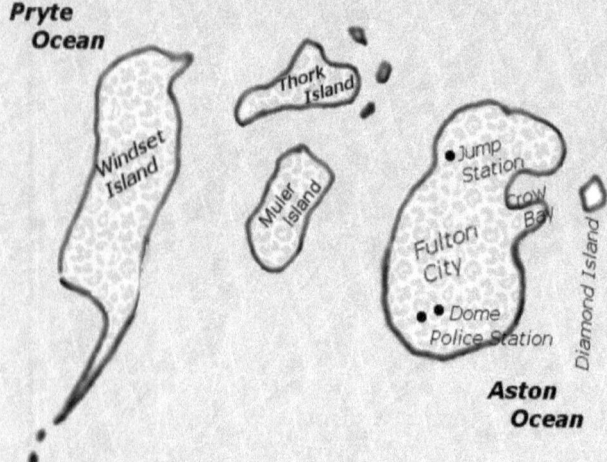

Planet Fulton Station
Land Mass Map

Chapter One

Fred Stoshingburg took up most of my office. He was one big guy; no fat, just big. My detective was handing in his latest case report. He was like a big loveable teddy bear but he was deceiving as he was one tough cop. Of course, he was like me, he could stretch the rules and that is why Lieutenant Judith Hill, complaining loudly, had also squeezed her slim little torso into my office. It was too hot to have so many bodies in my small room which had no window and of course a struggling, hardly working air conditioning system. I reached over turning my fan on super high. Now it sounded like we had a wind storm in with us.

Our planet, Fulton Station, doesn't have much land mass, but what we have is hot weather almost year round reaching 120 degrees and then our winter season drops to a balmy 95 degrees. Due to the winds off our oceans, it keeps the humidity down, thus it made it bearable - just bearable. It was an early engineered planet made only for supplies and housing workers to cultivate our sector. Thus the engineers didn't spend a lot of time on temperature control and it shows! They abandoned the planet when more convenient Jumps were found but when the sector needed a central government, they re-found it. Lucky us!

The whole planet of Fulton has only a series of relatively small islands. The largest island, holding the city of Fulton, has a regular population of about 40,000 strong but with the transient inhabitants of the other dozen sector planets that run the central government, it adds another 60,000. When the government isn't in session it actually feels almost deserted.

Inhabitants of Fulton Island live on 2,500 sq. miles. Fulton City contains the government offices, all modern with the Golden Dome as the official sector representatives' chambers. Across and down the street was our centralized sector Police Force's dilapidated five story yellow brick building - housing all 300 regular police and 20 detectives. I wear the "Sector Chief" badge. Lucky me!

"Well, you see Chief", Fred seemed to be hesitating, not sure how to break the news to me but Hill had no qualms telling me exactly how she felt.

"He's a big oaf!" She sternly pointed her finger at him, "he, he..."

Now she was having trouble, her face getting red, her cheeks burning, her foot angrily tapping away. **"Okay, anyone just tell me!"** When my voice booms, I usually get results and now I had both of them talking at once.

"He shot someone and then..," came from Hill.

"It was a total accident, I broke a vase..." came simultaneously from Fred.

"Whoa! **Where the hell is Carl**?" I loudly barked which brought in Captain Carl Issam, who was trying to hide right outside my door. He stepped in. Thank god he was a small man, not many more could squeeze in. Now we were really tight and hot! Carl's bald head was shining with sweat; his face red with what I guessed was frustration. I wasn't sure I wanted to hear this.

"Fred, you first!" I figured to give the big guy the first chance because once Hill got going he'd not get a word in otherwise.

"Well, you see boss," Fred was shuffling his feet and not looking at me, bad sign. "We chased Carliango into the museum. You know the one on Franklin Street."

I waved at him to hurry up, "just spill it, Stoshingburg!" I have little patience, well really I have none.

"We saw Carliango get the drugs and he saw us."

"He's so damn big," she pointed at Fred, "how can you miss him!" Hill just had to interrupt, again shaking her finger angrily at Stoshingburg. I glared at her, she got the message and shut up.

Fred hurriedly talked, scowling at Hill, "Well, Chief, we chased him into the Fulton Antiquity Center. We knew he had all that Supfline on him." He hesitated, that was all Hill needed.

"He shot him, right there, with everyone around. That is totally unacceptable, totally against regulation." Hill was now yelling at me. One of my looks and she lowered her voice a couple of decibels, but she kept right on going. "He shoots Carliango but then backs into a pedestal with a vase and it falls. An antique Minga vase!" She made it sound that the breaking of the vase is what really ticked her off.

"Aw, come on Hill." Fred lamented. "I only stunned him. I didn't mean to get the woman next to him...."

My head hurt. Issam, who is my lead detective, spoke up, "I talked to the curator of the museum. You'll have to call him, just a courtesy call. The accidentally stunned woman is alright, she works there. I've already sent her some flowers with a card from her grateful police force."

"What about Carliango?" Had everyone forgotten the drug dealer? He was one of the scums of Fulton City, not only the city but the entire planet. In truth, the entire sector! Although, I had to admit, on this hot miserable insane planet I didn't blame the residents for taking drugs. Just keep them legal!

"They took him to jail via the hospital; he was kind of out of it." Stoshingburg guiltily half smiled. I have to admit that I half smiled too. This brought a damning frown from Lt. Hill.

I ignored her, quickly moving on. "Well, let's be thankful he didn't run into the Dome," which I knew was right next door. Our government was in session which meant the new ultra-modern building was full of important sector dignitaries making laws for the entire sector planets. I didn't need that problem. If he'd tasered one of the senators, I'd be out of a job!

"Oh," Hill was talking again, I wasn't going to like this. "Senator Hollebrandt was there! She was having a special meeting at the museum on its funding. The delegation saw it all!"

Now my head really hurt. "Issam!"

Carl frowned and waved his hand trying to tell Hill to shut up. "Don't get upset, Chief. I explained to the Senator about Carliango. The Senator is from Hilda, she seems to understand," Issam clarified. He scowled at my rookie lieutenant.

Issam is also my second in command and he acts as my diplomat, considering I am terrible at it. My captain is always smoothing ruffled feathers, including mine. His cellbutton beeped and he stepped out leaving me with my two sweaty detectives.

"Stoshingburg, give me the report!" I grabbed the tab stick and before Hill could say anything else Issam had returned.

"Hey," he announced, "the Consulate is on his way up from the lobby. He wants to talk to you. I'll meet him at the elevator." He disappeared from my doorway, but so did Stoshingburg and Hill. Laren Borger was my boss and since this was the first time in four years he'd come to my office, it must be trouble. Hill and

Stoshingburg were betting it was them. I was betting on it too. Shit! We didn't have the budget for tab sticks, how much was a Minga Vase gonna cost!

I heard Issam direct him to my office and in he came! He looked around my dingy small work space before he settled in my nice folding metal chair. I could tell he was not impressed. Well, neither was I. I wasn't about to get cushiony furniture when my police and detectives didn't even have up to date tabloids. When the chair creaked, he jumped back up, looking down at it.

"Don't worry, it hasn't dropped anyone on the floor yet." I motioned for him to sit. Borger was a tall thin man with a rather small face for such a tall frame. His large bulbous nose made him look lopsidedly disproportionate. Although he was in his forties, he looked older with lots of peppered gray. His job was showing on him. He was the liaison officer with the central sector government; in charge of overseeing the important departments that ran the Crab planets.

We didn't agree on priorities, especially on the purse strings, but we did agree on fighting crime. He'd always been there to back me on pursuing criminals; in our courts, on the streets, against politicians. As far as I knew he was incorruptible. However, he obviously paid the price in stress. Fulton Station, being the center of the sector's government, was full of powerful politicians and corrupt lobbyists and so far Laren Borger had stayed above it and gone for the law and nothing but the law.

"How is it going Skip?" He looked uncomfortable but not mad which was a good sign.

"I'm hanging in there," I told him and got a wide weak smile from such a small face. I decided the best strategy was to get right to the point. Hit the problem head on. "I know the vase is probably worth a lot but so are the supfline drugs that come down here from that damn planet, Skantie Row." That planet was a pain in my side despite it being the farthest out in our sector. It was a hell hole even though it was smaller than Fulton Island. The drug families have their headquarters there and they make my life miserable with their high stakes casinos and classy high priced bordellos, not to mention their drug trafficking. They did it from a small piece of land. When they had engineered the planet Skantie Row, they kept it small, easy to control their corrupt businesses.

A strange look came over his face. "I don't understand. Are we having trouble again with Skantie? I thought we'd brought them under control when you got the Blithie family's files late last year. I thought we put a real scare into the other mob families."

Now it was my turn to be confused. Obviously, he wasn't here about Sloshingburg's museum incident. "Let's start over. Why are you here? I misunderstood. I thought it was about an incident that happened this morning?"

"Oh you mean the museum?" He shook his head. "Minor. Senator Hollebrandt was rather amused. Good thing the vase was a fake."

I felt my mind shake. "A fake?"

"Yeah, the real one is being fixed, had a crack in it. The curator was rather glad about the police helping to keep drug dealers out of his museum. No, I'm here about Moss."

"Moss?" Now my heart started thumping. "The Medical Operation Space Station?"

"Yes. Dr. Kel Hibnet called me. Are you up to snuff on what happened out at the medical space station?"

"No." I wasn't sure I wanted to know. I'd spent my first eleven years growing up on the huge space station. I spent another year when, at eighteen, I was hurt in my racing accident. It was a dangerous place for me. My parents had been killed there, murdered, although it was never confirmed by whom. I knew who, but there wasn't any proof. Of course Laren Borger had no idea. I had a new identity with my Uncle's adoption of me at age 11, however Dr. Hibnet did know! "What does Dr. Hibnet want?"

"He specifically asked for you. He thinks highly of you." Borger wasn't looking at me, bad sign. "Let me explain. There was an explosion in one of the labs on Moss, in one of the research labs. It was deemed an accident, gas leak. Two assistant lab technicians were badly burned."

My heart raced again. I had a feeling I knew which research lab. I just nodded, Borger didn't even notice as he just continued on. "Well, he thinks there is something suspicious about it. There is an important conference being held next week and he's worried about something else happening. This symposium is their biggest fund raiser. They hold it every common Federation year with lots of dignitaries from every sector. He'd like you to send some extra security, including yourself."

"Lont Pol is a very capable superintendent of the police force out there. I'm sure if she thought help was needed from us, she would have told me." I also knew, but didn't mention it to Borger, that my superintendent Pol was always fighting with the head administration on Moss. They often went over her head interfering with her authority and supervision of her own police force.

The highly educated research personnel on the space station, including Dr. Hibnet, were hard to handle. I hated to admit it, since my parents were researchers, but they tend to think of themselves as experts on everything. I've dealt with these highly educated scholars on every planet and it seems most intellectuals gravitate to the same cockiness. Their research comes first and very little else matters to them. It is hard to wrestle power from them. I didn't envy Lont Pol having to deal with all those doctors and researchers on Moss.

"Oh, I'm not questioning Superintendent Pol's capability but you know how those doctor administrators can be." He seemed embarrassed and I realized why he'd come, Dr. Hibnet was calling in a favor. I knew Borger's youngest daughter had been sent to the medical space station for treatment of a brain tumor. They had saved her life. I wasn't surprised, after spending a year with them for treatment on my own brain damage. They did phenomenal work and the whole cosmos came to them.

He looked at me, reading my thoughts. "I really do owe Dr. Hibnet's team a lot."

"You don't have to explain to me." I told him. "I owe him myself. You know I spent time after my accident with him. His whole team did a lot for me." Of course Borger didn't know I'd grown up on Moss, that was pre Skip Brown. It was something I'd hidden; my life depended on hiding it. Dr. Hibnet knew but only because he knew my parents and he also knew the importance of keeping it quiet.

"He's amazing," Borger commented. "If you could put a crew of your detectives together and send them out there and if you could just go and supervise…"

"I really don't have the time to go out there," I interrupted him. I didn't mention I had no desire either. It was bad enough I had to go out a couple of times a cycle to meet with Pol.

"Well, at least talk to him. He's here visiting the Dome on budgetary meetings. Hibnet wants to talk to you before he Jumps home. I would appreciate it - you meeting with him."

"Of course." My stomach churned. Dr. Hibnet was an intense type person, not one easily denied anything but then he'd have to be as Moss depended on his fundraising. I was sure the good doctor was here for the opening of our session of congress. He'd be lobbying for the funds necessary to run the space station.

Borger stood up, extending his hand. "Thanks, Skip." He looked around; the fan was blowing hot air around my office, giving little relief. I noticed beads of sweat on his brow. "Gee, doesn't your air conditioning work?"

"Most of the time, no." I told him as I wiped my forehead with my sleeve. "It's an antiquated system, left over from the days when this was a storage warehouse."

"Oh," he looked around, frowning. He cleared his throat, "Well, what a quaint building. I'll see what I can do about the air conditioning." He nodded then left.

See what he could do, yeah, right. I leaned back, extending my feet under my desk and relaxed like my doctor/therapist had taught me. Still my fingers went into my pocket and got a little blue pill, popping it into my mouth. I reached for my cup of java to swallow it when Issam, Stoshingburg and Hill's heads came around my office door. All three of them looked at me with big question marks on their faces. Time to have some fun.

"Well, he is only docking your pays," I nodded to Hill and Stoshingburg, "only for the cost of getting the vase fixed, a moderate 25% amount each week for about a year should do it."

Both yelled, "WHAT!" together and then started yelling at each other. Hill was blaming my big detective for shooting and he blaming her for getting in the way.

Issam glared at me, he knew I was pulling their chain. "What did Borger really say," he commented, "what did he really want?"

It brought both my arguing detectives to a silent standstill. Hill put her hands on her hips and Stoshingburg leaned on my desk glaring at me.

I laughed, "It was a fake vase but that doesn't excuse either of you. I pointed my finger at Fred, "You need to spend some time at the firing range." Then I nodded toward Hill, "You need to take some time and relax, perhaps some cooperative management courses?"

Both opened up their mouths to argue but the scowl on my face shut them up. In a shouting match, I would win and they knew it. Hill stomped out and Fred slouched out.

"What did he really want?" Carl Issam sat on my metal chair, he didn't weigh enough to even make it creak. Castorians aren't big people.

"It was about Moss." I sat back trying to relax but not really succeeding. This was not going to count as a good day, not even coming close to decent.

"He came here to talk about Moss, the space station?" Issam cocked his head having trouble believing what I said. "What problem do they have? Pol runs a tight ship. The station has a low crime rate. I know she'd love to murder those head administrators. They are constantly giving her a hard time or completely ignoring her. I can't tell you how many reports come through without her knowing about it. I automatically now just copy her on everything that comes from Moss."

"I gather there was an explosion at a lab that the head of the space station, Dr.Hibnet, thinks is suspicious and not an accident as first reported. Get a hold of Lont Pol and see what she has to say on it. Don't make a big deal of it. Make it a routine check. I guess Dr. Hibnet is in Fulton City, he's stopping by to discuss the incident with me before he heads home. He's requesting we send a team out there to make sure his big fund raising conference gets extra protection. I guess the accident at the lab spooked him."

"Not a good time, we are really stretched thin," Issam commented. His slanted amber eyes were unhappy and his pointed thick ears turned slightly red. Being from Castor in the Casteroid Belt, every emotion showed in his features, so typical of his race. They were short slim intellectuals. Castorians were known for short bodies but big brains. Issam was no exception. Carl hadn't let leaving his home planet and moving to Fulton Station change him. He kept to his strict Castor vegetarian diet and his Castor religion. No sweets, only dark tea and high morals. His wife and two daughters were his world, although he blamed his baldness on his two teenage children. Those that took his shortness for weakness learned a hard lesson as he had earned the highest possible level in the Federation Martial Arts. He certainly could whoop my ass.

"I know," I answered him. "We've had a rash of homicides lately. How many personnel have we got off planet?"

"Fifteen and Oleg Lawerson just got back from maternity leave. I can't send her off planet yet. Plus we need detectives here, the Dome just got back in session."

I nodded my understanding. Besides being my second in charge, he was my friend - he and his wife. Dr. Lily, his spouse, was my doctor/therapist. She had been immensely helpful when I moved to Fulton Station. They knew my history and kept it to themselves, for which I was extremely grateful. Besides them only Lieutenant Hill knew of my roots on the medical space station and then my life on the Planet Nestor. Hill and I had been investigating a murder on Nestor, known as the center of intergalactic car racing, when she learned of my past. My newest detective also had not breathed a word to anyone.

Hill came from the far off Orion Sector, from the planet Orbo, known for their serious mindedness. Orbo was Orion's government sector center. The sector encompassed a huge area and although not well known here, it was a progressive sector, a growing sector. The Lieutenant had been tops at her law school and tops at the police academy and had come right straight into our detective division. Of course, she came cheap - a big budgetary help as Borger had pointed out when he recommended her to fill my latest detective spot.

Hill had learned that I had been "rookie of the year" on the Intergalactic racing circuit and had taken the racing championship at age 17. No one had ever done that before at such a young age. The next year I won the championship again but on the last race I had crashed. One driver was killed by my car and I spent a year on MOSS (Medical Operation Space Station) and had finally recovered mostly.

My injuries were so serious I had been rushed to the highly rated medical space station for treatment. When I had finally woken up, I was at first alarmed to have returned to my childhood home, but Dr. Hibnet had taken good care of me. He had not said a word to anyone that I my parents had actually been Helen and James Masters; the famous research doctors who were searching for the cure to free the slaves on Ligithia. Slaves, who were blood bonded to their masters, the Highblood Laositians, slaves that died if they left their masters. It was reported that my parents were close to solving it when their family was killed in a space shuttle explosion. So technically, I was dead.

Although we had been scheduled to go with them, I had been sick, so my parents had at the last minute left me and my brother Ray at home with our nursemaid Killa. Killa, a Ligithian who was blood bonded to my mother, took us immediately to my mother's brother Jack on the racing planet of Nestor. He adopted us, giving me a new name - Skip Brown. My brother became Ray Brown and Uncle Jack had also taken on Killa's blood bond. When he had died, I had taken on her bond or she would have died.

The Ligithians only have about twenty days to bond to another who has Laositian blood - blood that is related to the original bond. So Killa was on Fulton Station, acting as my superintendent of the apartment building which I had refurbished for the disabled. It kept her busy on something important to me, thus the bond was actively satisfied. Being my superintendent also acted as a cover for her since few in our sector knew what a Ligithian was; she posed as a Casey dwarf and no one was the wiser. Of course, Hill had spotted her right away. Why was it always Lt. Hill? Being from the Orion sector, my newest detective had spotted what she was right away but had kept it to herself, even becoming a good friend to Killa.

Ligithia is a planet in the farthest reaches of the Orion Sector. It is a mining treasure chest making the ruling Laositians very wealthy. The most important was the mining of methanilum. It is used in the sparking of the Jumps. It has been suggested that the "slave issue" was used by the Federation to provoke a war to get easy access to the methanilum and that the war was easily settled once the Laositians came up with a deal on the precious Jump fuel. Whatever, the slaves came out the worse for it.

The Orion sector is over a two day jump from the Crab. Little is known of the failed war outside of Orion vicinity, it wasn't something that the Federations Ruling Body was real proud of. The humanoid Federation had tried to free the slaves from their masters on Ligithia. The soldiers found that killing the masters, Laositians, also resulted in the Liggis dying within 20 days. That is why they were called the *blood slaves*. The war ended with a treaty that left the slaves not freed until a cure could be found to undo the blood bond. The methanilum continued to flow. It was a Federation disgrace that no one talked about.

My mother was given Killa as a nursemaid when she was a young girl on Ligithia. My mother became a Doctor of Biochemistry. When she fled Ligithia, she took Killa and my uncle Jack with her to Nestor, taking on a new identity. She later married Dr. James Masters and they both went to work on Moss, trying to find a cure for the blood bond. Unfortunately, the Laositians later found my mother and believed they killed all of us.

Issam left my office to put in a call to Lont Pol. I searched the files for anything recently reported from Moss. Sure enough, the lab accident filed the screen. It was dated over a week ago.

M.O.S.S ACCIDENT causes burns on the **station.** *It was reported yesterday that the medical space station had a bad accident in one of the research labs. First reports indicate that the lab research technicians left a gas line open which caused a lab explosion. Two research assistants were badly burned and taken to the Ring Four level on the station, their famous burn unit. Due to the delay in Jump line news, the names have not reached the newsroom but we will publish names as soon as we get them. It has not been reported which lab was involved but it is rumored to be on their level Eight ring - the highly restricted area of the space station.*

I scrolled down to the next article appearing three days later.

M.O.S.S ACCIDENT NEWS CONFERENCE *held finally three days after the event. Dr. Kel Hibnet held a news conference on the explosion on the Moss space station. He confirmed that the research lab was just about completely destroyed but no structural damage was done to Ring Eight. The station sustained no damage; it was all contained within the lab.*

"No one outside of the lab was in any danger. Two of the lab assistants have sustained considerable burn injuries but have been taken to our Burn Unit, Ring Four. It was an unfortunate accident which is being thoroughly investigated by our police Superintendent Lont Pol. We will release the findings when our police

investigators are done." Dr. Hibnet announced finally three days after the initial report.

The head administrator, Hibnet, would only say that the research lab was "classified" and would not elaborate further. Since news on the space station is delayed because it must first be digitally sent to the orbiting satellite moon so no Jump lines interfere with the space station's delicate instruments, the families of the burn victims are just now being notified. The names of Richard Stone, age 33 from Casey and Elizabeth Ryserl age 30, from Hilda were just released. Both are in stable condition. None of the families have yet commented.

I pushed the button for Daisy our administrative assistant. After a long pause, I heard, "Yes, Chief". Why Daisy always sounded like she didn't want to talk to me I couldn't understand, although I have from time to time barked at her.

"Did Lont Pol send her latest reports from Moss?" I asked.

"Well, you know her reports are always late due to the line Jump delay?"

"I'm aware of that, Daisy. Has she sent in a report about the lab explosion?" I honestly tried to sound not annoyed, I succeeded a little.

"Well…" she stuttered, I heard her typing her keys. My fingers tapped, I was really trying to be patient. "Well…" More typing came again. My fingers went faster. "Well…" I was now gritting my teeth. "Ah, NO." she finally said. No more typing.

"THANK YOU." I said a little too loud and I heard a whimper before she clicked off. Damn the woman was too sensitive.

I looked up to see Hill standing in my doorway, cutting off my fresh air. "Yeah?" I frowned as deep as I could. Hill was the last person I needed to see.

"You really should learn patience," she said. Obviously, she'd been listening in. "Since I have to sign up for that cooperative management course, how about joining me?"

"Yeah, well your sarcasm will only get you assigned to foot patrol." That shut her up. "Now, what do you want?" Again I gave her my deepest frown.

"I'm picking up Killa, we're going to attend that lecture on *How to Grow Plants Successfully on Fulton.*"

Hill had learned that a healthy natural diet helped epileptics, like me, and had been conspiring with Killa to make me eat better. Lucky me! They'd been trying to feed me high protein, healthy fiber and natural vegetables. I'd given up trying to stop them. Now they had it in their heads to try and have a garden on my apartment building roof. The only plants that grow on Fulton are cactus.

"Well, have a good time." I gave her by best smirk, "Knock yourselves out."

"I don't want to be late," she countered. "Make your own supper so she's not late."

"I never make Killa make me supper. Lately I prefer she didn't!" I was thinking of the spinach salad with some kind of fish bites thrown in that I'd had last night, probably a recipe straight from Hill. "She has her own apartment; I don't need her to do anything for me."

"You know she feels obligated!" Hill had her hands on her hips as if it came quite natural for her to lecture me. "You know she feels responsible for your health. It's not like you help her. Your eating habits are horrible! She worries!"

"Ligithians are natural worry warts. It is something they do! It must be something about the Orion sector since you suffer from the same symptoms. Mind your own business," I growled, giving her my best scowl to go with it.

Hill sputtered something that I didn't quite hear, but probably didn't want to hear anyways. She started pointing her finger at me but Daisy chose this time to walk into my office. Daisy Totel, my administrative assistant, had the natural ability to dress in the worst possible clothes that she could find. Often in bright color patterns that didn't match. Today was a green polka dotted skirt with a red striped halter top. She finished it with yellow stripped high heels. Her bright orange hair just did wonders for her pale white complexion which sat on a tall thin body; she was from one of the moons on Logan. They looked weird to begin with and ditsy as all hell so I guess she just decided to emphasize it more.

She slapped a tab file on my desk, half crying, her eyes red, she said, "Satisfied, I found it!" and turned heels and abruptly left. I gathered it was Lont Pol's accident report.

Hill just looked at me, a pleased grin on her face, "Told you, sure you don't want to go to that management class with me?"

One look at my angry face and she beat it quickly out of my office. I glared at the door, hoping someone would come in for me to yell at, but I realized just about everyone had headed home. *Time to go home.* Of course I still had to call the curator of the museum for my "courtesy call" and I had to finish filing my day's report. And I needed to call Killa to make sure she didn't make me supper. Damn that Hill!

Chapter Two

The ride home seemed long although I only lived twenty minutes from the station on the outskirts of Fulton City. With the Dome in session, traffic getting out of downtown was brutal. We have 33 senators (3 from each sector planet) and 11 Parleys (1 judge from each planet) and they tend to all have large hover limos with their own drivers. They have a tendency to park where they want and to tie up traffic without a thought to us poor working stiffs trying to get home. I had brought this up with Consulate Borger; a few traffic tickets would be embarrassing but an effective deterrent since our representatives live in fear of bad publicity. But it wasn't a fight he wanted to fight. The Consulate has enough head butting with the higher ups about things much more important. Still, as I inched through the intersections I was tempted to jump out and give tickets on my own. Add to the congestion thousands of government staff members and the streets became a nightmare at rush hour. Tonight was annoyingly slow, slow.

Normally I'm out after the worst of the traffic has past but it was the beginning of the week and it had been a wicked bad day, so I left pretty much on time. My apartment building overlooks Crow Bay. As I drove around the once Industrial section, now turned residential, the sun bounced off the bay encompassing my little Ant hover craft. It was only the two-seater version but despite the size discomfort, it cost little to fuel charge and easy to park even if my large body had to squeeze into it.

I ran through the drive up at CosmicSub and got a couple of cheeseburgers, fries, onion rings and a chocolate shake. After a wicked bad day, I figured I deserved it and since Killa wasn't around I'd truly enjoy my total diet slipup. No health food tonight; it was justified I told my guilt ridden brain. The smell emanating from the fast food bag was heavenly, especially in the confines of my small Ant.

By the time I arrived at Crow Bay, my guilt was totally gone and my stomach rumbled in anticipation of the contents of my food bag. In my neighborhood, almost every apartment complex had been a former storage facility from Fulton's early days. Given a financial break to convert them to apartments had been a great incentive. The city built new walkways, roads and parks around the bay area and the buildings' owners fixed up the former warehouses to reasonable rents. I had purchased one of the buildings when I moved to Fulton with the money I had left over from my car racing winnings. I hadn't that much left after law school and my ex-wife had ended up with a big chunk of it. Well, most of it. Sore point, I let the thought go, water over the dam.

I pulled into my underground parking lot and put the Ant next to my red Dugante turbocycle. I fondly touched its seat on my way up to the entrance ramp. Lately I'd only gotten to ride the cycle on Sundays; my work schedule had been brutal recently. I entered the lobby. At the desk was Artchie Mcaster. He was filling in. Killa had hired him as an assistant superintendent. Working for her paid his rent and let him have a little left over to live on. He stood up when he saw me. His wheelchair actually let him stand so he could talk to me face to face. The chair quickly unfolded upward, lifting him vertically. It had meant a lot to the young man when I had gotten our local veteran's disability chapter to fund it for him.

"Hi, Chief," he grinned at me. He'd had his legs damaged in the Cathian War but there was nothing wrong with his brain. He was attending Fulton University, majoring in economics. He is a top student on full scholarship. He wants to work at the Dome as a staff member to the Majority Minister's office.

"How goes it?" I asked him. "Killa gone out?"

"Yeah, she left with Ms. Hill about an hour ago. Told me to tell you she'd be back in a couple of hours. The lieutenant left you some boxes. She said to be careful with them, they're plants for the garden."

He helped me take the boxes in the crook of my arm. One hand held the fast food bag and my other hand had my briefcase. Artchie followed me to the elevators, pressing my elevator button for me.

"Thanks." I told him as I punched my code in for the top floor using my elbow. I live on the top fifth floor, the entire fifth floor. All the other sixteen apartments were on the lower floors. The door opened onto my apartment. Bear and Hoover were faithfully waiting for me.

"Hi Guys," I said to the two immense Hiberlan Hounds, all 356 lbs of them. They bounded forward, almost knocking me over. "Whoa." I tried to tell them. Before I could catch my balance the boxes started to slip out of my arms. I tried to recover but lost my equilibrium. Everything went flying. I landed on my rump with the dogs bouncing around me. Their tails hurt as they accidentally hit me. It was like being beaten with two whips.

"Stop!" I yelled. Immediately they sat. Both looked so confused that I took pity on them, reaching up, rubbing their ears as I sat on the floor. Both dogs were gray with dark black spots. They almost looked like someone had painted camouflage on them. I hadn't had their ears cropped but let the large ears flop down. The breeders always crop their hound's ears as they were originally bred to hunt Hiberian boars. The shortened ears kept the boars from grabbing onto the dogs heads. Here on Fulton, I didn't think they'd be chasing any boars.

The two were brothers; still puppies being under two years old. They'd fill out to over 200lbs each when they were done growing. Both dogs had been brought to the animal pound to be euthanized. Because they were born spotted, they couldn't be professionally shown. Thus the breeder thought them useless. They were so big that the animal control office had called the police station for help in handling them. When Issam had told me of the request, out of curiosity, I went over to see them and fell in love with the two, taking them home with me.

I slowly got to my feet. I grabbed the boxes and put them on my kitchen table. Unfortunately, the bag of food scattered everywhere. I tried to get to it but the two dogs had gobbled up the hamburgers and were finishing off the fries before I even got back. They left the onion rings for me to pick up. The milkshake was all over. They were over by the elevator slurping it up. "Stop it!" I yelled but it was too late, there wasn't much for me to even clean up.

I shook my finger at them, "You both will be sick!" Usually they ate only dry dog food, their stomachs were finicky. They cocked their heads at me wondering why I was yelling at them. *"Wasn't that a treat for us?"* they seem to say.

"Well, at least the day has finished like it started." I moaned. I walked over to the part of the fifth floor I had semi-finished. I had a large kitchen with a good sized table. Next to the kitchen was a cozy den. It held all my trophies and racing memories and a large telescreen that I didn't get to watch much. Huge couches circled the screen. I usually fell asleep watching the early news, waking up when the late news came on and then dragged myself to bed.

Next to the den was a bedroom with a bed and a half-finished closet. The only bathroom was at the other end near the stairs going up to my roof. The rest of the fifth floor is unfinished with its left over storage facility large windows from ceiling to gray cement floor. The remaining part of the apartment looked like what it was - a storage warehouse. Still I get great panoramic views of the city and on the other side Crow Bay.

I had splurged on the bathroom. It is spaciously luxurious with, besides the usual toilet and sinks, I had a long shower with many shower heads as my crowning finish. I had put in a shower-drying room in the back part which also could serve as a sauna at the touch of a button. In an alcove was my washing machine and dryer; the only practical part of the room.

"Come on guys, up we go." I took the two hounds through the canvas flaps covering the stairway up to the roof. I trudged up the twelve stairs, coming on to my half of the roof. The other half, which was separated by a cement wall, I had fixed up for the residents. They have picnic tables and lounging chairs with grills for barbequing.

On my side I had fixed a run for the dogs with a place for them to go to the bathroom. Every third day, a large bag dumped by chutes automatically into the dumpster down below and was automatically replaced. I had put in a hot tub but kept it cool and a picnic area for myself. The dogs immediately started to run around chasing each other.

Evening was just about making its appearance so the heat on the roof wasn't too bad. The evening winds off Crow Bay were stirring, making it even more comfortable. I stood by the four foot side walls and watched the sun setting. The seagulls were silhouettes dotting the sky above the bay. The Aston Ocean could be seen this high up sparkling beyond the bay. It is the biggest ocean on Fulton. We only have two; their water took up 96 percent of the planet, leaving us a puny 4 percent land mass to live on.

My stomach growled, reminding me that I hadn't eaten. "Come on, let's get downstairs, I'll bring you up later tonight." They did one more race around, Bear won, of course. He is the bigger and faster of the two but Hoover is the smarter one. It was Hoover that thought of opening cabinets, of getting any food left on the counters and Bear just followed behind; his faithful assistant. They are mischief makers and I had picked up plenty of their pranks. One time they were mad that I had left them for a week with Killa in charge. When I got home they had dragged my mattresses in front of the elevator and were sleeping on them. When the doors slid open I was greeted with guilty mugs welcoming me home.

There wasn't much in the fridge except a plate that Killa had made up. I winced, I had told her not to bother with supper but there it was - a plate of green vegetables with pieces of chicken on top. "Heat up the chicken," was the only note. I left it on the counter and took out some bread and cheese. I went to the back of my refrigerator and got the pepperoni I had hidden behind the soy bean milk that Killa had gotten. I climbed up to the cabinet above the refrigerator and grabbed the bag of chips I had also hidden. I made myself a thick sandwich and a cup of java. I was thinking of watching the local news when I heard the buzzer for the elevator.

The dogs heard it too and started racing toward the lift, deep growls as they expectantly looked at the doors. "Whoa guys." I patted them as I pushed the intercom button. "Yeah?" It probably was a tenant or a salesperson.

"Skip?" I knew that cultured voice. It was a deep bass with a hint of off planet accent. I reached for a pill but they were in my suit jacket on the back of a kitchen chair.

I actually thought of not answering but shoved the immature idea out of my head. "Yes, it's me." I answered.

"I hope I haven't gotten you at a bad time. I thought we could talk more privately if I came here." I hadn't heard that voice in a long time, my spine shivered.

"I'm sending the elevator down. Come on up, Dr. Hibnet." I punched in the code that would let him get in and back up. I heard the grinding as it lowered, it sounded like my stomach. "Sit, both of you." I ordered the dogs, the two immediately sat on their haunches, their powerful tails swishing behind them. They knew the drill. I had actually sent them to training school. Some things they learned, some they didn't, but "sit" they got.

When the doors opened a heavy set man stood there. He looked older but then he would, I hadn't seen him in several years. I avoided any visits with him when I went to meet with Pol twice a year. His hair was graying; strikes of white hair lay at his temples and sides. His intense dark brown eyes looked weary and like always had a hint of sadness. I imagined he saw a lot of difficult situations being the head of the medical space station. Very much like myself, I'd seen a lot of hurt too. As I got every brutal crime possible, every illness, mental and physical, came to his hospital.

He stepped forward, saw the dogs and stopped. It's probably the only time I'd seen panic cover his normally calm features. The dogs had let out a low growl. "It's alright," I petted them, "he's a friend." They knew that word and immediately stopped growling but stayed close to me as I stepped forward giving the good doctor my hand.

He shook it but his eyes never left the dogs. "What in god's name are they?" he finally managed to get out.

"They are Hiberian Hounds, although born here." I told him. "They won't hurt you. I'm not saying they couldn't, but they won't. Great watchdogs."

"They are magnificent." He cautiously came into the apartment. He looked around, "You own this building? I was told it houses disabled tenants?"

"Yup, including me." I laughed.

"You're not disabled Skip, perhaps a little damaged but definitely not disabled." He walked over to the immense windows looking out at the bay. "What a great view."

I showed him the apartment and the roof, making small talk; something I'm not real good at. Offered him a drink but he declined. "I was hoping we could go for a walk and a chat. I saw some nice walking trails as I pulled in along the bay with convenient park benches."

In other words, he wanted to make sure we were alone. I went into the kitchen to get my suit jacket. I popped a little blue pill in my mouth, taking a swig of my now cold java to swallow it.

"Let's take the dogs, they'll enjoy the fresh air." I quickly slipped their electronic harnesses on them. They were all excited. "They need to run off hamburgers and fries," I informed him, getting a strange look from him in return. I explained further, "I dropped my supper and they ate it before I could stop them." He laughed, it was strange coming from him; he was always so serious.

It was a crowded elevator as we headed down. I had the dogs well trained to sit quietly, no wagging hurting tails. They had accepted Hibnet as a friend and brushed up against him. He scratched their ears and got a grateful "Woof" in return.

I told Artchie I was taking the dogs for a walk if anyone came looking for me. I wouldn't be gone long. I expressly didn't mention Killa and he just nodded. He was doing his homework.

"He's a cripple," Dr. Hibnet mentioned as we left heading down the walkway to the park.

"Yes, his legs were damaged in the Cathian Offensive." I told him.

"We got a lot of damaged young people from that conflict." Hibnet sounded sad. "I remember they filled the sixth ring completely. My nephew lost his life in that damn war."

I remembered Hibnet was originally from the Pinwheel Sector. The area had been caught in a civil war with half the planets wanting to opt out of the sector. The Federation had denied their claim and war had ensued with the final battle on Cathia's capital. The sector stayed intact but a lot of the soldiers didn't. "Sorry to hear that," I told him and got a curt nod as a reply as if he'd felt he had said too much. The doctor was a very private person. I knew very little of his personal life. On the other hand, he knew mine very well.

We walked along the bay. The tall lantern type lights came on giving the trail a safe homey feel. We passed joggers, families out for walks, other dog walkers. It is a popular trail. Hill drags me with the dogs on the weekends when she can catch me before I'm off on my turbocycle. We finally took a seat at a bench that has a long lawn between us and the shore. It was peaceful with the head winds brushing us. I adjusted the dog's leashes letting them romp in front of us.

"I don't know how you can stand all this hot weather. At least here by the bay you have the breezes coming off the water. Even the breezes have a warm feel to them." Hibnet wiped his face with his handkerchief. It actually seemed cooler to me, Fulton gets much hotter in its *summer* season.

"It's something we either ignore or move off planet. It isn't going to change. They can't reengineer without taking the population off it. Can't see that happening, after all there is air conditioning which is what most live in." *When you have it,* I thought but kept to myself.

"True." He shook his head. "I guess I'm use to the controlled climate we have on Moss. I forget sometimes how artificial it is but then you've experienced the space station too."

Yes, I'd experienced it. I wasn't much for small talk, being a cop left me little patience for polite conversation. "Why did you want to see me? Consulate Borger came in today and mentioned something about an explosion in a lab and that's made you nervous about the upcoming Moss conference?"

"We had an accident in a research lab facility on Level Eight Ring. Two assistant researchers were badly burned. The interns are lucky to be alive considering it destroyed the entire laboratory." His fingers brushed through his hair, a nervous reaction. He wasn't sure how to tell me, so I jumped in.

"Let me guess, since you want me to investigate, it was the research on the Ligithian blood bond." I looked over at him, he just nodded. "You don't think it was an accident but that someone sabotaged it. Correct?"

"I'm fairly sure of it." He still didn't look at me. "I have actual proof that the gas line was tampered with."

"What does Pol think?" I asked and got a blank stare from him.

"Pol?" His face finally registered what I was asking. "Well, I haven't discussed it with her yet. I don't need any more people to know. It was Dr. Lawry that discovered the tampered line and she came right to me."

"Lont Pol is my Police Superintendent on Moss. She's the first person you should have told!" I guess the anger shown in my face as Dr. Hibnet drew back, sitting straight up on the bench as far away from me as possible. I am known for my temper but he'd never seen it before and it took him by surprise.

"She does the day to day policing, I just didn't think of her…" he stammered.

"Well, you need to think of her, that's why she's there!" I calmed myself down. Once again I reminded myself that intellectuals live in another world. "Look Dr. Hibnet…"

"Please call me Kel." He said.

"You'll always be Dr. Hibnet to me." I told him. He smiled, I suppose he'd heard that before. He was too an imposing figure to me. It was like calling my parents by their first names, ain't gonna happen. "Who do you think is responsible?" I asked, although I really would have preferred not to ask. I'd rather not be involved but then that wasn't gonna happen either.

"I think it is someone who is an integral part of the space station's staff," he reluctantly admitted. "I have been over and over the video security tapes and I see no one unusual around the lab at the time of the explosion."

"Could someone have tampered with the videos?"

"I don't think so, but I'm no expert." His hands went up in a shrug.

"Another reason Lont Pol should be involved, she's more qualified to know," I reminded him.

"I really don't think she'd know any more than I do."

It was like hitting my head against a wall, so I gave it up. I would fill Lont Pol in personally. "I'm not sure I can do much myself."

"Well, there's more." He sat back, not looking at me. His shoulders slumped as he seemed to look across the bay that was now in deep shadows. My eyes followed his, taking in the playing dogs with the backdrop of the small waves hitting the beach. I wasn't going to like what was coming next, I could feel it. I stopped my hand as it automatically went to my coat for another pill. "Okay, let's hear it," I told him.

"Well, you see," he seemed to stumble over the words. "Dr. Ditterset is close to duplicating your parent's results. I think that's why the lab was sabotaged." He turned to me now, as if he wanted to emphasize his meaning, "I think she's found the cure!"

He must have seen the surprise on my face, my thoughts going to Killa. How much it would mean to her to be free of the blood bond; to have her family freed on Ligithia. "Please don't tell me all the results were destroyed in that explosion."

"No, of course not," he sounded annoyed with me that I'd even think that, "we are not stupid, Skip. We have duplicate records stored elsewhere but it did destroy some of her physical work."

"Some of her physical work?" Now we were getting to the part I was not going to like.

"We need some blood and tissue work done on Killa and since we also lost your Uncle's blood and DNA samples, we need some from you. I need you to bring Killa to Moss. That's why I asked Borger to let you come to Moss. It wasn't just to help with the security of the conference."

"NO!" I almost shouted it. He looked really annoyed now but I didn't care. "I'll not subject her to that danger. If someone did blow up the lab, then it's even more dangerous for her. Get another Ligithian."

"She's what your parents were working with. We need her!" Now he was almost shouting. "We will protect her as best we can. It is worth it! Besides, there is more."

Now my instincts were on high gear. "There is more?"

"Well," he was stammering now, unsure of my temper, he was hesitating to tell me.

"Out with it!" I was past being patient, "What else?"

"I had a special security feature added to the files. If anyone made copies of any files it would set up a flag that only I would see. Well, someone has made copies of the lab's files. Yours included. I'm afraid someone knows of you and Killa."

I just sat there stunned. "And my brother, Ray, too?"

He nodded, "I'm sorry. It wasn't just the explosion I was concerned about. The whole project has been compromised."

I sat stunned. The darkness was complete, I could only hear the waves slapping on the beach, their white caps barely visible. The dogs sensing I was upset had come over, their heads pushing my shoulders. I instinctively put my hands on them finding comfort in their presence. I hadn't realized how much they'd come to mean to me.

"Have you talked to Ray?" I knew my brother was off sector over in the Sol Clusters racing.

"Yes, I stopped over in Nestor before I came here. I talked to him before he left for Sol. He is the one who told me where your apartment was. I told him not to contact you, I don't want whoever it is alerted that I know. He's taking precautions."

"I'm not letting Killa go to Moss. It is just too dangerous. Can you get what you need here?" My head was swimming. I was relieved that my brother knew and was protecting himself and Julie but I was still stunned. All the years of protection my Uncle Jack had provided - gone.

Hibnet sat back. He nodded. "Alright. I can have my contacts at White Memorial Hospital here in Fulton do the lab work. But…"

I knew what was coming and beat him to it, "I'll go myself, I'll get some of my people to go to Moss. I'll find the god damn traitor."

He smiled and I realized it was what he had planned all along. Dr. Hibnet was a cunning negotiator and I fell right into his plans. "There is one more thing." He seemed to hesitate.

"Tell me!" I was sick of playing games.

"Well," he stood up, looking over the bay, "I got a note that says they will kill me and cripple the space station if I continue with the blood bond research."

I was stunned. A medical hospital being threatened? Time for me to go to Moss.

We walked back to the apartment in silence. I just waved at Artchie on my way to the elevator. He looked up briefly, and then went back to his books.

We were by the elevators when the dogs bolted back towards the front of the lobby. Killa came walking in, all four foot two inches of her. She saw the dogs; they almost dwarfed her small body. Hoover and Bear bounced around her. She looked over at me. It took her a few seconds to realize who I was with. "Dr. Hibnet?" Her eyes went wide as she looked at me then back at the doctor. "What?" she seemed to only be able to get the one word out.

Hill, who had been walking behind her, put the bags she'd been carrying on the front desk and then quickly left; going back out the door to the garage. She must have left something in her hover. I was glad she wasn't there to see Killa's eyes go from light lavender to total black, her pointed ears twitched rapidly and her white hair frizzed, actually standing on end. Ligithians were highly psychic and emotional people and their bodies react as such.

The dogs were sensitive to my moods, they were extra sensitive to Killa's, being with her most of the day. Both started barking. Their barks are deep throaty *woofs*, resounding deep *woofs*. I went over grabbing them by their actual collars and pushing Killa toward the elevator at the same time. Artchie looked up, surprise written all over his face. Thank goodness Killa's back was to him.

I put her in the elevator. "Skipper", she managed to gasp.

"Never mind, he's only visiting. Take the dogs up to the apartment." I pushed the button that sent her upstairs. Her eyes were returning to purple as the doors closed.

"I'm sorry," Hibnet began, "I didn't mean to alarm her."

"It's alright." I said, glancing over at Artchie, who had gotten his wheelchair up. "It's all set Artchie," I yelled over, "the dogs got too much fresh air. Killa just surprised them."

"Fresh air!" he laughed, "No such thing on Fulton, probably got over heated!"

"Yeah, right!" I waved at him, watched him settle back down to his books. I breathed a sigh of relief, thank goodness no one else had been in the lobby.

"I'm really sorry." Kel Hibnet whispered to me, keeping his eye on my front desk, "I didn't mean to cause any trouble."

The elevator had come back down. I looked around for Hill but she hadn't returned. Maybe she had been in a hurry. I pressed the fifth floor button along with my code and we went up to the apartment.

The dogs greeted us as we got off the elevator. Killa was over in the darkened part of the unfinished section of the apartment by the windows facing the city.

In the dim light her worried look reflected in the glass. I could tell her mind was far away, perhaps thinking of our life on Nestor, or perhaps our life on the space station. I walked over lightly tapping her arm, she looked over at me coming back to the here and now. "Skipper," worry dripped from her voice , "why is he here?"

"He came to warn me that someone might know about us." I answered her, "and a lab fire destroyed all the physical evidence mom and dad left of their work."

"A fire?" she echoed. I saw her eyes deepen to a dark purple.

"Killa," I touched her arm. "There is nothing to worry about. He just wants you to go to the hospital and take some tests, to replace what they lost. The fire destroyed physical evidence they had of us. Good news," I told her, "they think they have found the cure for the blood bond."

Her eyes softened, her eyes teared up, "That would be good, Skip." The dogs had come over rubbing against her small frame, trying to get her attention. Her hands automatically reached to scratch their floppy ears calming them. They sat on either side of her. "If you think it is necessary, I will do as you say."

I looked over to Dr. Hibnet standing by the elevator. He must have heard, he was smiling slightly, "Thank you Killa. I appreciate it."

"I don't do it for you." The anger in her voice was evident, it took me off guard. She'd never said too much about Moss, certainly never anything about Dr. Kel Hibnet.

The doctor seemed to be taken aback, "I never met to hurt you Killa. You have to believe me…"

"I don't believe you." Her body was rigid with rage. The dogs felt it and their attention focused on Hibnet. Suddenly, they stood up, growling at him sensing he was a danger.

"Stop it!" I yelled at both of them. They stopped growling but still stood on either side of Killa, crouched as if protecting her.

"I'd better go." He backed to the elevator pushing the button. "I'll be in touch Skip."

I didn't know what to say. I watched in silence as he got into the elevator and the doors closed. I listened as the elevator descended and then heard it land on the first floor. I looked over at Killa. She was looking out the windows toward the city of Fulton. Her mind was miles away. I could tell her thoughts were far away in the past.

"Why do you hate him?" I asked. Her violet eyes seemed to shine in the darkened part of my apartment, her white hair just emphasized her small delicate oval face. I had never seen her have just plain fury toward anyone, it wasn't in the Ligithian nature. Although sensitive and emotional they had a peaceful nature about them, a sharp contrast to their Laositian masters; who were reported to be cruel and hard. I had often wondered if my temper had come from my Highblood Laositian ancestry. Both my parents had been kind, generous and even tempered but I didn't know what my relatives had been like. My mother's mother had died shortly after Uncle Jack was born. I never knew her, and neither my mother nor Uncle Jack ever talked of her. My father had been from beyond the Sol sector and I knew little of his background.

Killa turned to me. The big long industrial windows in the unfinished part of the apartment let in enough light behind her to frame her tiny silhouette in an almost halo outline. In the distance I could see the top of the Dome, the glass building standing out above all of Fulton. I repeated my question, "Why the anger, Killa?"

I didn't get an answer as the noise of the elevator rising got my attention. The dogs bounded over to my surprise they weren't barking but only seemed excited. Still, no one knew my security code. I reached inside my jacket getting my gun out.

When the doors opened Hill stood there, her arms held the packages she'd left downstairs. She looked at me, giving me that disapproving look I knew so well. "Really, Chief, put that gun down and help me with these packages."

"Hill! How the hell did you get up here?"

Anyone else would have withered under my scowl, not my lieutenant. She shoved the bags in my arms, walked over to Killa, turned to me and without the least bit of guilt said, "I've watched you punch it in!" As if I should have known she was a snoop. The worse thing was, I should have!

Chapter Three

"You are not to just let yourself in!" I yelled at her in my strongest authoritative voice, pointing my finger right at her nose.

"Please Skipper, I told her to come up." Killa looked over at me, pleading Hill's case while the dogs jumped around rubbing against my lieutenant, licking her hand. They seemed to agree with Killa but then Hill had often given them bones. So their opinion was slanted by treats! Damn! I knew Killa was stretching the truth but I couldn't bring myself to disagree with her, not with all that had happened tonight.

"Just don't do it again!" I growled. "Where the hell did you go?"

"I forgot something." She didn't look at me but had turned to Killa, "Are you alright?"

Killa shook her head yes, but her eyes said no. Hill put her arm around my delicately small superintendent. Killa responded by hugging Hill and crying into her shoulder. My lieutenant glared at me as if I was responsible. "Why was Dr. Hibnet here?"

"How would you know Dr. Hibnet?" I walked over toward them. Hill had handed Killa a tissue and was ignoring me. "How did you know who he is?" I repeated the question in my strongest Chief of Police voice.

"Chief, everyone knows him. He's in the news all the time, he heads the medical space station, Moss." She sounded like I had accused her of being an idiot. Well, if the shoe fit. "What was he doing here?" She asked.

"He's a family friend." I told her.

To my dismay Killa angrily spat, "He's no friend of ours."

I hit my forehead with my hand in exasperation, "Killa!"

It was like giving a Ziltilian vampire the smell of blood, my lieutenant pounced, "Why, what has he done to you?"

"Nothing!" I snapped.

To my dismay, again Killa spoke up, "He's a bad man. I cannot talk of it." She turned to the dogs, "Come." She commanded them and headed up to the roof, leaving both Hill and I glaring at each other.

"You have to be more sensitive to her." My newest detective had the nerve to lecture me.

"You don't know what you're talking about." I snapped. "I have no idea why she hates the doctor. He's always been good to me. When I was on Moss for a year recovering from my racing accident he made sure I got the best of care and kept the reporters away from me. He was my parents' best friend."

"Well, he did something." She countered. "Killa is a kind soul, not one to hold on to hatred. It's not like a Ligithian to hold a grudge, they're sensitive beautiful people."

"You know," I found myself pointing my finger at her again, "just because you're from the same Orion sector doesn't make you the expert on Killa. I've known her all my life. I know what's best for her. I'll take care of it."

My lieutenant was sharp, "It? What does he want of her?"

Damn. "Nothing." I remarked, but Hill wasn't going to let that go.

"Hibnet always wants something," she dryly commented. "What's got her so upset?"

Killa had come back down. "The dogs are all set." She sounded her old self, calm and in charge. "I'm sorry Judy, I did not mean to get everyone upset. I'll have all the tests done and be done with it."

"Tests?" Hill was on high alert, "What tests?"

"She's going to go to White Memorial and have some lab work done to replace what was lost in the fire on Moss. It shouldn't take too long."

"You mean the fire that they had on the space station destroyed some data on Killa?" She walked over to me, "Has this something to do with what your parents were working on? Does this have something to do with the Ligithian blood bond?"

"It's none of your business!" I growled, turning my back on her. I walked into the kitchen, my stomach was reminding me I hadn't had anything to eat. Of course, Hill brazenly just followed me in. She had found out how my family went into hiding when she had been investigating a murder on Nestor. Now there was nothing she felt wasn't her business, especially since becoming close to Killa.

"You and your family hid on Nestor because your parents were killed. Is Killa in any danger? Are you in any danger?" She was just full of questions. I wished she'd shut up.

Killa, who had followed us into the galley, suddenly became alarmed, "Is that why he was here Skip? Does someone know we are alive?"

I couldn't lie to her, "It's possible. He thinks someone has been into his files."

Killa gasped and sat down at the table, stunned into silence. Hill sat next to her, trying to comfort her. I just stood there, not sure what to do as the dogs began to bark. They could feel the tension in the room.

Hill suddenly looked at me, pointing at the counter she said, "What are those chips doing on the counter?" Killa's eyes went to my pile of potato chips and my pepperoni sandwich that lay where I left them untouched.

"Skip! Your diet!" Her tone took on that nursemaid tone of disapproval and for a moment I thought I was six years old again and caught with my hand in the cookie jar.

"I was hungry." I started to explain.

"What is this!" The dogs were playing with my CosmicSub bag that I must have missed throwing in the garbage bin. Hill held it by her finger tips as if it was some kind of poison, waving it in front of me. "I don't believe it!" she sounded as if it was a personal affront to her. Killa gasped.

"I never got to eat it, the dogs tripped me and I dropped it on the floor. The dogs ended up eating it!" I moaned.

"You gave that kind of food to Hoover and Bear," Killa chastised me as if I was some kind of criminal.

"It was an accident..." But I didn't get to finish as my cellbutton rang with its emergency tone. I was actually relieved as I answered it. Issam was on the cell. I was needed at a robbery at the Dome. Within seconds Hill's tab was buzzing. She took it out, typing some reply. She was being called in too.

"Listen Killa," I told my superintendent. She was use to me being called out at all different hours, "Please stay here with the dogs. Don't go to your apartment. Sleep in my room. I don't know how long I'll be gone and when I get in I'll sleep on the couch. The dogs will stay right near you. Please." I tried never to order her to do anything. I knew and she knew that I could order her. I was relieved to see her nod. "How long is Artchie at the front desk?"

"A couple of more hours and then he'll lock up." She told me. "Mrs. March is on at seven tomorrow morning."

"Alright, lock the elevator, I'll override it when I come in," I warned her as I strapped on my gun harness and grabbed my suit coat off of the back of the chair which still had my badge and medicine in the pocket.

"Wake me when you get here, although the dogs will tell me." She smiled at the two Hiberian Hounds, scratching their long noses. They weighed more than she did by far but they were gentle with her, sensing her slight build vulnerability. Unlike the wrestling bounces with me, they were slightly brushing against her. They would keep her safe I thought as I the elevator doors closed and the two dogs book ended her.

Sharing an elevator with Hill is torturous as there was no escaping her. I tried to ignore my detective but she didn't get the idea.

"You haven't told her you are going to Moss, have you?" she demanded and even though I didn't answer her she continued, "She'll take it hard."

"I just decided tonight, how do you know I'm going to Moss?" Despite trying to ignore her curiosity her knowing got the better of me.

"I heard why Consulate Borger really came to your office today. Issam said you told him that we didn't have the manpower to go to Moss. But you are going now, aren't you?"

I was going to kill Issam for telling her but then there wasn't much Hill didn't find out. "You know, Hill, you are much too nosey for your own good. Yes, I'm going, Dr. Hibnet isn't easy to turn down."

"You mean he's good at blackmailing," she spat.

I looked at her strangely, she wasn't telling me something but I didn't get to pursue it further as the elevator doors opened and Artchie looked up from his books.

"Get a call, Chief Brown?" he said

"Yep, duty calls." I nodded to him as I went out the door, followed by Hill who just waved at him. I got into my Ant, Hill got into her hover and we head out to the Dome.

~~~~~~~~~~~~~~~~~

I got home after 3 in the morning. The dogs came running out and bleary eyed Killa came out to see if she could make me anything. I didn't dare tell her I had stopped with Issam at the all night Muffin Café and had eaten a sausage filled pancake. My Captain had his tea and a fresh fruit cup but this time I didn't feel the least bit of remorse as hunger conquers all guilt. I sent my bleary eyed old nursemaid back to bed and flopped down on my couch until my cellbutton woke me a couple of hours later.

As I drove Killa to the hospital my head was thumping and although I'd changed into another of my standard police suits and had managed a long shower, I felt crumpled. Killa sat quietly buckled up in the seat next to me, her hands folded on her lap, not saying anything. Despite the smallness of my little hover, she still seemed tiny. Even though I hadn't had much choice, I felt guilty having to put her through this. As we were sent up to the third floor, I was surprised to see Hill sitting in the waiting room.

She ignored me completely going to Killa. "I'll go in with you."

"No." I growled, "What are you doing here?" I was in no mood to be disagreed with and it angered me to see my lieutenant, who had been at the Dome's crime scene last night with me, showed no signs of having hardly any sleep. She was impeccably dressed with no hint of fatigue about her. Her nicely wrinkled free suit fit nicely on her trim body. Her light auburn hair was pulled back in a tight bun giving her an authoritative air while my half combed mop only seemed to emphasize my tiredness. She even had her tie on straight, while mine limply hung around my shirt collar.

"It's okay Skip," Killa touched my arm, "I don't mind her coming in, they won't let you in, you're a man."

Hill smugly took a seat. I told her smug look, "They won't let you go in with her. You're not a relative, even if you are a female."

"They'll let me in," she told me, confidence dripping with every word.

I didn't get to argue further as a nurse opened the office door and called Killa's name. Killa went through with Hill at her heels. The nurse went to stop her, "Sorry, patients only." I smirked, trying to keep the *I told you so laugh* from coming out of my mouth.

"Dr. Hibnet sent me, I'm to observe that everything is done correctly," she announced with some authority showing her badge as she did so.

"Oh, of course." The nurse stepped aside. The backwards glance Hill gave me was *I told you so smile*. Damn, how the woman could lie with such a straight face amazed me. Once again I was astounded at Dr. Hibnet's authority.

I settled down in one of the waiting seats. I rang Issam. We had talked last night at the Café about putting a team together to go to Moss. He wasn't happy about it but promised to have some names for me by mid-day. I checked in and he was working on it. He also assured me that the incident at the Dome had been resolved fully. It had not gotten to the news reporters, no mention of it in any of the media. I breathed a sigh of relief.

Last night the Senator from Hilda had walked into his office and found the Senator from Casey going through his desk. He immediately called the Dome Security Police who immediately called Issam, who then called me. It was a political hot potato. Hill was on call duty so she got called in as backup.

When I got there they were both yelling at each other. Senator Tutz wanted charges brought against Senator Cruse. Cruse was claiming he was looking for his cuff link that he'd dropped earlier when he was in Tutz's office. Tutz wasn't buying it and wanted Cruse arrested. Hill had gotten on her knees and searched the area and found a cuff link, handling it over to Cruse and shutting up Tutz, especially when I reminded the senator that it wouldn't look good in the news if he was falsely accusing another senator. Of course, I knew that Hill had handed over her own cuff link but kept it to myself. I would have Consulate Borger have a talk with Cruse. It was now a political issue.

I leaned my head against the back of the chair and immediately fell asleep. It was Hill's rough kick that awoke me. Killa had several Band-Aids on her arms where they had taken blood and skin. I swore under by breath. She'd have bruises. Ligithians skin wasn't as thick as others and they easily bruised. Some researchers felt it was their slavers that had limited their breeding to a small pool that were to blame.

Hill walked out with us. "I'll take Killa home," she announced.

"No. Don't you have to get back to work." I snapped. I didn't make it a question but a statement.

"I have plenty of time coming, Chief." She stared me down, knowing I knew she never took any time off but worked long hours. I almost felt guilty about snapping at her, almost. I was going to snap again but Killa interrupted.

"It's fine, Skip. We're going out for tea at the TeaGarden, would you like to come too?" Her purple eyes sparkling, knowing I would rather be anywhere else.

I hated tea. I hated the dainty elite atmosphere of the TeaGarden. I preferred the workman's black hearty java or nothing. I gave in; let Hill take her home. I declined the invite, helping Killa into Hill's craft. I watched them leave, I could see them jabbering away in the front seat.

How had Hill injected herself into my life? Then I felt guilty again, a feeling that was occurring a lot lately. Killa had few friends, most thought of her as a Casean Dwarf, not realizing her Ligithian heritage. Hill was from the Orion Sector and knew who Killa really was. My lieutenant knew of her heritage and her psychic sensitivity. I was being selfish and needed to try harder to be more attuned to my old nursemaid's feelings. It was the least I could do after all Killa had done for me and my brother. Perhaps Hill was a necessary evil. I shuddered at the thought. Oh well. Such is life.

The office was abuzz, as usual. With the Dome in session, it was always busy. It was really hot, over 110 degrees out and every fan was on high causing even more noisy chaos than normal. Issam had the list of who he thought was needed for the Moss security team. He had canceled their present assignments, making them available to go with me.

Carl sat in my office going over the list. He wiped the sweat off his brow that was seeping into and stinging his wide slanted amber eyes. He opened his tab, putting the screen up in front of me. On the top of the list was Elly Gren. She was my explosive expert.

"You might need her if they try to disrupt the conference with explosives." Issam was pointing to her name. "She just finished up over in Logan so she's free."

I agreed with him. Although a rather plain short dumpy woman, who no one would notice in a crowd, Elly was the best in her field. They had nicknamed her

"Dynamite", in reality she was rather drab in her dress and her only interest outside the office was bird watching. She was an expert on avian life throughout the planets. Yet despite her rather calm life, Elly's eyes lit up when defusing an explosive, or when she talked of the new techniques criminals were using in the art of bomb-making.

I was also bringing Marcus Nettleson. He was an older man near retiring but with tons of experience. He was a data analyst expert, up on all the latest computer technology. There wasn't much he hadn't seen as a regular cop and as a detective. He was a mentor to many of my younger cops. How often I heard "let's ask Marcus". He'd be a good second in command. I could count on him to keep things organized.

The third name was Lara Null. She was originally born on that hell hole, Skantie Row. Her mother was a prostitute. Lara left at fourteen, or should I say escaped. She lied about her age and became a soldier. Excelling in marksmanship, she earned her way up to Captain of her own squad. Leaving after a few years she became a highly paid mercenary and then took the money she made and went on to better herself by getting not only an undergraduate degree but also did graduate work.

Being a sharp shooter before helped her become one of my top detectives, she'd probably make Captain soon. She was alert and relentless in her pursuit of clues, besides being a weapon expert. She was also absolutely gorgeous with long legs and long blonde hair. She had advanced degrees in psychology and often would discuss the whys of cases; getting into the criminals' minds. She'd also spent several years on Moss doing her graduate work in psychology. All this and she was barely into her thirties.

The last name was Fred Stoshingburg. Issam thought Fred would be good as pure muscle. Although

Fred was large and seemed clumsy, he could also fight with the best of them and he was an observant type individual. He had to be, as a drug enforcer he needed to keep his wits and senses about his surroundings. He also knew a lot about the drug trades, if there was a hint of anything going on he'd know and he knew criminals; their records and their faces.

They all sat in the conference room. The two overhead fans were wildly turning and several other fans were blowing hot air from the corners. With all the wind blowing, I was lucky I could stand up. "Hey, guys shut a few of the fans off." I remarked and got moans in response. At least the Medical Operation Space Station was totally climate controlled. I'd point that out if anyone gave me a hard time about going.

No one, however, gave me a hard time. They were professionals ready to do a job. Lara was the only one beside myself that had been to the space station. Issam set up a screen and I described the station itself.

It looked almost like a small world made of moving rings with the two smallest rings at the tips then fanning out to a large middle ring. Even just a picture of it was impressive. "It has nine rings. It is the middle ring, Ring Five, that the city of Eupepsia is located. It contains twenty-five thousand inhabitants over an equivalent thirty miles around and two miles wide. This is the ring we will be spending most of our time in. It is at their Herriden Convention Center that the conference is being held. Five hundred VIP's plus their entourages from all the human sectors will be attending, including our own Dome representatives."

Lara spoke up, "When I was there, it took a little while to get use to life on the space station. The city is divided into two sections Eupepsia One and Eupepsia Two; when one is in daylight the other is on the other side of the ring in night mode. The reason is that the space station is in constant hospital use, which means they need full time, all time operation. Thus there are two twelve hour shifts. It's quite unique, but believe me it works well. They joke as the medical staff calls themselves either Eupies1 or Eupies2. It's almost like there are two similar societies, yet separated by sleep time."

I nodded acknowledging what she said. "We will most likely be Eupies1," I told them. "As long as you are on Ring Five you'll not need any special equipment. That ring is what I call "normal" living. Its gravitational pull is exactly as most of our Sector worlds; no grav boots, oxygen equipment or other adaptive equipment is needed. All the rings are basically "human" oriented. They'll let you know if any special equipment is needed to go onto a certain area."

Lara spoke up again, "Eupepsia One and Eupepsia Two are almost identical. Each has schools, hotels, and even matching manmade lakes. It really is two societies with the same purpose - supplying and servicing the space station as a hospital."

"How long is this going to take? When can we tell our families we will be back?" Marcus commented, always the common sense older guy.

"Well, we have an early morning Jump tomorrow, so be at the Jump port before seven. We Jump to Logan's Moon and then have a layover so we won't be getting into the ferry relay station until late afternoon."

"Ferry relay station?" Fred blurted out, sounding totally confused.

"They have a satellite that circles Moss. Since they are worried that the energy from the Jumps may interrupt all the sensitive instruments on the space station, all traffic has to go there first and take a space shuttle to the hospital. It is also why there is a communication delay on the Space Station. Warn anyone you may want to keep in touch with that there is a delay. No cellbuttons work for 'off planet' calls. They do have one Jumpline that goes directly to the hospital but it is tightly controlled and used only by top officials and for emergency use or for informational medical records they need."

"And how long do you think we'll be there?" Marcus asked again.

"Well, we will arrive two days before the conference which will last two days. Unless we have problems we should be back within a week."

Marcus nodded, followed by all the others. Issam passed out a tab folder to each of them. "Our main players are all in these folders, study them before tomorrow." My Captain opened his pointing to the first page. "You all are aware of Dr. Hibnet, he's the main administrator on Moss. Important guy, so pay attention!"

"Isn't Lont Pol the head of the police out there?" Lara Null asked. "She was here last year, she's really sharp. I really liked her."

"Yes, she's on page two." I told them. "She'll be our main contact. We are to work with her and Lorna Lune, her second in command. They have a regular police force of about fifty. Let's not step on their toes but work with them. I repeat, *with them*, folks."

They all nodded but I wasn't really concerned because they were used to going to all the sector planets and working with other police forces. Of course, Moss was a different equation with their highly educated hierarchy. I hadn't told Lont we were coming. I'd send her a message from the Ferry station to give her a slight heads up. I didn't want her storming into Hibnet's office until I was there to defuse it.

"I heard that some get space sickness?' Elly said. "Is this true?"

Lara answered her, "Not many, just bring some disorient pills. It passes quickly if you get it. Some think it's because of the complication of the different gravitational pulls. Some are sensitive to it."

"Gravitational pulls!" Fred didn't like the sound of that, his big frame making his seat creak as he sat up in alarm.

I tried to explain, "Listen, I'm no scientist, I've read several articles on it. The bottom of the center stem of the space station is made of positively charged atonimum; it causes a "heavy" effect. I've heard that black holes work on the same principle. Anyways, each of the rings spin at a calculated rate causing a gravitational effect. Consequently, each ring is regulated the way they want it to be. An example, Ring four is the burn ward. They actually keep it with less gravity, thus helping the burn patients heal better."

Fred went to ask another question, but I cut him off. "I really don't know anymore. You'll get a feel for it when you are there. Or to tell you the truth you'll not feel a thing, it's an amazing place. Just go with it, Fred." He nodded at me but I could tell he was skeptical.

I decided to tell them of the year I spent there. "Look, as most of you know or don't know, I was in a racing accident, I spent a year recovering. I was only eighteen." I heard a few gasps but no one said anything. I continued, "They were great there and put me back together. So know that the work they do is phenomenal, so let's help them out. They provide a great service for the entire Federation, especially to humans."

They all looked down at their tab folders as I explained the lab explosion and how Dr. Hibnet felt it wasn't an accident but actual sabotage and how he was afraid that someone would disrupt the convention. Lastly I explained of the death threat to him and the threat to do damage to the space station. When we left the conference room everyone looked comfortable with our mission, all clutching their tabs to study before the Jump tomorrow.

I passed Hill's desk. She was busy on her computer, talking on her cellbutton. She ignored me. Oh well.

Issam followed me back to my office. "I wish you weren't going, I don't mind going myself. It really isn't safe for you there, Chief."

"I'll be fine. Hibnet wants me there, I really do owe him." I shook my head at my Captain, "just remember it'll be hard to get ahold of me so I've told the Consulate you have full authority. Call on him if you need him."

Issam nodded his head, "I'll do my best."

I had no doubt he would. "I need that Killa is protected." I told him. "If Hibnet is correct then someone may know of her and finish off what they started with my parents."

"I'll watch her," came from Hill who was standing in my doorway. If looks could kill, she'd be dead.

"Hill, have you no shame? You have no sense of privacy, of decorum, of knocking to let me know you are there?" I shook my head at her. I noticed Issam smile.

She actually blushed a little when she answered me. "Killa trusts me. I'll stay at your place. She'll stay there instead of her apartment if she knows I'm there."

Before I could bark at her to mind her own business, Issam spoke up, "She's right, Chief. Killa will be as protected as if you were there. Killa will listen to her. Let her do it."

Of course he was right. I swallowed my pride and nodded my head, "Okay, just alert the cops in the neighborhood to keep their eyes out during the day. Check in with Issam each night."

"Will do," she said, then smiled, "we'll practice on our healthy recipes for when you return." She scuttled away before I could say anything. Issam left laughing. I just turned my fan on high and scowled. Somehow I think I lost another Hill battle and I had no idea how. Worse, I couldn't remember winning any.

Chapter Four

I heard noises, it was still dark out. I was sleeping on my den couch. Killa was sleeping in my bedroom. The den telescreen monitor said it was 04:30. I jumped up, someone or someones were in my apartment. I grabbed my gun under my pillow. I didn't dare make noise just in case it wasn't Killa, instinctively I knew it wasn't her. Ligithians are super quiet, being small they don't have heavy footsteps. Where were the damn dogs? I had ordered them to sleep in my bedroom with Killa. They should be going wild right now.

Shaking my head, getting the sleep out of me, I inched forward. The sliding den doors were closed, my heart skipped a beat. I hadn't closed them.

Slowly opening the doorway, the noises became more distinct. A light was shining from the galley. Someone was searching the draws of my kitchen. My head flashed with pictures of dead dogs, of Killa being hurt. I jumped out, racing around the corner, banging my knee on the entranceway. "Freeze, right where you are!" I pointed my gun at a small figure that was in one of my kitchen drawers.

A shocked Hill turned around; her back was to me as she was fiddling with my silverware. Killa was sitting at the table, a cup of tea clutched in her hands. Bear and Hoover were sleeping underneath. "Chief?" My lieutenant half smiled at the gun, "don't you think you should turn the gun on? Is it even charged?" Her mouth was in a half smirk.

"What the hell!" I growled lowering my gun, rubbing my knee. "It's four in the morning! I don't turn the gun on until I shoot. Regulations, remember?" I sarcastically grumbled.

"It's 4:38 to be exact, glad to see you follow some rules." Hill quipped, "What are you doing up?"

"What are you doing here?" I growled, also including Killa in my displeasure. She just stared back at me, sleep dust still filling her purple eyelids yet there was amusement in her eyes.

"I'm going to stay here." Hill looked incredulously at me, as if I was loony. As if she was reminding a child. "Don't worry, I didn't use your code. Killa let me in."

"I know you're staying here!" I spat as I pointed at the clock on my java maker. "I'm not leaving until 6:30!"

"I just wanted to get settled before I have to leave for work." She pointed at several large suitcases that were by my elevator. My one small suitcase that I'd packed the night before looked tiny compared to her big luggage.

"Really, Hill?" I looked back at her, "It isn't a permanent move you know." I also noticed a large portable bed she must have brought with her. How she had managed to lug that up the elevator was anyone's guess. My head hurt. The dogs stretched under the table as if they agreed with me, one big loud "woof" as they settled back down. Even they knew it was too early for any sane person.

I noticed Hill's grin as she took my almost naked body in. I only had a pair of boxer shorts on. I felt my face reddened, she just grinned even more. "Nice shorts," she quipped.

"Thanks," as I turned and headed into my bedroom. I wasn't giving her the satisfaction of knowing how embarrassed I felt. Of course, I had on the pair that said "Chief" inside big hearts, a joke gift from my detectives a few Yuletide seasons ago, pre-Hill. Perfect timing I chided myself, I had never worn them but I hadn't wanted to wake Killa up when I'd gotten in at midnight and these were in the den drawer where I had shoved them two years ago.

I grabbed my bathrobe, took a shower and dressed in my suit. I didn't even dare have a cup of Java as my stomach had trouble on Jump trips. I took another disorient pill, although it wasn't going to help much. I hadn't eaten since yesterday and that didn't matter much either as I just wouldn't have anything to throw up, but would still heave my inners anyways. I took one of my little blue pills; I didn't need to have an episode, although the last one had been on Nestor six months ago and before that almost two years had passed. I usually controlled it myself thanks to Dr. Lily Issam's calming exercises. I should be fine. I grabbed my gun, my spare was already in the suitcase, both were fully charged.

Hill was now dressed in her work suit. Her hair tied tightly in a bun, her regulation tie just right, and her standard shoe pumps shiny; the perfectly dressed rookie detective. Unlike myself, no matter what I did I looked crumpled and wrinkled. Give her a few years, she'd crinkle up under the pressures of fighting crime, of the senselessness of it all, especially the homicides.

"Killa, don't go out without Lieutenant Hill." I warned my blood bond carefully not to make it too strong to be taken as a command. "Stay inside. Have you got enough people scheduled for the front desk?"

"Yes, Skip. Artchie helps a lot. He knows everything that has to be done. He even helps me with the dogs. So don't worry!" Killa was double checking my suitcase. Even though she is blood bonded to me, she still feels she's my nursemaid. She thought of my brother Ray and me as her own sons. She was all we'd had for a mother after my parents had been killed. "Please don't worry, Judy is very capable policewoman." Killa reached up patting Hill on the arm emphasizing her point. Hill was helping her refold my clothes. I bit my tongue, now was not the time to lose my temper.

It was amusing to have a Ligithian telling me not to worry. They are the biggest worry warts in the universe. Killa was very sensitive, feeling everyone's feelings in a psychic way. Consequently like all the slaves from Ligithia, she was always on the alert, taking everything into her senses; trying to "serve" as best she could. It could be maddening sometimes.

"Just remember, communication with Moss is slow." She nodded, she remembered. "Still, Captain Issam will get word to me if you need." She nodded again.

"Please be careful, Skipper, please." She came over and hugged me, her eyes going deep purple. "Do not trust him, please."

"You know me, I don't trust anyone," I told her, hearing a guffaw from Hill. I glared at my Lieutenant but it, of course, had no effect.

I grabbed my suitcase. They both waved at me as I headed towards the elevator. I heard them laughing in the kitchen as I left. I felt guilty, Killa never laughed with me, Hill was good for her.

In my underground parking garage I could already feel the coming heat. The outside temperature was already over a hundred. I looked wistfully at my turbocycle. I wouldn't be riding it this weekend. I ran my hand along the seat, feeling the beauty of the bike, my one really big extravagance, spending way too much for it. It was the closest I'd ever come to feeling the speed I had loved so much in racing. Oh well.

I climbed into my small Ant hovercraft and headed to the Jump Station. I parked in the long-term parking lot and caught a shuttlehover to the main entrance of the Jump Station. The heat made me hurry to the entrance. The rush of cool air as I entered the station felt great. It was just seven but the station was full, a lot of early Jumps. The huge schedule board told me my Jump was on time at gate five. I zipped through security as I was well known by the guards and took my seat in the lobby waiting to be called to my gate. Lara was already there as were Elly and Marcus. Of course big Fred came rushing in as they were calling our Jump. He was all crumpled with his hair sticking out at all angles.

"Sorry, over slept," he mumbled as he followed me down the ramp entrance. I noticed pieces of his clothes hanging out his suitcase. Oh well, at least he'd made it.

We all settled in adjacent seats. The white soft cushioned seats slowly conformed to everyone's body, supposedly relaxing its occupant. It was a useless exercise for me. I made sure I sat on an aisle. It gets tedious stepping over someone as I rushed to the lavatory.

"Welcome everyone." Our pilot came in on the speakers located in the top of the conform chairs. "We'll be at Logan's Moon in a couple of hours. You'll find your connecting Jump schedule on your cellbuttons or ask an attendant. As soon as we reach orbit and Jump, feel free to visit the Club Car and get yourself something to eat."

Fred, who hardly fit in his conform seat, smiled, "Great, I didn't get any breakfast."

I just moaned. I knew when we reached orbit and jumped, I didn't need the overhead sign to tell me it was alright to leave my seat; my stomach told me. Two hours later when we got out at Logan's Moon Station, I stumbled out, glad my stomach was returning to normal but knowing I had another Jump to make, a much longer Jump of six hours. My body moaned.

Logan's Moon station was bustling. It was a huge Jump hub with three times the gates that Fulton Station has. We had a three hour wait until our Jump headed to the space station. Our waiting area filled up with obvious patients heading to the medical facility. There were plenty of people in wheelchairs and some on gurneys with nurses checking their IVs.

Most of those waiting for the Jump seemed nervous. A high feeling of anxiety filled the waiting area. I had been used to it as a child. When we traveled with my doctor parents, we were taught to behave and be quiet and not to bother the anxious patients on our return trip to our home on Moss. Even Fred seemed effected, being unusually quiet. The big guy hardly said two words. Only Lara, who'd spent several years on Moss, seemed unbothered, typing voraciously in her tab, chatting with Elly as she did so. Marcus tried to sleep but I could tell he wasn't having any luck.

"Is it going to be like this on the station?" he leaned over to me so as not to be heard. I noticed his hair was almost all white now, his eyebrows were bushy gray but his eyes were still bright matching his intelligent brain. I liked Marcus, he was what he seemed, a nice guy.

"Not really," I answered him. "The City is normal, where you'll mostly be. The medical staff keep it as normal as they can for their families. Of course, the other rings are more of a hospital atmosphere; some of the rings are more intense than others. The fourth ring, the burn unit for instance, has some really awful stuff. "

"Where did you spend your time?" He asked me.

Medical Operations Space Station - M.O.S.S.

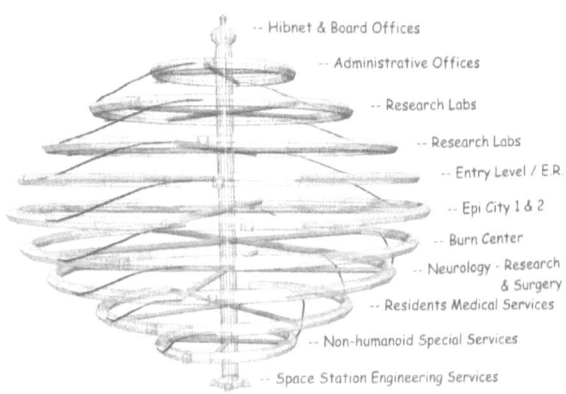

- Hibnet & Board Offices
- Administrative Offices
- Research Labs
- Research Labs
- Entry Level / E.R.
- Epi City 1 & 2
- Burn Center
- Neurology - Research & Surgery
- Residents Medical Services
- Non-humanoid Special Services
- Space Station Engineering Services

Of course, as a kid, I'd spent it on Eupepsia One, the first city, Ring Five but I couldn't tell him of that. "Well, I spent the first few months in the emergency ring - Ring Six. I had been burned badly in the accident but I'd also broken most of my bones. So they put me back together there and not on Ring Four."

"Gesh, damn," he said, "that's awful."

"To tell you the truth Marcus," I shrugged, "I don't remember much of that because I was in a coma. When I woke up, I spent the next eight months on the fourth ring recuperating. It's there that I learned to walk again, feed myself and overall become human again. At first, they thought I was going to be blind but that ended up being fixed."

"Gee, Chief, I didn't realize…." He was at a loss for words so I saved him from trying to find the correct words.

"I was only nineteen, I recovered fine. Went on to school and became a cop instead of a race car driver." I shrugged again as if it was no big deal. Of course it had been, but life is what it is. I didn't tell him of the time I'd spent on Ring Three, the brain operations and then learning to cope with my epileptic seizures, but it wasn't something I shared with many. Wrong or right, it made me feel lacking, not a good feeling to share with someone.

"Well, this sure will be an experience, I've never been on a space station before," he commented, his excitement was catchy.

"This is one of the biggest space stations in all the human sectors." I told him. "But strangely you'll find you get used to it real fast. They have done wonders with the city of Eupepsia on Ring Five. The inhabitants call the two cities Eupie1 and Eupie2.

Fred Stoshingburg, who'd been listening, just grunted and shook his head, "Crime is crime, anywhere you go. Criminals are criminals. Low life is low life." It was an amazingly introspected deep comment from him. The big guy constantly surprised me.

When we boarded for the last Jump I popped another disorient pill but it didn't matter, I spent the first three hours throwing my empty guts up and then finally had tired myself out so much I spent the rest of the time sleeping. Fred tapped me on the shoulder when the pilot announced we were coming into orbit around Moss's satellite station terminal. My head felt like it had been pounded against a rock wall, with my body not feeling much better. I gathered my suitcase and followed the rest of them out to the disembarkment lobby. Fred and I waited for Elly, Marcus and Lata to claim their luggage, we had just brought carry-ons. As we waited for the others, I was glad to have the time to recuperate. My stomach settled down and my head cleared. By the time the other three had rejoined us I actually was feeling a bit hungry.

We found the ferry heading to Moss and took seats. Again, we waited as the wheelchairs and gurneys were loaded. The atmosphere was a bit tense and everyone was quiet. The space station was such a sight that they all spent the half hour ride looking out the portholes, including Lara. We flew right into Ring Six's welcoming center. Only the truly bad cases were flown right to the appropriate treatment Ring. Ring Six was the patient entry and emergency level, I had been flown into that Ring but of course I had no recollection of it. Other Rings also catered to other species that were not human and could handle special shuttles depending on gravity needs and oxygen levels.

"Please allow those in wheelchairs and the gurneys to go first," an attendant announced. We were the last off. The tube entrance into the space station's welcoming lobby was all decorated in bright pastel colors with huge cascades of flowers flowing down the sides. It provided a much needed relaxed atmosphere. The cheerful atmosphere worked as I noticed my four detectives seemed less tense. I helped with the extra luggage Lara and Elly had brought. Lara had packed her long range sharp shooter guns and Elly had her explosives detection gear. I knew Lont Pol had her own equipment, but Elly and Lara had insisted on bringing their own. They trusted their own gear and I couldn't blame them.

At the end of the tube walkway was a receptionist. Her smile seemed genuine and she had a helpful cheerful attitude. Although she had a regulation lab hospital lab coat on it was a pastel blue instead of white. Unfrightening to the income patients was my first thought on seeing her. To my surprise, she knew who I was even before I had my badge out. "Chief Brown, we've been expecting you."

I noticed my picture had automatically come up on her tabloid register. "Great," I nodded to the others, "we'll be heading right in then."

"Well, Dr. Hibnet is going to send someone down…" she started to say, but I immediately cut her off.

"No need." I used my official Chief Brown voice, leaving no room for disagreement. After all, technically my authority overrides just about everyone including Dr. Hibnet, but I didn't need to tell her that I'd been here before since my level of authority shone brightly on her tabloid. I could read it from where I stood. Still, Dr. Hibnet was a force to be reckoned with, her eyes showed doubt but before she could say anything I headed into the reception area.

"Wait, you need your identification buttons," she was yelling after us.

I let my detectives hurry by me as I turned back, "No, we don't get those." And I hurried to follow them. The identification buttons were used to track anyone entering the space station. I didn't want my people tracked. I saw the receptionist speaking into her cellbutton but Lara had already gotten the four of them and the bags into a waiting tram and I jumped in as the door was closing and the train took off.

I saw her push the Eupepsia One Station switch in front of her seat. She looked at me, I nodded that it was where we would go. We headed out, the tram that could hold about twenty held only us. Fred took up most of the bench in front of me. I heard Elly in her seat behind me gasp as we entered Ring Six's clear glass tube that connected to Ring Five. For about ten seconds it felt like you were floating out in space with the myriad of stars' lights surrounding the space station glowing all around us. Then we came into the Eupie Station One and we all got out leaving the clear tube's view behind us and entered into a park-like area leading into the city itself. As we pulled the luggage down the ramps leading to the street I spotted a cab.

"Come on," I told them, but everyone other than Lara and I had stopped and were staring around them. "Come on I want to get to Lont's police station before Hibnet realizes it," I yelled back at the three gawking detectives.

"It's a frigging city." Fred blurted out as he dragged one of Elly's big suitcases behind him.

"Yeah, watch that suitcase!" Elly roared at him, "I'll have your ass if you break anything! That's delicate equipment, asshole!"

That got Fred's attention and he slowed down before the luggage hit a side wall leading down to the cab but still muttered, "It's a frigging city."

"I showed you pictures!" I reminded them but I knew it still took everyone who visited by surprise. In the distance, several tall buildings could be seen. Although we were on the outskirts of the city proper, it looked like any urban street with traffic and people.

The cab driver looked puzzled at us, "I'm not getting a reading from you guys. Your identifications buttons aren't working." He was referring to the buttons that emitted a signal to him of who we were. He was talking about the identification buttons I had refused at the reception area.

I showed him my police badge. "We need to go to Center Level Crossover Five." He looked strangely at me, typing in his tabloid on his steering wheel which came up with the same screen the receptionist had; my beautiful mug taking up half the screen.

"Alright," he half stuttered, "Dr. Hibnet would like you to check in with him. That's what the message says on my tab."

"Thank you," I managed to say calmly, although I was annoyed it wasn't this man's fault. "Just take us to Center Level Crossover Five."

"Yes Sir." Lara and Elly sat next to him, while the three men sat in the back. It was tight, with Fred taking up half the seat. I could tell the driver wanted to ask questions but on Moss everyone was under orders to not ask questions. It was felt that patients and their families were going through enough and no extra burden was to be added.

Both Fred and Marcus were looking out the open windows, staring at the multitude of businesses we were passing. "Look at the sky!" Fred burst out, "It's a sky!"

I noticed the driver looked up; he probably was wondering what was wrong with the sky. "It's normal today," he said. "No rain coming today, no clouds either. They're giving us a good day!" He looked back at us, "You know it's controlled, don't you? This is a space station."

Fred snorted, "Of course we know!"

Lara and Elly were laughing. "Are you sure, Fred?" Lara yelled back at him.

"Funny." He slumped down in the seat.

"This is amazing though," Marcus pointed outside. "You'd never know it's not a real city."

"Of course it's a real city." The taxi driver proudly announced, "It's just a controlled city, we got everything everyone else has." The pride in his voice was so pronounced, it was inescapable. "We got everything that everyone else has in the Crab Sector, we're full citizens."

"Yes, you are." I assured him, "We're from Fulton Station and we know your representatives Butive and Everotl, both are highly respected at the Dome." I knew it was a sore point to those who were permanent residents of Moss. They felt they were not looked upon as equals with the rest of the sector planets. They should try living on Fulton, I thought. We didn't even get to vote but I still tried to placate the taxi driver.

"Ah, so you're from the government." As if that explained it, we were ignorant government workers. Ah, now who was making assumptions? He must have seen the look on my face as he shut up.

He took it upon himself to point out the schools, parks, theater, movie theaters. He pointed out the Herriden Convention Center with the attached ten story hotel. Elly almost said we were staying there but caught herself, we were supposed to be here on the Q-T.

He finally turned down a side road taking us to the Center Level Crossover Five doorway, it was a passageway to the space station's core. We got out and as we were getting our luggage out of the trunk, a woman came walking down the ramp that led to the center tube that led to the actual middle of the space station. The middle was a black cylinder made partly of atonimum. The heaviest particle ever discovered that held the space station not only in orbit around a distant sun but also was an intricate structural part of space station itself.

"Hi Lorna." I was glad to see Lont's assistant, Lorna Lune. She nodded to us, walking over to the cab, she gave him her card and he swiped it. He left, heading back into the city.

"Hi Chief Brown, Captain Pol is waiting for you." She looked at my four detectives. Lorna, besides being an excellent administrative assistant, was also a smart cop. I saw her assessing all four, her eyes lingered on Fred Stoshingburg. It was hard not to be awed by his size. "Let's go, she's anxious to see you."

"Let me guess, Hibnet's been calling." I remarked as we went up the ramp to two large glass doors that automatically slid open.

"Yes, he's been calling. I've been telling him Lont's not in yet. I don't think he's real happy." Lorna was as tall as I was. She was quite beautiful. Dark oval eyes matched her dark chocolate skin and made her white curly hair stand out. I noticed Fred was quite stunned by her, he hadn't said a word since she'd appeared but kept staring at her. Of course, that irritated Lara and Elly, who kept bumping into him, trying to distract him. Marcus brought up the rear. As we entered the passageway, he kept looking over the side. We were in a clear tube that led to the center black cylinder of the space station. It was in this center section that all administrative offices were located, including their central police station.

From the sides of the tube, you could look up the and down the cylinder along with a view of the back of the Rings. It was a confusing sight. We got into a tramway. There was no one but us on it so we comfortably sat as it accelerated toward the cylinder center. It was fascinating to watch the rings from the inside, although we could only see Tube Five with Six above and a little of Four below. Open space could be seen beyond, just slight glimpses of the stars. Somehow it was calming without knowing why it was. Fred was looking a little green around the gills.

"How you feeling?" I asked him.

"A little under the weather, I think I got that space station sickness." He seemed to get even paler.

"Here, you big baby." Lara handed him two pills. "You'll be feeling fine in a few minutes."

Fred swallowed them dry. "Thanks" he mumbled.

We came to a set of elevators. Lorna swiped her card and one of the doors swung open. It could fit all of us and then some. She pressed a button on the panel and we felt ourselves going up. When the doors opened it was onto a wide grey colored hallway. We followed her down to the first opening. We entered into a grayish reception room. Different shades of grays covered each wall. No windows, no paintings, just gray walls. The white reception desk stood out. Several uniformed police personnel were busy watching monitors and working on tabloids behind the long counter. I was greeted warmly by the main receptionist, "Well, welcome back Chief Brown." Seeing the others she nodded to them. "I hope you all had a good trip here."

"We managed," I smiled at Buntie. She was from Atlise, her drawling accent gave her away. Atlise was one of the friendliest planets in the Crab Sector. It took a five hour Jump from Logan's Moon. It was also the most exotic planet, its one large continent was covered in thick jungle and had the most fascinating animals and plants in the entire sector. No one hurried on Atlise. Life was slow but deliberate. Deliberate in the sense that life was to be enjoyed. It was originally built for the famous Thorne Atlise, a tycoon, who was the inventor of the original silent hovercraft propellant.

That was more than three hundred standard galactic years ago. Thorne Atlise had never married nor had children. Thus on his death, he gave the planet away to his several hundred servants. It was the last planet to be admitted to the Crab Sector and enjoys a booming tourist industry, only Hilda does better.

"Let me buzz her that you all are here." She drawled, although she needn't have bothered, Lont Pol was walking into the room from a side hallway.

"Hello Chief." She crossed the room extending her hand to me. She was a small woman perhaps ten years older than me. Everything about her screamed compact and direct. I knew like Issam, she had achieved several levels of combat achievement. She wore her black hair in a tight knitted bun letting her sharply pointed ears dominate her features. Like Issam, she was from Castor's Asteroid Belt. They breed them small but tough.

Although she wore her regulated grey suit, it was tailored to fit her, emphasizing her shapely curves. She wore tall black high heels that I would bet would bring down any foe within seconds. Her face wasn't beautiful but it had distinction, with wide slanted amber eyes and a rich full mouth and small but prominent nose. Her no-nonsense air let her dominate any room and probably scared the bejeesus out of her foes.

"Hi Lont. I'd like you to meet Elly Gren, Marcus Nettleson, Lara Null and Fred Stoshingburg." As I pointed each out, she nodded at Lara, whom she'd met on Fulton.

"Welcome." She clipped, "Lorna will get you settled in our back rooms. It contains cubicles for each of you and a main conference room for meetings. Chief, if you'll join me in my office, I'd appreciate it."

I followed her down to her office. I heard my detectives as they were introduced to the personnel and then led off to grab their desk stations. Elly was again yelling at Fred to be careful with her equipment. Stoshingburg was grumbling back at her.

When we were in Lont's office, she shut the door. Before I could say much of anything she turned, "Why are you here? Glad you gave me a little heads up. I got the tab message this morning!" Sarcasm dripped from her voice.

Just as I had suspected, Dr. Hibnet hadn't discussed the extra security he had requested and gotten. "I'm sorry Lont, if I'd had time I would have cabled you earlier but I knew with the communication delay, I'd arrive at the same time. I should have guessed Hibnet wouldn't tell you. I sent the tab note when we left Logan's Moon hoping you'd get it before we arrived." I didn't tell her I didn't want her to know too long before I arrived, she'd have confronted Hibnet and that wouldn't have gotten us anywhere.

She went around sitting at her desk, her hand pounded on the desk. "That bastard," she spat, "I'd like to take what little balls he has and kick them out into space."

I couldn't help but smile, she probably could do exactly that given her martial arts capabilities. I'd been in her office before; it was three times the size of mine, temperature controlled, modern with telescreens showing her outer offices. In one screen, I noticed a slew of police officer desks but most were empty as they were probably out on patrol. She had over fifty just regular foot police patrolling two twelve hour shifts.

"Does this happen to have anything to do with the lab explosion?" she asked. "I know it was deliberately set." My eyebrows went up and she continued, "I have my sources too, otherwise I'd know very little of the labs. Hibnet and the Directors feel it is their territory, the pompous assholes."

"Yes, but he also wants more security at the conference. He is somehow connecting the lab accident to perhaps trouble at the fund raiser. He also has received a death threat and they have even threatened the safety of the space station." I sat in one of the two plush chairs that faced her desk. I could feel the fatigue of the Jumps hitting me. In my office we'd be sweating bullets though, so I relaxed taking in the perfect temperature.

"I figured it was more than just the lab incident." She went over to her far wall pushing a button and the whole wall turned transparent. Below she got good view of part of the City, Eupepsia One. As the center cylinder moved slower than the outer rings, she'd sometimes see Eupepsia Two. She usually kept the wall solid gray as she had once explained to me, the outstanding view could be distracting but when she needed to calm down, she opened it. I could see the steam coming out of her head, anger permeated the room.

She stood there looking down. "Strange doings lately, Chief. The Bassodian are visiting us this week. Been years since they stopped here. Usually we don't even know they're nearby unless they happen to be dragging one of their damn planets through, disrupting the Jumps. They leave the Crab sector as soon as they can. Two days from now, they will be sending one of their ships to Ring One's port. The huge dock was built for them, with low gravity, more oxygen but they haven't used it in years."

"Why are they visiting the space station?" Of all the species, they had the least interest in any humanoid activities. It was frustrating as they also had the most power in the Federation Council.

"They don't tell us. They have never felt the need to inform us of anything." She turned, sitting at her desk, reaching over to a tab stick and handed it to me. "It's all in there, including lately some of the Laositian Highbloods have been visiting the hospital. They are officially in for patient services. Hibnet won't tell me what "patient services" claiming patient information privileges. Also, the Ligithian Ambassador Alphonso Medicinis will be attending the conference."

"What are they up to?" I asked. Evidently my distaste showed in my voice as she looked up with a quizzical look on her face.

"Ah, I think you're here because the Laositians are linked to the lab accident, aren't they?"

I wasn't going to keep Lont Pol in the dark, she deserved as much as I could tell her. "It's part of it. The lab that had the explosion was doing experiments on the blood bond on Ligithia. If a cure for the bond can be found, there is a treaty between the Federation and the Laositians that they must free the slaves. Of course, it is not something the Highblood Laositians want."

"I'm not so sure it something that the Federation wants either," she commented. So she knew of the Ligithian War. I wasn't surprised; Lont was a Castorian and like Issam was extremely smart. She surprised me more with her next question. "Wasn't it rumored that doctors Helen and James Masters were killed because they were close to a cure? Their whole family was killed, I believe in a Ferry explosion on their way out to the satellite quite some time ago."

I just nodded. "It was rumored but nothing could be proven," was all I'd say on it.

Her computer screen rang; with a frown she answered it. Buntie's concerned face showed up on the screen. "He is insisting on me finding you." Her voice was full of frustration.

We both knew who that "he" was. "Put him on." She looked up at me, anger in every feature of her face, her amber eyes actually glowing.

It was time to deal with Dr. Hibnet.

Chapter Five

A flustered Hibnet came on line. It was quite evident he was not happy. "Captain Pol, have you seen Chief Brown?" boomed out of the computer screen. I had had enough. I reached over and turned the screen to me.

"There you are!" He sounded like a King having found his misbehaving serf. I swear he was about to point his finger at me.

"Yes, here I am! What the hell is it?" I can sound extremely angry and annoyed when I want. Even when I don't want, it comes naturally. My temper usually stops everyone in their tracks and Dr. Hibnet was no exception. He stuttered, not used to being talked to in such a manner. He'd better get used to it; I'd had enough of his secrecy and bureaucracy, never mind his high handed manner. "What exactly is it that you want, Doctor, that can't wait until I finish here with Captain Pol?"

"We have to, we have to…" he was flustered, finally getting it out, "we have to go over the plans for the conference security. I am very worried."

"Well, so am I and doing the best thing I can, conferring with Captain Pol. When we are done here and have some sense of what we are going to do, we'll come up and meet with you. Until I get everything straight with Lont, there is nothing you can contribute to the plan."

"But... but…" he was red in the face. "I find this highly irregular…"

I cut him off. "You cannot find it irregular to have your head of security briefing me and me conferring with her. It is what she is supposed to be doing. It was what I advised you to do back on Fulton. I am shocked that I come here and she is not yet been briefed by you. I am losing precious time by you neglecting to inform Captain Pol of the discussions we had back on Fulton Station."

"I meant to." He knew I had him by the short hairs. His contrition was fleeting, however, "I'll expect you both here when you are done with full reports on what you expect to do!"

"We will do that. See you soon." I hit the disconnect button.

Lont's amber eyes were wide, her mouth half opened. "I don't believe you talked to him that way." She hit her head with her palm, "That was wonderful!"

"It was necessary," I told her. "He's getting in the way. He should be helping us, not trying to run the show. A show he has no idea how to handle."

"I have all the plans for the conference, including the schematics of the buildings and the rooms where all the meetings and activities will be held." She brought up her tab screen. I glanced at the floor plans. The whole Herriden Convention Complex was large. "I am waiting on the guest list and when they are arriving. They should start arriving tomorrow."

"Let's go show this to my crew," I told her. "They are all experts in their fields, might as well get them involved right from the start. Then we'll meet with Dr. Hibnet and get the guest list and all the info he has. Damn the man, you should have had this weeks ago."

"Good idea, let me get my guys that have been working on this." She was speaking into her cellbutton and typing on her tabloid when I left her.

Elly and Lara were assembling some of their equipment. We had been assigned a good sized room with large cubicle desks with a MOSS police computer stationed on each. Another room in the back led to a meeting room with a table and telescreen. It was luxurious compared to Fulton.

I noticed Fred and Marcus were staying out of Elly and Lara's way. The two men were over studying a mockup of Moss. The space station holograph hung in the air between the two of them. Marcus had his tabloid out; his screen was giving a tutorial of what they were looking at. Each level was being described.

"Wow!" Fred commented. "I never realized how complex this station is." He pointed to the black center cylinder, "Did you know it's made of almost pure atonimum which causes the pull of gravity and the Ring's spin to maintain the gravitational pull they want? They almost counteract each other."

"Well that simplifying it a little." I pointed to the cylinder, "We are here. Almost all the space station's executive offices, including the police station, are located in the cylinder. The actual mass of atonimum is located at the lower end of the cylinder, creating a downward gravity pull within each Ring."

Marcus peered closer, "Did you see all the space ports on the different levels?" His frown matched his next words, "We're going to have a hell of a time controlling what comes in and out."

"You and Fred can check each port, make sure the security at the docks is sufficient," I advised my senior detective. "Shut down any that aren't."

"Toby can go with them." Lont Pol had entered with four of her police force. I couldn't call them detectives as the space station was not commissioned to have detectives. I knew Lont used them as such, although crime on Moss was minimal. "Toby knows our systems inside out."

She introduced her security team. "This is Evie Melca, our security equipment specialist." A middle aged woman, whose hair was going gray early, stepped forward shaking our hands. Just a little stout, she had a sweet nature about her. Elly took to her right away, showing her the equipment she'd brought.

"This is Toby Graciea, oversees the patrol police. He knows the city like the back of his hand and the layout of all the Rings extensively." He nodded his head. Toby was a young, bronze skinned Abbisian from Abbis, the planet that is the most populated in the Crab but was also the poorest in the sector. They were usually tough individuals, many with chips on their shoulders from having to struggle so hard to make it. I would, however, reserve judgment. I noticed Fred frown; he had had many a run in with Abbisians, many of them drug dealers trying to get out of the poverty of Abbis. I hope Fred wasn't giving Toby a bum rap just from his experience.

Captain Pol went over to a large man, almost as large as Fred and well built. From his dark complexion and his completely white eyes, I knew he was from Casey. A Crow Clansman, very intimidating, he was from one of the tribes from the Casey Plains. I would not like to get on the wrong side of him in an interrogation. "This is Pat Telexis. He is my best investigator. He can find out anything you'll need to know." He shook my hand and it was a firm grip. Yep, I wouldn't cross him.

The last member of the team was dressed in a nice tailored suit. "This is Lans Aroro. He's my liaison with the medical staff. He has a medical degree in general practice. I rely on him heavily in handling the administrative staff on Moss. He has the most experience with dealing with Hibnet's office."

"My sympathies," I told him as I shook his hand. "We will probably be looking to you as we try and get some information out of his office. We need the guest list, we needed it yesterday."

"Yes, he is usually not forthcoming with info." Lans half laughed, shaking his head in frustration, "we'll do our best."

"Can't ask for anything more." I assured him.

We spent the next couple of hours going over all the contingencies plans. It was Lans that started handing out Moss cellbuttons. "As you know, your Fulton cellbuttons won't work here. We programmed these just for you. Here is a booklet explaining the commands or numbers to use. For instance, to get right to the police headquarters say "police" or number 3. To get hold of Chief Brown, it's "Chief" or number 7.

"What about these identification buttons we are supposed to be wearing?" Lara knew Moss and how they keep track of everyone. "The cab driver was confused as we didn't register."

It was Lont Pol that answered her, "As you know, being a hospital it's important to be able to find people when they are needed. Thus everyone wears identification buttons. However, your cellbuttons are police issued that will register as several "fake" people. You'll never be the same person twice and it is randomly created each time." She laughed. "You'll have to trust me, I'm the only one that has the lists of names so not even Dr. Hibnet knows. It essential no one is aware of where our on-duty law enforcement personnel are. So be assured no one will be tracking your whereabouts."

She looked over at me, "You will also have a special feature on your cellbutton that will hook directly to the emergency teleport line. Although it will be a few minutes delay, it will connect you with your Fulton Police Line. Be aware though that it is monitored, as all high speed data Jumps are. Our medical personnel are very nervous about interference with our high tech instruments, or at least Hibnet is!"

"I understand" I assured her. "I think we'd better head to see Dr. Hibnet before he comes looking for us." I turned to Marcus, who would be in charge when I wasn't around, "I'll be back in a couple of hours. Set up a schedule for tomorrow. Then when I get back we will get checked into our hotel and get some supper."

"Right Chief," he said, "we have plenty to do here."

Lont Pol and I left, crossing through her main police office that I had viewed earlier on her office televiewer. Now it was busy with many of the police officers having returned and busy at their desks.

"It's near the shift change so many are switching," she pointed out as we headed out into the hallway. "How did Hibnet get you to come here with your team? I know how you hate even the annual visit required every year. I know it brings bad memories of the year you spent here recovering."

This time, as we left the police offices, we went right to the small elevators that dotted the entire center cylinder. Lont used her card and pressed the top button. Up we started.

Lont Pol was just a regular foot policeman when I spent the year being fixed up here. I couldn't tell her my parents were the murders she had mentioned before, that my childhood had been spent in Eupie1. It wasn't just my life, it was Ray's and Killa's too. So I just nodded. "He asked me and reinforced the request through Consulate Borger too. Let's just say I couldn't refuse."

"Ah, he's famous for his persuasive methods. In other words, he blackmailed you with something. I've never seen Borger have much influence on what you do."

Lont was sharp. I just didn't answer her. She smiled as we got into the elevator.

"If you hate the man so much, why didn't you take the Chief of Police job when it was offered to you?" I asked her.

"So you know they asked me?" she leaned against the elevator wall as it started up. "My life is here. I came here when I was just out of law school. I hadn't intended to stay, it seemed a good jumping off place for my career. I had every intention of returning to Castor."

The doors opened we had gone to the very top of the inner cylinder where the executive offices were.

She stopped in front of the door that led into Hibnet's office suite. "The work they do here, the amazing medical wonders that occur here, keeps me here. I feel I'm needed, I feel I make a difference. Being part of something that is so important makes it all worthwhile and why I put up with the administrator's bullshit."

"You would have made a great Chief." I told her. I also knew she was involved with Dr. Dan Bolker, a neurosurgeon, who had worked on me when I was recovering.

"They have the right person," she told me as we walked into another gray office similar to her own headquarters. This one, however, had rich furnishings; plush chairs and couches in the waiting room, with several office assistants behind a glassed in reception desk. A receptionist, who looked like she could grace a fashion magazine cover, was obviously waiting for us.

"Captain Pol, Chief Brown, please follow me. Dr. Hibnet has been waiting!" She sounded like we were delinquent children about to be brought into the principle. My temper thermometer was rising. Pol touched my arm bringing my ire back to controllable warmth. How she dealt with these pompous assholes was way beyond me.

We followed the swaying hips of the receptionist into Hibnet's inner large office. He was standing by his opened wall. The view was magnificent. His office was at the top of the tower. The top Ring Nine was evident right below but the view of space was outstandingly fascinating. The glass must have been made to enhance into the outer reaches as everything seemed magnified. Their distant sun was quite large in his view when in reality it was over a four hour Inter-Jump. The space station, unlike the other sector's engineered planets, didn't need their sun's energy. I'd heard that Moss did use some of its sun's gravitational pull to keep it in place, to keep it exactly in the right orbit. Mostly all the energy needed to run the station came from the tower's bottom core of atonimum - the most expensive part of the whole station.

I'd never been in the good doctor's office when he's had the wall open. I couldn't help but gawk, it was so magnificent. He was deep in thought and didn't notice us until his receptionist interrupted him. "Doctor, they are finally here."

OHH, I'd like to turn my angry foot to her swaying arse but one look from Pol and I shut up; the retort burning on my tongue.

"Thank you Marshie." Hibnet turned giving her his biggest smile. Did I catch a blush? She turned her cute ass, giving us one last wiggle as she left.

"Well, do you have some results for me?" He pushed a button on his desk and the wall became darkly opaque, turning to the same gray as the rest of his office. The room now seemed gloomy.

I didn't trust my temper, I was still steaming. Pol knowing, answered. Jumping right in, "Chief Brown's team and my security personnel are coordinating to cover every contingency we can think of." She handed him a tab, "You'll find a complete schedule of our combined efforts for the next few days as we check every possibility of someone sabotaging the conference."

"Thank you Captain Pol, I really must apologize for my lack of judgment in not including you immediately upon my return as Chief Brown had encouraged me to do. I arrived just as the Loamar freighter collision had taken place. As I'm sure you are aware, it collided with another freighter when they came out of a Jump at Hilda. We were quite busy with the casualties and I let it slip from my mind."

Pol just nodded, probably as she had nodded a hundred times before when he'd left her out of the loop. "We will have extra personnel at the conference dinner ball."

He interrupted her, "Just make sure they do not stick out, I don't want our guests to feel uncomfortable."

What he really meant was that he didn't want his financial donors to know there were any problems, heaven forbid. I looked around his office. He had several telescreens showing him sector news including even one that was off sector. Well, the good doctor also had a sports screen with the annual Sector Futball game. He saw me looking

"I have a data high speed Jump line. We are at the top of the station; it is the least likely place to bother our equipment. We have enough of a Jump band that we can then broadcast to the rest of the station on a limited basis. We have a very limited line. If we are transmitting out we have to cut some of the data coming in. All other regular communications come from our orbiting satellite but it is always at least several hours behind the rest of the sector since it is a slower digital data link that will not affect any sensitive equipment. Of course, the data comes in per importance and sometimes our regular communications may take a day or even two days."

So Dr. Hibnet controlled what the entire station saw and he could monitor all the incoming and out coming lines. I noticed that he had a big enough data Jump line to choose to watch the game. That was what Pol had warned me about. If I used the emergency line to call Fulton, he would know of it. I had never realized what a complete control freak Hibnet was, but maybe he had to be that way.

"Yes, I understand." I told him, "It is unfortunate that the sensitive equipment can't be shielded someway. I know it is one of the biggest complaints on Moss - that they feel the delays strongly. We hear it all the way to Fulton Station."

"Yes, yes." He waved his hand as if to dismiss the complaint. "Helping the sick is by far more important." He made it sound like the residents of the space station were crybabies, not humans with human needs. I could tell from Capt. Pol's frown that she did not agree with him and her next statement proved it.

"Well, it is rumored that they have perfected a shield…" she started to say but was cut off with his raised hand.

"It would take away critical funds. I know what they think. As long as I'm here our priorities will remain on the hospital, not on frivolous issues." He scowled at her.

Speaking of frivolous issues, as long as it's Dr. Hibnet's frivolous issue, it was time to get back to the conference. "We need a list of the guests and when they are arriving."

"I will have Marshie give you a tab on it. Please, for your eyes only as I assured all donors of their privacy. These are high profile people; you know how the press can be." He looked directly at me as if to remind me how he had protected me when I had been here as a patient. As I had been a rather prominent race driver who had been accused of manslaughter in the death of a fellow race driver, I was a prime news target. The doctor had protected me from the press, not letting them near me as I lay broken and battered. Yes, Hibnet was good for reminding of past favors for future favors he needed.

"I will be extremely careful with it but know my detectives need to check every contingency including who your guests are bringing with them and where they are coming from." I stood up emphasizing how serious I was, "It had better be a complete list!"

I walked over to the telescreen showing the game that was in its final moments. The sound was off but I could tell the excitement as the crowd was on its feet. "For instance," I pointed at the screen, "Puso Pelimi is one of your donors, will he be coming directly from the game or is he going to go to his home planet Abbis first?" Pelimi was the top Sector futball player; a big sector hero. I'd seen his picture with Dr. Hibnet at fund raisers. He was also retiring after this season and running for office. He wanted to be the next Crab Nebula Sector Federation Senator. It would be to his opponent's advantage to cause a scene at the conference.

"I have no idea." Kel Hibnet sounded indignant, "I do not want you bothering Puso with questions!"

"My detectives are better than that, they have other ways of getting the information but they have to know what they are dealing with."

"Just keep it to a minimum," he grumbled.

"You have my word on it." I assured him making a mental note to have Marcus do most of the guest list inquiries, Fred would fumble through it.

The door opened and my heart stopped. She was tall and slender with long beautiful shapely legs. The doctor's white lab coat she wore didn't hide her nicely shaped figure either. She smiled and the room lit up. I found myself staring into deep blue intelligent eyes. She wore her blonde hair tied back which only accentuated her perfectly shaped face. Given that she was a doctor, she must have been close to my age but she looked like she was just out of her teens.

"Ah, Dr. Lawry." Hibnet grinned from ear to ear; obviously Dr. Lawry was a favorite of his. "I'd like you to meet Chief Brown. You know Captain Pol."

She shook my hand. She had a firm handshake, warm and soft. "Oh, Chief Brown, I've seen you in the news." Her voice was lyrically pleasant. "Please call me Gale, I'm glad Kel has you here. I'm sure Lont is glad of the assistance too. The conference is so important to Moss."

"Dr. Lawry is the head of Level Eight. She's our top biochemist. The lab that the fire was in is under her supervision. I thought you'd like to question her." Dr. Hibnet grinned from ear to ear again as he went over and stood next to Lawry, putting his hand on her arm. "Gale is the one that discovered it wasn't an accident."

I saw Lont stiffen, Hibnet so casually had left Pol out of the information and here he was openly bragging. It was my turn to touch my Captain's arm, I felt her relax. I turned my attention to the biochemist. "Nice to meet you. My explosive expert would like to go over the laboratory tomorrow."

"I don't mind." Her voice was hypnotically pleasant to listen to. I hadn't realized I was just staring at her, she was fascinating. After a few moments, "Chief?" she asked, breaking the spell.

"Oh, yeah, sure. Lt. Null will be there tomorrow." I could see Lont Pol smile, obviously Dr. Lawry had this effect on other males and Lont found it amusing.

"We haven't told anyone yet that the lab wasn't an accident, so you'll keep it under your hat." The good old doctor was lecturing again and I found my ire up again.

"We're in the business of keeping things quiet, remember that and keep me and Lont up to date on everything. I mean it, Dr. Hibner." I was the one pointing my finger now right at his pompous head. "It will behoove you to tell us everything! It will be on your head, I repeat, *your head* if I something happens and I find out it was due to a miscommunication!"

He looked embarrassed, "I have already apologized to Captain Pol. I will keep you fully informed."

"Good," I growled at him. You could tell he was not use to being told anything, he actually indignantly stepped back.

"We have to at some point tell the board that it wasn't an accident." The gorgeous Dr.Gale spoke up, "we have a steadfast rule that if a laboratory accident occurs, the responsible lab assistants must leave our program. I will not stand by and let those two lab assistants be thrown out of their graduate programs. It was not their fault! Dr. Ditterset agrees."

"Of course, my dear," Hibnet spoke right up, patting her arm to reassure her. "I totally agree. The two interns will be a while on Level Four recovering from their burns. We will clear their names before the board hearing."

Her face relaxed, making it even more enchanting. "Well, then I'll see you tomorrow. You will be coming with your detective, won't you?" she turned to me, giving me her full wonderful attention. All I could do was nod. I was smitten, what can I say; male hormones gone wild.

"Brilliant researcher!" Dr. Hibnet exclaimed as the door shut. "She has done a wonderful job on Ring Eight." I was thinking other things, but said nothing. Lont Pol just smirked, taking my arm, pushing me towards the door. She'd had enough of Hibnet.

"We will be getting back to you, Doctor." She nodded to him as she dragged me out the door. She stopped at Marchie's station and got the list of conference attendees. I followed her out to the hallway. We were at the top of the tower which was quite narrow, the elevators were nearby. It wasn't until we were in the elevator that she turned to me, "Really Chief, not you too!"

"She's quite fetching," I said feeling my face blush. "I will try and get my hormones under control."

"She seems to have that effect on most males. I haven't seen one male that didn't trip all over himself to get her attention. Don't get me wrong, I admire and like Dr. Lawry. The best part about her besides her brilliant work is she seems totally unaware of her effect on the male species. She doesn't seem to be that interested. I'm not saying she hasn't been seen with a few of the doctors but over all she seems to be too engrossed in her research. The personnel on Ring Eight adore her."

"I'll try and keep a level head when I next see her," I laughed as we reached Lont's Level. The police station was now busy; the second shift or the "Epies2" were actively getting ready to head to patrol the space station. My detectives were still huddled over the conference maps. Marcus had already scheduled everyone's activities for the following day almost to the minute. I explained to Elly that we'd be spending the morning with Dr. Lawry up on Ring Eight going over the lab explosion site.

"Good," she exclaimed. "Let's meet at 06:00. I also have to go over the conference facility to check out possible danger zones there. The earlier we get started the better."

"Let's make it 07:00," I winced. "I doubt Lawry will be even there that early."

"Oh, she'll be there," Lont Pol interjected. "She's a workaholic. So is Dr. Ditterset. Lawry heads the entire Ring 8. Ditterset runs the actual lab that was destroyed. Angi Ditterset just moved into a newly built lab, replacing the burnt one.

"Chief, you might even make it 08:00. Tomorrow will be your first day here and you'll be recovering." That got everyone's attention; they all looked at Moss' superintendent. "Let me explain, although Chief Brown and Lt. Null know, having been here before." We both nodded, we knew what was coming next. "You see, the regular gravity on Moss is just slightly more than you are used to, not much more pull, but your bodies will be affected."

"I don't feel any different," Elly spoke up and the rest agreed.

"As I said, it is only slight, your muscles will be sore tomorrow. In everyone's room you'll find a packet of pills. When you get up tomorrow, take them. By noon, most of you will be fine. By the next day, you'll not even notice."

"Great." Fred Stoshingburg exclaimed, "I already feel like shit."

"You're a big baby," Lara told him, "take the damn pills and you'll be fine."

"Alright," Pol interjected, "you all have your new cellbuttons. As I've explained they are set up for voice commands. Look at the booklet you've been given for further numbers and instructions. Only Chief Brown and I have access to your locations. As I've told you, the cellbuttons will not be tracked as others are. No one will be aware that you are cops unless you explicitly command it to ID you. You'll not even be identified as visitors either."

"That's spooky that you track everyone." Elly said, "I don't think I'd like it."

"You have to understand," Pol assured her, "this is a medical facility, and personnel are needed for emergencies. The tracking is only used for that need. See you all tomorrow."

We gathered our suitcases and headed back to the City, Ring Five. Once again dragging our luggage, we took the large elevator onto the connector corridor to the outer ring. As we rode the moving tram to the city's entranceway, conversation was minimal. Fatigue was setting in. The cab driver read our IDs, this time no problem, our cellbutton identifications were obviously working.

Eupie1 was just settling into nighttime. This part of the Ring 5 was slowly darkening. Eupie2 on the other side of the Ring would be experiencing morning. The Conference Center was on the far side of Eupie1, making it easy for Eupie2 inhabitants to also use it. The cab drove us up to the circular driveway that led to the lobby's entrance.

"You'd never know that this wasn't some city on a regular planet," Elly said as she climbed out, looking up at the ten story luxury hotel. The huge conference center was attached by a skyway bridge over to our left spanning the Main Avenue. I also knew that a tunnel lay underneath the avenue also leading to the Center. The square attached building was just as large as the hotel. Big tall windows graced the entire complex whose light glowed up into what looked like a starlit sky which in reality was just a mock up, a well done illusion

Lush gardens filled with high shooting water fountains graced the entire complex. Pathways with flowers decorating each side were filled with people enjoying a warm evening. A slight breeze ruffled hairdos.

Whichever way you looked, stores and restaurants lined the sidewalks off the main street. People were out strolling, couples laughing with some dragging children along. The sounds of the city were normal city sounds. The space station was forgotten by normalcy. It was what the planners had worked diligently to achieve. I remembered a very normal childhood filled with parks, cinemas, schools and friends. Ray and I never felt we were deprived of anything. I knew just a mile away were single family houses with yards and neighborhoods. Ring Five was made as a refuge for normal living for all the medical personnel that it took to run the rest of the rings. It did exactly that, I knew from my own childhood experience.

We checked in. We had a suite of rooms on the sixth floor. They were some of Dr. Hibnet's rooms that he kept reserved for himself for entertaining when he had medical functions going on. It was probably the only open rooms left, as the hotel was booked solid for the conference. They were a nice suite of rooms with a living room that had five bedrooms and two baths with a small kitchenette. A fully stocked bar was in one corner. The living room had big windows looking out over the city. On the table was a supper of sandwiches and salads. Everyone helped themselves.

"Even though I spent several years here," Lara Null said looking out at the landscape, "it still amazes me. I'd never guess that sky was an illusion."

"I believe that was the idea when they built this," Marcus remarked. "I'll be curious to see the other Rings." He looked at me, questions in his tone.

"The other rings are more like a hospital," I remarked. "Each Ring is unique. Some have different gravities, temperature variances - in other words, controlled atmospheres for different species, diseases, wounds, experiments." My detectives would see tomorrow as we began our investigations and readied our security enhancements.

We each retired to a bedroom. I thought of Killa. I hadn't received any messages but then communications were so delayed, sometimes as much as two days if they had a backlog waiting to be transmitted. I wondered how Hill was managing. Were Bear and Hoover behaving? Hill and the dogs would keep Killa safe, not to mention Issam. Still I worried. I understood the concern of Moss's inhabitants. The Jump lines kept us connected, made us part of the Humanoid Community. It was why the engineers kept all the planets on manageable time tables. We all shared a common time, making us all a community. I didn't blame the resentment of being left out of everyday sector news by the Space Station's community.

I thought of Dr. Hibnet's futbol game. I admired the man greatly. My parents admired him, yet was he so pigheaded that he couldn't see the forest for the trees? Was he extremely self-centered or was he the lifeline that kept the hospital space station the best hope for the sick? My head hurt from too many emotions that were crashing in on my brain. I popped a blue pill - being back at the space station stirred up memories. I couldn't help but think of my parents; my mother's soft intelligent eyes, my father's slender strong hands that could fix my bike that I crashed so often. I swallowed another one of my blue pills and let sleep settle everything.

Chapter Six

I was glad when I awoke from dark dreams. It was early, dawn hadn't appeared yet. I stood in my boxer shorts looking out of my bedroom window onto the quiet city of EupepsiaOne. Way below I could see the early risers - small hovertrucks delivering supplies to start the day. Muffled sounds filtered up as the restaurants and some of the shops were opening. The city street lights were going off as the simulation of dawn was rising. It was just after 05:00.

I quickly took a shower, letting the hot water massage my aching muscles. I had taken the muscle recovery pills that were by my bedside. I could feel them start to work. Most of me felt much better as I dried off and got into my gray suit. My fingers did ache though, still I managed to draw my tie into a presentable knot. I slipped out the room, careful not to wake anyone, and headed down to the restaurant in the lobby, hopeful I could get a good cup of java. My brain needed it.

The lobby, with its big wide open atriums and lush carpeting, was almost empty. The front desk was just changing shifts, getting ready for the day's busy schedule. It would really be bustling come tomorrow when most of the conference guests would start arriving. The "Sunlight Café" was in the far corner. I could smell the java brewing which hurried my steps along.

I sat in one of the tables with a window overlooking the main street. Shadows still hid most of the buildings but rays of sunlight were starting to filter down. Even though I knew it was artificially created, my brain believed it to be a real sunrise.

I ordered a glass of orangeade, oatmeal and a large pot of java. Issam and Hill would be proud of me. No gooey chocolate muffins today - maybe tomorrow. I took out one of my little blue pills, better to be safe. I couldn't afford an episode. I was putting it in my mouth when I heard, "Can I sit here?"

It was Lara. I nodded as I swallowed my pill. She looked trim and curvy in her gray suit yet very professional. With the heels she wore, she was almost as tall as I was. Her blonde hair was in one long braid down her back. My weapon's specialist wore little makeup, she didn't need it. A sharp angled face accentuated by gray eyes didn't need any enhancement. Lara's eyes were shining like two gemstones, bright with intelligence. I knew she was a few years older than I was but she wore her years better.

"I didn't want to disturb you," her voice was deep and clear. I'd bet she had a great alto singing voice. My detective sharp shooter took off her suit coat, carefully making sure her firearm was hidden, then she took the seat opposite mine.

"You aren't bothering," I told her, "you're up early."

"I never sleep much." She said ordering a fruit cup topped with granola. It reminded me of Hill who ate the same fare.

She saw me looking at it. "I need to keep fit and trim, my trainer keeps me on a short leash."

"Nothing wrong with healthy," I commented not really believing what I was saying. My lifestyle was anything but healthy. Beer and pizza were my agenda.

"Did you get the methozine pills from here or from Dr. Lily Issam?" Lara must have seen me swallow my little blue pill.

I knew she had degrees in psychology but I didn't know she knew Issam's wife Lily. "How do you know about Dr. Issam?" I asked cautiously.

"Oh, I wasn't snooping. I see her myself and I saw you coming out of her office. She's my therapist too. So did the anticonvulsant drug come from Moss or Issam?"

So she knew what my little blue pills were for. "They come from Moss. Issam believes more in calming therapy. I used to be addicted to the methozine, now I take half of what I use to take."

I saw her nod. "You must have damaged your frontal lobe in the accident. How often do you have a seizure?"

"I hadn't had one in over two years until a couple of months ago when I was on Nestor, and that was an unusual circumstance." Perhaps because she had degrees in psychology, I didn't mind telling her. It was unusual for me to say anything about my epilepsy since I kept my seizures to myself.

"Did the Jump aversion come with the epilepsy?" Lara cocked her head, as if she was totally engrossed in my problems. She would have made a good doctor with her trait of making you feel at ease. It also helped her be a good detective.

"No," I laughed, "I've had that since I was a kid. My poor mother tried everything, so did one doctor after another. Although Dr. Hibnet has a hypothesis, pointing to my sensitivity to the Jumps, that my seizures were just controlled before and that my accident just brought it out."

"Ah, Dr. Hibnet." Simply said but I could tell there was a whole bunch of meaning behind that statement.

I raised my eyebrows. She smiled, "Water over the damn."

I left it. So Dr. Hibnet liked the girls. "You were an intern here?"

"Yeah, young and impressionable. I learned fast that titles don't mean high morals." She smiled. "Like I said, I see Dr. Lily Issam, she never brought your name up. She would never discuses clients with me."

"I never thought she did." If there was one person in this whole universe I thought was above reproach it was my therapist, Dr. Lily Issam.

"You know I was a soldier?" Her long wide eyelashes hypnotized. I just nodded, letting her continue. "I was trained as a sharp shooter right out of secondary school in the Federation Army. I served in the Cathian War." Her breakfast lay untouched, her java getting cold. Her face was full of pain as she looked up at me.

"Yeah, not a pretty war. I have someone in my apartment complex that lost the use of his legs in that war. He's going to school on the Veteran's bill." I thought of Artchie, his face would show the same pain as Lara's when the war was brought up. Lara must have served at the beginning of that senselessly long war; Artchie more recently.

"I used the same tuition credits to attend Moss and get my degrees in psychology. I thought I could cure myself. I was wrong." She was playing with her food but she wasn't even aware of it. Her mind was far away in that war that had left so many of our young crippled in mind and body. The war had lasted way too long and took too many lives.

"You don't have to tell me..." I assured her but she put up her hand, to stop me.

"I don't mind." Her eyes lifted to mine, they were wet at the corners. "I was one of the best snipers that my command unit had. I love my work, the preciseness and intricate workings of weapon systems excites my mind. I've always been a good shot, even as a kid. However, some of the horrors of the war settled too deeply in my soul. I saw too many atrocities on both sides. I have horrible nightmares."

Well that explained the little sleep she said she got. "Is Lily Issam helping you," I asked?

"Oh, yes. We are making slow but lasting progress. You seem to have adjusted well." She looked questioningly at me. "You were very young if I remember correctly to take up racing. Youngest Rookie of the Year and took two championships before your nineteenth birthday."

So she knew of me. She must have seen me wince, I don't like to think of my past racing life. "I'd rather…"

I didn't get very far before she interrupted me, "I was here doing my internship, remember? You were rather a famous patient. You're a fascinating subject to study for a psychologist."

"How so?" I asked, amused at the thought of me being a *psychological interest*.

"You are what we psychologists call an *alpha over-achiever;* even after experiencing some brain damage you still strive to be the best at what you do without realizing the pressure you put on yourself. I've never come across a more blatant example. Does it run in your family? I know your brother just took a championship." She saw the doubt in my eyes. "No, really! At seventeen you were the youngest driver winning two championships to boot and now you are amazingly young to be a sector Chief of Police. You must realize this when you attend the annual Chief Sectors' Federation meeting every year. I have a feeling you're not done achieving yet."

I did indeed feel young at the Federation meeting. Most of my Police Sector Chief peers were an average of fifteen years older than I was. "It was just being in the right place at the right time," I told her. "I'm very happy where I am, thank you, any higher and politics come roaring in."

She laughed, "I don't think so. Alphas can't help themselves. It's almost like it's something automatic in your nature. I remember you as the best patrol cop, then an aggressive crime detective. Your audacity overwhelmed everyone. I know you use that famous temper to compensate for how young you're perceived. You've got everyone leery of you including Consulate Borger. Yet you don't overdo it. You've done an amazing job organizing the whole Fulton Police operation and everyone knows it."

"You don't seem to be frightened of me." I glared at her.

She laughed. "I'm petrified," then laughed again. I couldn't pursue it further as I saw Elly and Marcus enter the café. I waved to them and they sauntered over. Elly walked across the restaurant dragging her equipment behind her. The attached baggage wheels squeaked under the strain of what was in her bag.

"I'm ready Chief, let's go," she told me out of breath, "can't wait until I can try this new equipment out."

I touched my cellbutton, it was only 06:50. "Calm down Elly, Evie Melca isn't meeting us until seven thirty. Have some breakfast."

She sat down looking downhearted. Elly was a work alcoholic. Only her bird watching hobby could interfere. She was the best in the sector on the latest research on explosives especially chemical explosives which seemed the popular way to go today among criminals.

"You are just bored because you have no birds to watch," Marcus commented.

"Your wrong Marcus," Lara interjected before I could tell him, "there are plenty of birds on the Epie level. I believe there are about fifty different species. Look it up on your Tablet Elly, you'll see."

Elly immediately brought out her Tab stretching the screen in front of her. Sure enough she pulled up a whole section of *Medical Operation Space Station* birds. "Why look at this," she pointed to one of the birds, "an Offlet Owl. Wow!"

"I'll find out from Lond Pol who you can get to give you a bird watching tour," I told her, getting a big smile which made her look less frumpy. I resisted the temptation to tell her so. Instead I got right to business. "Let's go over your schedules."

Marcus spoke up first, "Fred and I are checking out the entry ports on each level with Toby Graciea. He's knows the layout of the space station really well. It's gonna take all day and probably into evening. I need to check all the computer port data outlets."

Speaking of Fred Stoshingburg, as if he'd heard his name, he came stumbling into the Café. His tie was undone with his shirt collar open. His shirt was half hanging out of his pants. His hair was sticking out every which way. His face was pale and his eyes half opened.

"You look like hell," I growled. Normally on Fulton with the heat I didn't care but off planet I wanted my detectives to project a professional appearance.

"I feel like hell," he mumbled. "I was worried I was going to be late."

He half fell into the chair next to Lara. "You're an ass," she berated him. "Did you take your pills?" She got a nod. She reached into her pocketcatch and handed him some more of the pills she'd given him yesterday. "Here take this, you'll feel better in a few minutes." He swallowed some using her juice.

Then to my surprise, she grabbed his hand and led him off. We saw her take him into the Ladies Room.

A woman came out, looking shocked and I saw her join her husband, rambling away to him but she didn't get the manager. I had no doubts Lara had used her badge.

A few minutes later, Lara came back hauling Fred behind her. His tie was on straight, his face washed, his shirt neatly tucked in and his hair was combed. She shoved him into the seat next to her and waved to the waitress. "He'll have breakfast One and Two," she ordered for him.

"I don't think he should be eating," Elly leaned over speaking softly to Lara.

Lieutenant Lull shook her head. "Nonsense, he's feeling better, aren't you Fred?"

Fred nodded. "A little," looking at the six pancakes, three eggs, several pieces of toasts and home fries the waitress was putting in front of him. He then proceeded to eat it all; downing two cups of Java to boot. Lara put a napkin under his chin, shaking her head.

I was speechless. What could I say except, "What's on your agenda, Lara?"

"I'm heading over to the Convention Center. Pat Texis and Lans Aroro will be meeting me. We are going to check on police positioning for the Conference. I'll look for the best locations for placing the sharp shooters to view the conference activities and lookout for points that may cause us trouble."

"Just remember Dr. Hibnet wants low key and unobtrusive security. We will follow his wishes as best we can without compromising the guests' security. Elly and I will meet you later this afternoon. She'll check out all potential hiding places for combustibles."

"Got it!" She finished off her java then stood up and put on her jacket with its hidden gun holster, once again becoming the sharp looking professional. I saw Elly's envious glances. Lara patted Fred's shoulder, "Good luck big boy." She patted him again, "You'll be just fine. Remember to duck in those low hallways."

I noticed Stoshingburg had finished both the breakfasts and his color was returning. "Thanks for the pills Lara, I'm feeling much better."

She smiled and patted him one last time as she left. I noticed many of the men in the restaurant looked up as she went past their tables, following her with their eyes until she was gone. Lara was not only good looking but emitted an air of danger which only enhanced her overall beauty.

"Wish I could look like that." Elly moaned over her java cup.

"You look just fine." Marcus lightly brushed her hand, ever the older fatherly type. He probably had daughters he'd had to comfort for the same reason. Women were never happy with the way they looked, even if they are drop dead gorgeous.

Fred just loudly "humpfed", slouching down in his chair. "Sure feels a lot better. Lara's pills really helped."

"Then let's get going." Marcus stood up getting his wallet out.

"It's on the department, I'll get it," I informed him. Fred followed the older detective out; *cripes*, Stoshingburg was a big guy.

Elly and I headed out the front lobby. Evie Melca, Lont Pol's explosive expert, was waiting for us in an official "cop" car which on Moss is an oversized golf hovercart. I helped Elly stash her equipment in the opened back and let the two women have the front while I sat in the back. My head just barely missed the top. I couldn't imagine how Fred had managed if they had been picked up by one of these.

"I'm worried about my equipment, it is not supposed to get wet," Elly said looking back at her bags in the open trunk section.

"We aren't scheduled for rain today." Evie smiled. "I have a rain cover I take when precipitation is expected."

"Oh, I forgot it's all controlled." Elly looked back at me, I suppose hoping I'd be as surprised but I already knew of the space station's climate control. When I was a kid my mom knew exactly when to send us to school in rain gear. We also knew the temperature varied from 68 degrees to 88 degrees depending on time of day and what scheduled season the weather people had to deal with. Everything was ecologically planned out for the plants and animals that populated the Eupepsia Cities. My mother use to have a chart on our refrigerator with the whole "weather plan".

Evie weaved easily through the heavy morning traffic. Every Epie inhabitant had someplace to be. Within an hour though, most of the city would be depleted of its medical staff heading towards their levels. Most took mass transit to the train stations which then hooked everyone to the ring levels. It still left all the residuals; kids going to school, teachers, shopkeepers, city workers so Tube Five never was deserted.

When we arrived at one of the train terminals, Evie parked the cop vehicle in a designated space. At the train stations, parking was at a minimum that is why most everyone depended on the buses and trolleys. I grabbed Elly's bag finding it quite heavy as I rolled it up towards the train. There were plenty of stations, train cars were abundant. We easily found seats, giving one seat to the baggage.

The trains ran in tubes on the outside of the Rings then up or down through tunnel-tubes and repeated the process on every level. We were going up to Level Eight so we were on the outside of the Rings twice. On the outside the stars were magnificent. As many times as I've seen the universe through the clear wall of the tube, it still left me speechless. Even moving at a good clip, one got the sense of the immenseness of the surrounding star systems.

Of course, we were the gawkers, most everyone riding the train was either reading on their tabs or writing on their tabs. They saw this every day. Amazing, familiarity dulls the senses. Let them spend some time on Fulton Station and they'd wake up! I had to drag Elly off when we reached Ring Eight. Level eight being one of the small Rings, only six people got off.

We walked down the ramp from the train platform and we heard our names. A man sitting in a golf cart type vehicle was waving to us. On either side of a wide hallway were sidewalks with moving platforms. We crossed over to the driver. Evie nodded to him and climbed into the front seat. "Lab Three please.'

"I know, Evie. Dr. Lawry told me yesterday to be here early." Then he turned to us, "Hi, I'm Ed." He grabbed our bags and threw them in the back opened area of the cart. It brought a slur of curses from Elly on how to handle her equipment. He apologized and we both got in the back seat bench while Evie got in the front next to him. "We only have a little way to go," he explained, "but Dr.Lawry figured you might have equipment."

He was right as it seemed only seconds before he turned into a small side corridor. I glanced up and down the pathway. This was one of the smaller rings, I knew the layout of the space station, and this layer was all biological labs. It had been designed as research lab space. The main corridor was non descriptive gray walls with side roadways. The constant curving of the main corridor was the only indication that we were on a ring.

When we reached the end of the corridor there was several "golf carts" parked facing two large sliding frosted glass doors. Ed, going up to the doors, put his hand on the lockpad; the entranceway slid open. Harsh lights made me squint. I immediately felt like I was in a hospital. Elly, who had been following behind me, bumped into the back of me.

"Sorry Chief, these lights are disconcerting." She put her arm up trying to shade her eyes.

"Lower lights," Ed blurted out and the lights notched down to normal. "Sorry, the damn maintenance guy always does that. I swear he's half blind. The receptionist comes in at eight and she turns them down to normal, although the receptionist is now over at the new lab since this one was destroyed in the blast."

With the harshness of the lights gone the room looked a lot more hospitable, a more reception-like atmosphere. On the far wall was a glassed in receptionist desk, on all the side walls were comfortable waiting chairs and in one corner a telescreen. The walls were broken up with photographs taken at several key areas of the space station.

Elly immediate started investigating. "Which is the burnt lab?" She looked inquiringly at Ed. "This room is totally fireproofed. Good thing, as any explosion would not reach in here."

"She's right." Dr. Gale Lawry had entered the room from the large sliding door entranceway. "All the labs are fireproof and soundproof by the way. In this case if you look at that door," she pointed at one of the five doorways, "you will see a little scorch area near the top. One of the intern students was just entering the lab when the explosion took place. She fell backwards, thus the door slammed shut but not before the top scorched. Although the intern has extensive burns on the front of her body, she's not as bad as Eian, who was actually entering before her and got the full blast. It's too bad the interns had come back early, they would have missed the blast otherwise. Dr. Ditterset was at a meeting with me. My office is further down the corridor. We both heard the blast and came running."

Elly hurried over, checking out the door. It was locked.

"Here, I'll open it," Gale said. Turning to me smiling she added, "I'm sorry I'm late but I was needed in Lab Eleven. We are near a breakthrough in finding a treatment for radiation cancer that can occur to Litonia miners."

It didn't matter what she said I would have forgiven her. She felt like sunshine reigning down on me on a cold day. I just shook my head at her, my tongue was not working. Elly and Evie were right on her heels when she opened the door. I was surprised to see the lieutenants had changed into investigative gear; into white plastic coveralls with matching gloves and booties. I hadn't even noticed them get dressed. I had been too engrossed by the doctor's presence. I shook myself, mentally scolding my emotions. It was very alien to me. I usually had my feelings under control.

Evie had my gear draped over a chair. I quickly changed and joined them. It hit me, the smell of burnt plastic, chemicals and the remnants of smoke still lingered.

Dr. Lawry was standing by the door. "She won't let me come in. I tried to tell her, I've been in here several times."

"It's regulations," I told her, taking Gale's arm walking her out back into the reception area as Elly glared after her. *Keep her out of here!* Elly mouthed to me as I left the damaged lab.

"I'm sorry, you'll have to stay out." I couldn't make myself use my official harsh cop's voice. Instead I asked her out. "How about lunch today?" I felt like a school boy, what the hell was wrong with me?

She smiled, "Sure, I'll meet you here around noon?" She waved at me as she left through the glass doors. She turned back, "Dr. Ditterset's new lab is next to my office. It's number 10, but she's off station today, she should be back soon."

Elly was at the door, looking rather strange at me but she didn't say a word, just turned back into the lab. I followed her, blushing. Damn, now she'd tell the rest. *The chief has a crush on that doctor.* I could hear her telling my detectives back at the hotel tonight. Damn.

It put me in a bad mood. I walked over to the two woman investigators. They were bending over some wires, taking samples of some of the ash that surrounded the melted cords. "What have you got?" I grumbled. "Let's have it! Don't keep it to yourselves, share!"

"Glad to have you back," Elly slyly uttered. Evie just giggled. I cringed.

"There is definite evidence that this safety gauge was tampered with." Evie pointed to one of the wires that had solidified into one big mess. "The safety valve was disconnected, thankfully it didn't melt." With her gloved hand, she picked up a relay switch I recognized as an emergency shut off valve. The wires had been cut. "They cut this out and wired the system around it. Then they overloaded the system with extra current, causing it to heat up and explode the chemicals."

"They weren't taking any chances," Elly commented, "see this burnt up mess?" I nodded. "It's an incendiary device, maybe a small bomb. I'll know what it was in a minute." She reached over getting her equipment and attaching it to some of the burnt wires. Then she set a small vacuum to some of the other ash that fed into another one of her machines. Elly's eyes sparkled, she was enjoying herself.

I stood up, looking around the good sized laboratory. All the tables had been blown over, the walls were all marked in scorch streaks. Upside down desks with office chairs were blown all over the place. It had been a good sized effective explosion, even the cabinets had been blow off the wall spilling their contents every which way.

"The fire extinguishers did kick in but made it one big mess of wet ash," Elly told me, pointing to the crusty ash that covered the lab floor. It had dried hard enough that we didn't leave foot prints. "I wish they hadn't restored the lighting system. I could have gotten some clues as to how they set off the whole thing."

"They didn't call in Lont Pol until it was too late," Evie interjected. When we got here, Dr. Hibnet's people already had the maintenance personnel cleaning up. Pol had a fit!"

"Assholes!" I couldn't help blurting out. I was so angry, I reached in and took a blue pill. I wasn't going to take a chance on an episode. "Damn Hibnet." I could smell his interference. He was so damn worried about bad publicity!"

Elly shook her head. Evie nodded her agreement with me.

"I'll figure it out, Chief," my explosive expert assured me. "Not much gets past my analytical equipment. Evie, let's get busy. I want to comb this whole area, every inch of it! I bet they left something that will point to where the explosives came from!"

We worked all morning. Elly covered every inch with Evie and me feeding her our findings. At one point Evie was by the far wall. She was playing with something. I walked over to see her pushing a button. "I guess it was damaged, it's not working." She looked puzzled. Elly walked over as Lont Pol's security expert was taking the button switch apart. "This opens the wall. This lab is on the outside of the ring, they can view outside but the button seems to be broken, probably damaged in the blast."

Elly reached into her front pocket and started helping with the now exposed wiring. All of a sudden the gray back wall turned opaque then cleared. Although not as spectacular as Hibnet's office and I doubted the glass magnified like his, but it still was stunning. "Well, look what we did!" Elly laughed advancing on the clear wall. "Wow!"

We had a good view of the surrounding stars. Their own star, Silis, was way in the distance. I pointed it out to Elly, explaining they used it only for the slight gravitational pull the space station needed. The main atonimum core of Moss did most of the work of heating and controlling the space station's rotations.

One of Elly's machines beeped. She stared at it for a long time, looking from her tabloid screen to the machine's screen. "This is strange, Chief." She looked so confused which is not an Elly look. "According to this all the data banks in this room have been wiped clean and I mean clean!"

"Well with the blast, how could any of it survive?" I asked her.

"Something always survives. It may be jumbled but it leaves traces. I have none. The tabloids and main terminals in this office were wiped clean." She paced in front of her equipment.

Evie spoke up, "That means someone took the time before blowing up the lab to get all the data contained in the computers and then blew up the lab to cover it up not realizing we'd track that they'd done it."

"But you know the data has to be somewhere else. I'm sure it is stored in Moss's main memory banks." I was trying to follow the reasoning, it didn't make sense.

"We need to know if the main Moss data banks have been compromised." Elly looked at me. Dr. Hibnet is going to have to let Marcus check them out or at least someone he can trust to see if the files have been changed or erased."

"The files have been erased, I checked." A voice came from the doorway.

I looked over, a tall lean woman in a white laboratory coat was standing in the doorway. She had black hair tied in a tight bun which left her black eyes the center focus of her face. I was guessing but I'd bet she was a Modite, an inhabitant from Mody; one of the farthest out planets in the Crab Sector. It was a ten hour Jump from Fulton. I dealt with all the Dome representatives and the Modites were the hardest to deal with. Highly intellectual, they were always questioning everything and never satisfied with the answer, always wanting more information. They prided themselves in being one of the most educated inhabitants of the Crab, not that they looked down on all of us but it was close. They rarely and I mean rarely married outside their race. It was highly frowned upon. They rarely even associated with others. Not unfriendly, mind you, but just a little cool. Standoffish was the best I could call it. Let's just say tourism on Mody was nonexistent.

"And you are?" I asked.

"I'm Dr. Angi Ditterset. I headed this lab. I'm in the process of building a new lab. I just got back to the station this morning."

"And what exactly did you do here?" I asked, although I knew.

"We were researching the chemical DNA bond of the Ligithian/Laositian people. We were continuing the work of James and Helen Masters."

She knew who I was. Her smile confirmed it. Her dark gray eyes were only on me. "I'd still like them analyzed by a computer expert. I brought one with me." I forcefully told her. Whenever I dealt with a Modite I was firm.

"By all means, if you can get past Dr. Hibnet." She smiled again, her thin lips in a tight line across her face. I got the feeling she hadn't consulted the good doctor when she had done her analysis.

"What do you think happened here?" I asked her.

"It is quite obvious, although it looks like an accident, someone wanted my research to come to a halt and thus blew my lab up." She looked over at Elly, "You'll find they attached a fuse to a low grade explosive but put it right at the best place, near the most volatile chemicals."

Elly looked at me, "She's right, Chief. It's exactly what my analysis says."

"You said 'they', who's 'they'?" I walked over to her; she was about two inches above me. I noticed how large and thin her fingers were that clutched her oversized scientific tabloid. Everything about her was thin and boney. Her cheekbones were high on her face, pushing up her large black eyes. Her legs were pencil thin with protruding knees. Not for the first time I wondered if they were related to the nonhuman avian Itlites species. The bird-like Itlites were also known for their intellects. They were considered allies to humans, often helping us with the Federation Assembly.

"I figure it's someone who sympathizes with the Laositians or at least does not want the slavery of the Ligithians to end, like the methanilum fuel companies. The Xil company is the most powerful of those. Heaven forbid we don't have cheap Jump fuel." One of her boney fingers went to her face in a thoughtful gesture, "Yet they did not want to hurt anyone, the lab technicians were supposed to be at lunch."

It was a good point and a typical analytical Modite conclusion. "Where were you when it happened?"

"I was up reporting to Dr. Lawry on our progress. I was ready to announce significant strides in our research. I wanted Dr. Hibnet to help me get you here, along with your bondee." I glared at her; she got the idea as she shut up.

"What's she talking about Chief?" Elly came over to stand by me.

"She's got me confused with someone else." I answered her in the gruffest voice I could manage, a voice that I knew wouldn't let her question me further. I have a temper for a reason, it helps when I don't want to be questioned.

"Yes, he's right." Dr. Brock interjected, "I meant Dr. Hibnet was going to elicit your help in finding me an appropriate subject."

It seemed to satisfy Elly who went back to her machines and her evidence. I walked out to the reception area leaving the two lieutenants still combing the lab for clues. "I would appreciate it Doctor Ditterset if you'd keep any confidences that Hibnet told you to yourself!" I was mad. I'd worked hard to keep Killa's situation quiet, our lives depended on it as did my brother and his growing family.

"I'm sorry, truly," Angi Ditterset contritely said, "I didn't realize it was such a secret."

"My life and the lives of my family depend on it. My name is Skip Brown!" My temper was getting the better of me. "Dr. Hibnet had no right telling you!"

"He didn't." I could tell she was sorry now, she'd lost the condescending manner that Modites carry on their shoulders. She explained further, her hands dropping to her sides almost in a submissive way, "I've gone all over your parents' files. I found your mother's diary, and I saw an entry about her brother on Nestor and I investigated further. I knew she'd had Killa bonded to her as a child. I did not expect to find the Ligithian, nor you and your brother with him. Everyone thought you died in the accident."

"Let's keep us dead! This explosion is nothing compared to what they would do if they thought us alive!"

She actually apologized, "I'm truly sorry Chief Brown. I have erred, my apologies, I will not mention it again!"

I didn't get to say anything more as my cellbutton lightly beeped in my ear. I touched it, getting Lont Pol. "Chief, come immediately to my office."

"Can't you tell me over the cell? I'm busy and I have a noon appointment."

"NO!" came strongly in my ear. I was startled by her vehemence.

I yelled back into the lab, "I have to go to Pol's office, emergency. I'll call you as soon as I can." Stripping off the protective clothing, I dashed out of the lab's reception area, a golf cart was leaving somewhere, I got a ride to the center pathway and took the tram across taking the elevator down to Pol's office three floors down. What now!

Chapter Seven

I tried to walk as fast as I could without looking like something was wrong. I hurried past Pol's receptionist, Buntie, waving as I half ran down the police station's hallway. I just barely heard the confused woman say "Chief Brown?" I didn't even knock but charged into Lont Pol's office.

She was sitting at her desk, my Superintendent was talking to someone on her cellbutton. "I'll call you back," I heard her say and then she rolled her chair over to a corner cabinet. "No one must know of this," she immediately told me as Moss' head cop opened up the bottom draw using an actual key, pulling out a terminal output screen. "I'd get fired," simply said but with an intensity that impressed its importance on me. Of course I'd be the one firing her; awkward moment.

"We'll probably get fired together," I told her, releasing some of the tension. I looked down, over her shoulder, seeing the screen come alive at her touch. "What is this?" I asked.

"It's linked to Dr. Hibnet's communication Jump line. I monitor his incoming messages from off Moss." She said it with no apologies in her voice, "I would know nothing if I didn't go behind his back. I'd have no idea of what's going on since he tells me nothing."

I smiled, a woman after my own heart. We did what we have to do, followed regulations but followed what was best for the safety of the people too. It was a fine line we sometimes walked, but walk it we did. I just nodded.

"Something came in this morning. I thought he'd tell you but when I realized he wasn't notifying you, I called you." She looked up at me, her eyes full of questioning my approval or was I going to fire her.

"What is it?" I couldn't keep the alarm out of my voice, it had to be something serious or Pol wouldn't be taking the chance of getting fired.

She brought up a simple message that had come from Captain Issam, late last night. Damn that Hibnet, why hadn't he called me? I was just a few sentences long,

> *To: Chief Skip Brown*
> *From: Captain Issam, Fulton Station*
> *Re: Your message*
> *Got your message, Killa taking early*
> *Jump tomorrow, sending Lt. Hill with her.*
> *Arriving early afternoon.*
> *Congrat on Ray's car.*

For a few seconds I was so stunned I just stared at the screen. I pushed my cellbutton, *11:22 standard federation time,* it softly chimed in my ear.

"Oh, my god," I uttered, "what the hell."

"I didn't dare tell you over your cell. I couldn't chance he'd find out and figure I'm snooping." Lont sarcastically snickered, "The man's an ass. He's so damn secretive. I have no idea why he hasn't told you. I can call Jim, my supervisor on the Ferry Station but I'm afraid someone might be tipped off that we are aware of their arrival."

"No, don't call up there. Our only chance might be they don't think I know and perhaps Hibnet never saw the transmission. We have a traitor close to him."

My mind raced, I'd deal with Hibnet later, and right now I had to get a ferry going to Moss's satellite Jump Station. Hill had no idea that I hadn't sent for them. Who had? Was it a trap? Would they kill Killa the minute she got off the Jump? My mind was whirling with questions.

"Lont, call down to the Ferry Terminal, I'm on the next one out!" I rushed to the door, "Cover for me, let my people know I'll call them as soon as I get back!"

"Don't worry, but be careful." She said then I heard her call the Terminal as I ran out the door. I didn't care if someone saw me in a rush, my mind was totally on getting to the Satellite Jump station before they arrived. I heard Buntie call out to me again but I ignored her, running all the way to the elevator, taking it up to Ring Six. I jumped onto a tram that led me across to the train terminal. To my relief, the ferry stewards were waiting for me. I was rushed onto the next ferry bypassing a long line. It took only a few minutes and we were on our way. I was totally out of breath, Hill's chastisement that I need to jog everyday flooded my head.

I looked around; everyone was staring at me as the ferry had been delayed to wait for my arrival. It wasn't as tense as the ride in, as most were leaving Moss, leaving their stay at the hospital. The sadness still lingered as no one liked hospital stays. I had to sit with the wheel chaired patients as it must have been the only seat available. I felt kind of bad that I'd probably displaced a wheel chaired person but my fear of what might happen to Hill and Killa quickly swallowed up any guilt.

It was a long half hour ride. I didn't follow protocol of waiting for all the patients to disembark, but rushed out the minute the doors were opened. Again, feeling guilty but the concern over Hill and Killa took precedent.

The small Jump station was packed. It was the time of day that many of the incoming patients were arriving and since discharge time was often noon on Moss, many were leaving. I rushed over to the arrival board, looking for Logan Moon's arrivals since they'd have taken a connecting Jump from there. Ten incoming flights were blinking! Jiminy!

Most were in Terminal B. Fighting the crowds I headed toward the signs pointing to B. Issam probably didn't want to give too much information. He'd not want to give someone a heads up as to their exact arrival. "Ray's Car" what was he trying to tell me? Then it hit, Ray's car was number 15. I headed toward B15. Sure enough, a Logan Jump was coming in at 12:30.

I got in the corridor that pointed to B1-22. Should I wait, most of the B arrivals had to come through here? What if I'd misunderstood Issam's clue? I tapped my cellwatch; 12:45 softly entered my ear. The board said Jump B15 had arrived with time for unloading they'd get out just about now. My heart was pounding, what if I was wrong? I'd tried calling Hill's cell but got nothing. Damn Hibnet and his out dated Jump policies.

I was standing in the middle of the hallway. Passengers were bumping into me left and right. I stretched my neck. I looked for Lt. Hill's head as Killa was so short I'd not see her in this crowd. I saw what looked like Hill's auburn highlighted hair. I rushed forward, only to bump into a complete stranger, who looked at me like I was a crazy kook and rushed on past me.

"Chief?" I felt my arm being pulled. Hill and Killa were right beside me. I guess I make a bigger recognized target.

"Thank god." I muttered grabbing onto both of them. "Come on, let's get out of here." I dragged both of them down the hallway to the center. Hill, of course, was jabbering away, pulling back.

"Hey, I left my suitcase back there." She urgently tried to turn around.

"Forget it!" I growled, "I've got to get you guys out of here." She must have realized that I was serious, she gave up and rushed forward picking up the other side of Killa. With the tiny Ligithian between us we half carried the poor small woman to the terminal's security office. I opened the door, my badge already out and to the surprise of the guards turned left into their boss' office.

It was empty. A guard followed us in. "Do you need some help?" He glanced at Killa, "What's she done?"

Both Hill and I irritated that they would pick on a Ligithian, yelled, "Nothing!" making the guard take a step backwards and causing the other guard to come running.

Hill was not done though, "What is this all about Chief?" I didn't want the guards to hear so I ignored her and turned to the two officers blocking the doorway.

"Sorry, I need to use this office for a second."

"You're Chief Brown, aren't you?" the woman officer said from behind the man. Are you here to see Jim?"

I knew Jim Voste, the head of the terminal's security. When I came for my annual meeting every year, he joined us in Pol's office. "No, I'll talk to him later, I need some privacy right now."

Both left, I turned to see two very irritated women. Killa was the first to speak, "What's going on Skip? I came as soon as I could. You scared us half to death."

Hill, dressed casually in jeans and a plain t-shirt with her hair in a ponytail, looking more like a teenager than a police woman in her mid-twenties, glared at me. My lieutenant knew what was wrong, "You didn't send for Killa, did you?"

"NO!" I half shouted, the tension flowing right out of me in relief of seeing them, "I certainly did not. Why didn't you check first! You're lucky I made it here, I just got Issam's note!" I was pacing now, as I put a blue pill in my mouth, feeling the back of my neck tightening - a bad sign for me. "I was afraid you were walking into a trap!"

"Sit down Skip." Killa was talking to me like I was ten years old again, "Calm down. We're here, safe and sound, relax. You don't want to have an episode."

To my surprise I did exactly as she said, my old nursemaid still had that effect on me. "Well, at least you're here, I don't know about safe." I groaned. "Why didn't you check with me?"

It was Hill that answered, "For one thing, it's hard to get a hold of you here. The message said things only you would say."

Killa spoke up, "It said to come at once, to get Artchie to take care of the dogs and to supervise the front desk, that I'd be back within a week."

"What the hell!" I exclaimed, someone had gone to a lot of trouble to know our life. "I'm glad you didn't come alone."

"Issam saw to that," Hill remarked. "Although I would have taken personal time anyway, I wasn't going to let her come here unescorted."

"I've got to get you to Moss as quietly as possible," I exclaimed as a rap on the door came. Jim Voste's head came around the door.

"You need anything?" he asked. He was in his early thirties, nice looking clean cut guy who unlike me, spent time in a gym and lived on Epie1 when not here supervising the security at the terminal.

"Thanks Jim." I waved him in. "I need to get on a ferry back as soon as I can but with as little fanfare as possible. "Do you have a direct line to Lont Pol?"

"Yeah." He handed me a phone off his belt. "You have to actually punch the nine button on it." He laughed, "It's an old fashioned digital line. You'll have a six second delay. It was the best Pol could get out of Hibnet's office. I'll arrange for you to get on the next ferry, when you're ready. I'll walk you down and let you in the back way. Will that do?"

"Thanks. This is Lieutenant Hill and my Aunt Killa Brown." I saw the look on his face when he looked at Killa but he didn't say anything. He did say something to Hill, "Welcome Lieutenant. Have we met before?"

What a come on line. It annoyed me, he'd hit on my cop right in front of me. Hill looked startled, "No, I don't think so," she nervously fidgeted. Don't tell me she found him attractive!

"Well, maybe we should." He laughed. I just glared at him.

It didn't help that when he left Killa whispered to Judy, "He's not bad looking," and grinned.

"He's too old!" I grumbled, getting a disbelieving look from Hill.

"He's about your age, saying you're old, Chief?" Hill quipped and Killa snickered.

"Not the same." I couldn't think of anything else to come back with.

I picked up the old fashioned digital phone, pressing the number nine button. It took at least two minutes before Pol picked up. "Jim?" she asked.

"No, it's me, Skip." I could picture the surprised look that the Moss' superintendent of police probably had on her face. "I'm at the satellite ferry terminal. I'm leaving shortly. Jim's going to escort us to a ferry."

I had to wait ten seconds before I heard her answer, "Fine. I'll be down there waiting. Still be careful." The phone went dead.

We followed Jim to the back entrance to the ferry leaving shortly for Moss. We were the first seated. I felt Killa's tension as we watched those going to the hospital space station. My old nursemaid hadn't been back since she'd fled with me and my brother twenty years earlier. Her purple eyes were darkened, her small delicate slightly pointed ears were twitching - a sure sign of a Ligithian's nervous state. Hill, who was from the same sector as Killa's origins, knew the signs and took Killa's hand.

I was so tired. Even though the ferry trip was only half an hour long I felt my eyes closing. The seats were comfortable. Killa touched my arm. I forced myself to open my eyes and look at her. My former nursemaid, my responsibility to protect, now blood bonded to me, was worried, all four feet four inch of her. Her purple eyes held nothing but uncertainty and fear. I didn't blame her. The last time she'd been to Moss (Medical Operative Space Station) was when my doctor parents had been killed. Years ago, she'd left the space station as quickly as she could, running with me and my brother to Nestor to hide us with my Uncle Jack. She had never come back, not even when later I'd spent almost a year here recuperating from my accident. If the Highbloods of Ligithia knew she was alive, they would try and kill her. Me too, for that matter but we hid under my Uncle Jack's name. My mother's brother took Killa's blood bond until he died. I went from John Masters to Skip Brown and it was all I'd known since I was eleven years old. Killa wasn't a spring chicken and I worried this was too much on her. I patted her hand and got a half smile that was strained.

I looked over her to Judy Hill who was looking out the porthole window in the seat on the other side of

Killa. This was not a good situation. I silently thanked Pol for snooping on Hibnet's Jump line. Now that we were on our way back from the Jump Satellite station heading to the mammoth space station I reflected I had done everything I could to keep Killa away from, but had obviously failed. Rushing to the satellite, I hadn't had the time to be angry, now sitting here anger flooded my brain. Someone had duped Killa to come here using my name and I was going to find out who!

"Chief," Hill was pointing out the window. "What a sight. I'll never get over its immenseness. The rings are beautiful. The hospital station in my Orion Sector has maybe four rings!"

"Besides being a regional medical center it's also a research hospital that is respected by most of the sectors, humanoid and others." I didn't want to mention that Hill's Orion sector was so far out that they were considered bumpkins, but then Killa also came from the same sector. My mother had been born on Ligithia, the slave planet. I'd never been there. It was over two days Jump and I didn't do spatial travel well. I shuddered at the thought of a two day Jump of hell.

"It is impressive!" Hill commented. "They have the most advanced medical techniques of the entire Federation. Only the best doctors come here!" She must have remembered my parents had been doctors there, she looked at me but didn't say anything further.

"It's okay," I turned away from her. Very few knew of my parents but Hill had found out when she had investigated a murder on Nestor where Ray and I had fled to and grew up on. It was a memory I'd rather not think on, I had enough troubles. Who had sent the message that I needed Killa to come to Moss? No one knew of her, at least I had thought no one did. Only Doctor Hibnet knew. Surely he wouldn't tell anyone. He had kept our secret over twenty years, surely there was someone else who'd discovered us but how? Was it from the doctor's stolen files but his files were old they didn't mention Fulton only that we had survived.

"Welcome to the Medical Operations Space Station folks," our shuttle ferry pilot voice came over the intercom. "We will be docking in about twenty minutes. Please let the passengers in wheel chairs out first. Please have your medical card out; it will help us direct you to the correct portal and onto transports to the right section. Have a great rest of your day."

It was the same speech I had heard over a day earlier when I had first ridden the ferry. "What a system they have here," Hill expounded. "They must have hundreds of shuttles going every day to get from the satellite to the space station. We aren't going to be able to communicate very well with Issam."

"No, he'll have to manage best he can." I explained it further to her, "They say that the space station with all its medical equipment couldn't have the Jumps interfering with their sensitive equipment so the Jump is pulsated to the satellite which really is a manmade moon that circles Moss. Then it comes digitally to the station. I'm beginning to realize it is more Dr. Hibnet trying to keep everything under his control than the medical staff's concerns."

I looked around. Most passengers were incoming patients. Killa's worried look fit in very well with this crowd, who were on their way for some medical procedure. A somber quiet atmosphere, uncertainty clung to the passengers' fears. I remember my parents making us sit quiet in the shuttle whenever we traveled, explaining that quiet reserved behavior was to be observed under the circumstances; out of respect for the hospital's patients.

An attendant was hurrying down the aisle stopping at our seats. "Chief Brown?" The nervousness in her voice was unmistakable, making Killa grab tightly onto my arm.

"Yes, that's me." I looked up into the pretty face that was all alarm.

"Could you come with me, please?" I swear she was ready to pull me out of my chair, I could see it in her eyes.

"Sure." I turned to Killa, "Please stay with Lt. Hill. I'll be right back." She reluctantly nodded. I got a glimpse of Hill crossing over to my seat as I walked up the aisle.

I followed the attendant up to the front of the cabin. Everything seemed smooth, a nice quiet ride. At the front, near the galley, I saw another woman bending over what seemed a small package. She looked up. Seeing me, her hand pointed to it. "Please come here," her voice was shaking.

I knelt next to what seemed to be almost a jewelry box; my mother had one for her bracelets - strange how that memory had entered my head.

"We found this in the pantry. I was just about to offer drinks, when I saw it."

I read the top of the box; "This is a bomb, go to seat 24 and get Chief Brown." What really caught my eye were the words written under it – "aka John Masters RIP."

Shit! Someone had planted this and they wanted me to know about it before they blew the damn ferry shuttle to pieces. I had seen bombs like this before. They were used as military mines. I carefully took the note off the top. Sure enough the timer was blinking, three minutes ten seconds to go.

The co-pilot was standing over me. "What is going on?" I heard the attendant whispering to him, she didn't want the whole ship in total panic. In three minutes it wouldn't matter.

I felt a tug on my arm, it was Killa. Her eyes were wide as she saw what I was bending over. "Get back to your seat, now!" I quietly but firmly told her.

Being a Ligithian and blood bonded to me, she had to do whatever I ordered her to do. I never had ordered her to do anything before. I saw her struggle, she didn't want to leave me. Having no choice she turned and went back. Hill, however, kneeled next to me. "I could diffuse it if I had my kit but we don't have time."

"We need to get it out of here." My mind was racing. "We can't open any of the doors. Even if we could, the cabin would decompress and kill us all." My mind thought of my parents, is this what had happened to them? Did they know they were going to blow up?

I had to do something! Sweat was coming down into my eyes. *Calm, keep calm.* The lavatory light was blinking empty. I rushed in, throwing the cover open, I threw the package down into the dark blue liquid and pressed the handle. I didn't wait for it to finish. I rushed out.

"Flush it out. Open the valves. Tell the pilot to dump the sewage." I tried to keep my voice steady but firm. I didn't need the passengers alarmed.

The copilot went to say something but stopped and then rushed into the cabin. I followed him. He went over to the panel pressing some buttons. "I don't know if it will work, we do this only on the ground, they hook up hoses. It may freeze shut before it can get it out." The pilot was yelling at us but we didn't have time to explain.

The attendant was telling everyone in the cabin to make sure they were buckled up. I saw her go to the back and speak to the nurses taking care of the incoming patients. I rushed back out but I never made it past the galley as the ship almost seemed to lift up, taking me with it. I think I hit my head on the ceiling and then I fell hard to the ground. The ship was shaking violently. *Why the hell did I come here, I should have followed my instinct and stayed home* - my mind became an echo chamber bouncing that thought around in my brain and then nothing.......

~~~~~~~~~~~~~~~~~~~~~

The angel smiled. Her golden hair was shining from a large glow behind her. She was smiling. Her white glimmering cape seemed to flow around her. "Are you here to help me?" I finally managed to get out.

I felt her take my hand. "Wake up Chief Brown. Wake up."

"Wake UP!" My mind tried to focus but my eyes weren't cooperating. The fog surrounding her seemed to swirl and then start dissipating leaving a harsh overhead light outlining Dr. Gale Lawry who was patting my hand.

I tried to get up but she forced me back down. "Easy Skip," she told me, "you've gotten a bad bump on your head."

"I'm sorry," I managed to get out of my mouth, "I didn't mean to stand you up for lunch…"

"It's perfectly understandable." Her smile was so beautiful, again I found her fascinating. "We'll do it some other time."

I managed to nod, then Lt. Hill's voice cut into my stupor. "I think he needs one of his pills!"

"No, it's a slight concussion, not anything related to his seizures." Lawry told my Lieutenant who was now standing next to her.

"Hill?" I mumbled, then it hit me; the ferry bomb, the explosion. "Where's Killa? What happened to the ship?" I forced myself up despite Dr. Lawry's insistence that I lay down.

It was Hill that answered. "We made it to the Moss port, though barely. There is a huge hole in the side of the shuttle. Killa is in the outer room waiting. They wouldn't let her come in."

"Yes, it is procedure that families wait outside. Your Lieutenant insisted it was police protocol that some officer be present."

I looked over at Hill, she at least had the presence to blush. Protocol, my ass. She just had to stick herself in!

The door opened and Dr. Dan Bolker walked in. His over six foot two stature was impressive. In his white lab coat he looked tall and lean. He had high cheek bones that gave his face a pleasant look even when he was frowning. He was smiling now though as he came over and shook my hand. "I hear you're quite the hero, Skip."

I just grunted but of course Hill had to get her two cents in, "The bomb wouldn't have been on the shuttle if we hadn't been on it." She came to stand next to him, not looking at me, as she knew my scowl well.

"Still, it was your quick thinking that saved the day." Bolker interjected. "I came to check you out." He checked my pulse.

"I've done all the brain scans." Lawry told him. Bolker smiled at her. It wasn't a smile I liked and withdrew my arm in protest. He didn't seem to notice.

"I'm sure you've done all the proper tests." He smiled at her again.

Lont Pol's voice cut across from the door. "Is he going to be alright?" She sounded irritated as Dan Bolker and my superintendent had been an item for a long time, although they never openly flaunted it.

"Oh yes." He turned to her, sensing something was wrong but not sensing what exactly it was.

"Well, I must get back." Gale Lawry stepped toward the side door. "I just happened to be close by when they brought him in." She slipped out the door and the tension eased. Dr. Bolker turned back to me. "I've checked the brain scans. You have a slight concussion. Gale already gave you some dilating medicine that should take care of that." Gale, he called her Gale? I looked over at Lont, her frown matched mine. He didn't seem to notice, however, "How do you feel? Any sense of a seizure coming on?"

"No. I'm feeling a lot better. I was a little confused at first but my head has cleared."

"You were mumbling something about your Uncle Jack." Hill was standing next to Bolker, a huge frown on her face. "Also, something about an angel?"

I scowled at her. "Well, it certainly wasn't you," I irritatedly barked at her.

"No, I didn't think it was me." She looked over at the door that Dr. Lawry had just left. Oh, the woman could be infuriating. I stood up. I felt fine. Hill came over to take my arm but I shook her off and walked out to the reception area on my own steam.

Killa jumped up off the waiting room chair and rushed over to meet me. She just stopped short of hugging me. "Skippy, are you alright!" Her eyes were deep purple, her ears were twitching, her hair seemed to statically stand on end.

"Yes, stop worrying, I'm fine," I told her, taking her arm, trying to calm her, succeeding just a little. It was my rookie lieutenant that set her at ease.

"He's fine," Hill dryly commented, "he's already snapped at me twice."

I glowered at her but Killa laughed, "I guess he is alright." It was good to hear her laugh, it wasn't often I got to hear it.

I looked over at my lieutenant, she was wearing our standard regulated suit but it was quite large. The suit coat hung down almost to her knees, her shirt was tucked in but couldn't hide the fact it drooped on her. Only her tie seemed normal. She wore her sneakers! Totally not regulations. Totally not Hill! I just stared, my mouth openly gaping. "Hill…"

"I had to borrow this from one from Elly. My suitcase was left on the Moss's satellite Jump station." She looked accusingly at me, as if I was to blame for the lost apparel.

The woman was incorrigible. It was her own damn fault she'd left it behind. I opened my mouth to retort but it was Lont Pol, who had been talking softly with Dr. Bolker, that cut in before I could snap at Hill. "I've got Jim looking for it Judy. I'm sure he'll find it. We don't have a high stealing problem. If we don't find it, you can borrow some of my clothes. We're pretty close in size."

"Lont, I have to get Killa settled in the hotel. We'll need to arrange for some protection coverage. Someone tricked her to come here."

"If you don't mind Chief, let me get a couple of my police people to take her over, I sure could use you at the Convention Center if you're feeling Okay. We are running out of time. I want Judy to run over the guest list for me."

Killa assured me that she was fine. "You and Hill take my bedroom, I'll move in with Marcus. The hotel is full up because of Hibnet's conference. I'll have them bring in twin beds."

Two burly men and an older woman surrounded Killa. After they were introduced Killa went off. "Don't worry Chief, they'll take good care of her," Lont assured me.

From the tram ship at Moss' greeting ferry station they had brought me to the regular hospital ER wards on Ring Six. It seemed so familiar as I had spent a good several months on this ward. We caught a tram and headed down one level to Ring Five, the city of Eupie and to the convention center.

The main room was fairly large. Two immense marble staircases flanked the room heading up to a balcony where I knew there were elevators and in the back more conference rooms. This large room would be the focus of the reception with a stage set up below the overhanging balcony where musicians of the Crab Sector Symphony (Hibnet had imported them from the planet Alise, our arts center of the sector). Long tables covered in white table cloths lay against the walls.

"Hors D'oeuvres will be served by attendants and the tables will also be full of delectables," Lont informed me. "Tables seating eight will be circling a dance floor. She looked over at Hill, "I'd like you to meet Lans Aroro, he's my liaison officer with Hibnet's office."

He shook Hill's hand, "Have we met before?"

What was this, pick up Chief's detectives week? I started to say something but Lont interrupted me. "Lans, she knows personnel files, show her the guest list. She'll be able to see an irregularity."

Before I could say anything, Lans Aroro headed up the stairs with Hill following close behind. "I'm not sure she can help you. She's from off sector." I explained to Lont.

"She can help Lans cross reference incoming guests. She's smart Chief, or haven't you noticed?" Pol looked strangely at me.

"I'm well aware of Hill's *smartness*," I quipped. I had the feeling I was missing something but there was too much to do so I put it on the back burner.

We went over the whole complex; where the reception line would be, where all the exits and entranceways were located. Pol was stationing security at each door upstairs and down. The kitchen was being monitored and the food tested. The ballroom itself would have twenty roaming undercover security personnel.

My superintendent showed me a floor plan of the hotel rooms. Each floor hallway was being monitored with extra police staff and cameras. Each room had been labeled as to the guests. I noticed the guests came from all over. In Sector, many of the Dome's representatives were attending including Crab's Senate President Lilson. Many had brought their spouses and a few aides. Off Sector, included Human Federation Representatives, there was at least one from each of the sectors. I noticed from Orion the Ligithia ambassador had a suite of rooms. Alphonso Medicinis had three aides and four Ligithian helpers, slaves really. I felt my temperature rise, anger flushing upwards. I reached for my pills popping one in, swallowing it dry.

Included in the Federation Representatives was Consulate Assembly Governor General Thorn Pinote. He was about as high an official that the humanoid sectors had. He was responsible for representing all the Humans in the entire Federation. He had to deal with all the other species at the Federation Assembly. I didn't envy his position. His presence at the conference was a good indication how important the space station was.

Fred and Marcus, looking tired and exasperated, had come in to report on their investigating of all the ports of entry. "Cripes, Chief," Fred Stoshingburg complained, "we've been bumping heads all day with Moss' security. They sure are touchy individuals."

I looked over at Pol, she shook her head in disgust, "They report to Hibnet, not me. He's a control freak. It wouldn't be so bad if he was any good at it. He just bumbles his way through, as long as he's in charge."

"She's right," Marcus explained further. "The ports aren't well tended. We found several incidents where they are lack-a-daisy on not only their record keeping but on checking if the ship has the authority to bring anything into the station."

It was Lont Pol's policeman, Pat Telexis, who had been assigned to help Fred and Marcus, who spoke up. "Lont, they literally ignored us. No surprise. We may have a problem with 'un-wanteds' coming in through the other entry ports, especially Rings one and nine."

"Damn, now you see what I'm up against." She looked at me shrugging.

"I'll take care of the son of a bitch." I grumbled and headed out. Time I had it out with the pompous Dr. Hibnet.

Chapter Eight

I left the hotel. One of Lont's police cars was waiting for me at the front of the convention center. They dropped me at the crossover. Sitting on the tram I stewed, my anger pumping adrenaline into me. *That stupid asshole* was running through my head. I'd had enough. He was playing with fire, lives could be on the line including my own and Killa's.

Using my card I took the elevator to the top of the space station. Entering Hibnet's luxurious office, I ignored the receptionist heading right for his office door. I heard one of his secretaries yelling after me but I didn't even look in her direction. I pounded on his office door once, and then physically pushed it opened. I heard something crack but I could have given a shit.

Hibnet was indeed in his office along with his receptionist Marshie. She was massaging his neck and her shirt was unbuttoned showing lacy underwear. I have to admit, it did stop me for a second but being a cop you see it all. I just pointed my finger at her and yelled, "OUT!"

Gathering the front of her shirt, trying to button it at the same time, but having little success, she ran out past me. I had broken the door. I knew most of the outer reception area staff was standing in the open doorway peeking in. They cleared the way for the half-dressed receptionist.

I've been told that I'm a fearsome sight when I'm angry. Hibnet just stared, his mouth opened. I was thankful I'd had the sense to pop one of my blue pills into my system as my blood pressure skyrocketed. No wonder he hadn't warned me of Issam's cable or taken care of the security of the entry ports, he was too busy getting his jollies from his personal secretary.

"You have no right!" he finally sputtered. He touched his computer on his desk, although all he had to do was yell at the broken doorway, "Get security! Help!"

"Oh please," I laughed, "I am your security, you asshole!"

"I have my own security, you're under arrest, barging in here." He tried to put himself back together. I noticed he had to zip his pants. Despite being such an asshole, I'd always held him in high esteem. He'd been best friends with my parents. I guess it's true, familiarity breeds contempt.

"Listen to me!" I sat facing him across his desk. "You are going to tell that "special" security of yours to fall into line with my people. It's imperative that we secure all ports of entry. Do you understand?"

"You can't order me around." He glared at me.

"Well, then I'll be forced to cancel the convention." I glared right back at him.

"You can't do that!" he almost screeched it. His eyes were wide with anger.

"I have the authority. Under section five of the sector emergency regulations I have the right and the duty to cancel any event that poses a danger to the public. I have no doubt this is one of them. Would you care to call your counsel?" I glared at him. "Furthermore, I will have to have a press briefing to explain it all."

I could see him weighing his options. I also saw him come to the conclusion that I wasn't bluffing. "Look Skip, we've gotten off on the wrong foot. Think of your parents, this space station meant everything to them. You'd do nothing to jeopardize its future."

"It's not me that jeopardizing this station's future. You are to call your 'dogs' off, they are to cooperate with us and I mean it. You are to disassociate yourself from their activities. You have already cost us valuable time."

"It was not my intent to cause problems, but my security force is highly trained. "

"Trained by whom?" I asked. Something wasn't ringing right.

"I'd rather not say but I can trust them. Lont Pol's force may be compromised and unreliable. I need these independent security people." He once again scowled at me, challenging me to disagree with him.

"I'll ask one more time! Who told you this and where do those security people come from." I was leaning across his desk, ready to grab him around the neck, the pompous ass.

"It was me." I heard from behind me. I turned to see Dr. Gale Lawry had come into the room. "I didn't mean to interfere, Skip, my brother is in the security business and I offered Dr. Hibnet the chance to have extra protection. I only meant to help." She smiled at me.

"Why didn't you clear it with me, Dr. Hibnet." I felt my anger slowly dissipate; it wasn't sinister after all, only misguided.

"Again, it was my fault." Gale Lawry seemed totally contrite. "I hadn't met you and I knew that Dr. Hibnet did not trust Superintendent Pol. I was coming here to tell Dr. Hibnet he should tell you."

"Dr. Lawry," I started to say but she held up her hand.

"Please call me Gale and my apologies, Dr. Hibnet, you should put those people under Skip. She put her hand on his shoulder, which seemed to calm him down. "

"Yes, I think you are right doctor." He turned to me. "Is that satisfactory?"

I nodded, calling Lont to give her instructions to send Marcus and Fred back down to the entry ports and to secure them with some of Pol's people.

"Now that things are all settled, how about we all go for a cup of java? You do owe me for standing me up." She laughed, lightly touching my arm. I nodded, a few minutes with a cup of java before heading back would help clear my head. She had a way of calming me down. I couldn't explain it but it was a pleasant feeling.

"I have a meeting, sorry." Dr. Hibnet seemed totally recovered. "Guests will start arriving soon. I need to make sure all is set."

"Remember what I said, anymore secrets and I'll cancel the conference. Do you understand?"

He frowned but nodded. I had the feeling he was hiding something but I wasn't about to challenge him in front of Dr. Lawry.

I followed Gale and we went down to Epie One. Near the hotel was a small café. It was slightly drizzling. She wore a light raincoat. I hadn't paid any attention to the weather report. "The rain will be over shortly." She laughed lightly, "We all know to keep tract of the rain schedule. I think they wanted it over with before the guests start arriving."

I remembered when my mother would have our raincoats out the morning of the scheduled precipitation. We had taken it for granted, part of the space station life.

"Your mind seems far away." Her soft voice cut into my thoughts bringing me back to the present. Her hand was touching mine. I looked up to understanding dark blue eyes, her delicate perfectly tapered face was surrounded by velvet yellow hair. I smiled, thinking of the angel in my dream.

"I really do want to apologize about suggesting to Hibnet to get his own personal security. It was to help my brother. He's been trying to get his security business started. It was wrong. I didn't realize how it would impact Lont Pol."

"It's alright. Dr. Hibnet should have known better or at least tell Lont. It's water over the dam." We ordered a mug of java and some cinnamon scones. The scones were smothered in butter.

"So tell me Skip, what's Fulton Station like? I've never been there." She sat across from me. She was very real, very interested in what I had to say. She must have really great bedside manners, I thought. Then I blushed at the thought.

"Well, it's hot." It was as far as I got. Lieutenants Null and Hill entered the café. If I could have been invisible I would have done so. Of course, Hill noticed me right away.

"Oh good, you can help us carry snacks back for the troops." Hill came right up to our table. Everyone's hungry. Come on and help us." She smiled at Dr. Lawry.

I wasn't going to introduce her to Gale but Lara had followed her over. "Hello, Dr. Lawry. This is Judy Hill. Hope you don't mind if we steal the Chief?"

What could Lawry say, "Oh, we were just done." She touched my hand and rose, "Call me when you get a chance." I watched her leave, the rain had stopped and she just carried her raincoat on her arm.

"I'm gonna kill both of you." I growled but only got a smirk from Hill. Lara, with a grin on her face, had already gone up to the counter, totally ignoring me.

"Really, Chief?" Lt. Hill commented. "Long distance relationships never work, especially from someone who has violent Jump sickness."

I just growled again but I felt my face blush. The woman was incorrigible. Something in the back of my brain knew she was right but I'd be goddamned if I'd admit it. I duly helped them get several snack bags back to the convention police command center. Lont Pol had commandeered a large office right next to the ballroom. The room was full of small telescreens showing every angle of the both the reception area and the actual ballroom.

"We will have at least twenty officers in formal dress roaming in the crowds but also we'll have these monitors covered. Observers should be able to see any unusual activities and act on it immediately.

"Nice job, Lont," I congratulated her efforts. "I'm still uneasy as I think Hibnet is hiding something."

"I wouldn't be surprised," she offered, "I'm still angry over the security he hired."

I should have told her about Lawry but I didn't. It was innocently done. It would only turn Lont Pol against the doctor and I didn't think that would accomplish anything so I kept it to myself.

"You better check your cellbutton," Pol advised me, "I've been calling you for some time and you weren't answering.

My hand went to my cell button. Nothing. On inspection it was turned off. How the hell did I do that! "Sorry, it's turned off." I turned it back on and I was flooded with messages. Shit, where was my head!

"Mind elsewhere?" Hill lamented, "I thought you told me you'd never get involved with anyone again after your first marriage debacle."

"Dr. Lawry is a friend," I told her "and it is none of your business! Stop sticking your nose in where it doesn't belong. She's just a friend!" I reiterated.

"Didn't look like it to me, google eyes." She smirked.

"Hill!" I exploded but it was Lont who spoke up. "All the men like her."

I was surprised, Lont Pol was the ultimate professional, very rarely expressing a personal opinion.

She must have seen my startled look so she continued, "It's not her fault." Lont went even further, "she doesn't seem to care. Lawry mostly ignores her admirers. So be flattered Chief."

"We're just friends!" I insisted.

"Well, at least it's keeping her away from Dan." My superintendent half laughed but I could tell she was also half serious. Pol had been going out with Dr. Dan Bolker for several years. I found it astonishing that she was so insecure with Lawry. I remembered though how Dan had looked at Gale. I blushed at the thought, was I jealous? I put it out of my head, of course not, I had just been surprised.

Of course it was Hill who had to put in her two cents. "I don't think she's that attractive, must be her electrifying personality. Men just love electrifying personalities."

"Hill!" I pointed my finger at her yet both Lont and Lara were chuckling their asses off. I decided to ignore them, putting it down to envy over Gale's attractiveness. Women!

We were interrupted by Lans Aroro, Lont Pol's liaison with Dr. Hibnet's office. "Sorry to interrupt but I just got a message from Ambassador Alphonso Medicinis."

"What does the ambassador to Ligithia want?" Lont Pol questioned.

"It's to Chief Brown. He would like you to visit him in his suite at the Herriden."

"I haven't got time to see him." I didn't say it but I also had no desire to see the slaver either. I was sure that my hatred for his kind would be extremely obvious causing Dr. Hibnet PR troubles.

"Well, he says if you can't see him, could John please call on him." He was looking at his tab message reading it with a confused look on his face. "Who is John?"

I caught my breath. Obviously, the ambassador knew who I was. He was referring to my birth name, John Masters.

"Don't go." Hill was at my side talking softly so no one else could hear. "Send someone else. Send Marcus, let the Laotian think he made a mistake." Hill was one of the few that knew and by the look on Lont Pol's face I guessed she knew too. My hidden past was forging forward and with it, any safety I had. Killa came to mind. I had to go. If they knew she was here it could be disastrous.

"Lont, I'll be back." I told my superintendent.

"Chief, be careful." She walked me to the door. "I know how dangerous this is for you."

I guess Dr. Bolker had told his courtesan of my past. When the neurosurgeon had treated me after my racing accident, Dr. Hibnet felt it important to open up all the files. Dan Bolker had become my friend over thirteen years ago. I trusted him. If he told Lont, I had no problem with it. My superintendent and my Lieutenant looked worried. I tried to allay their fears, "Don't worry. He's not going to do anything that would cause problems, not so openly."

I went over to the hotel. I knew which suites the Ligithian delegation occupied. They had quite a large contingent but most of it was made up of his slaves, his blood bonded Ligithians. I didn't have to knock as the door opened as my fist was reaching up.

I hadn't seen many Ligithians outside of Killa. Very few were let out of their Orion sector or even off their planet. The one that opened the door was tiny; a little over four feet tall with light yellow hair that peeked out of her slave uniform hat which half covered her delicate pointed ears. She had the light violet eyes that could turn much darker if she became alarmed. She bowed low, "Please enter, Ambassador Medicinis will be with you shortly."

I walked into a luxurious suite. The room was decorated in plush deep cushioned seats. Beautiful flowers adorned all the tables. I could see several rooms off the main - a dining room with bedrooms beyond that, an office with several computer desks. The small men and women were busy doing the ambassador's bidding.

Another slave, this time a small white-haired four foot male, offered me a drink or food but I politely turned him down. I walked over to the large windows looking down on Eupie1. I tried not to stare at the Ligithians but I could see them in the reflection of the windows. All wore the light green uniforms with the ambassador's emblem. I knew it was a law that outside the Lightia it was required to show who they belonged to. I felt my face become flushed with anger. At least they didn't wear collars like some of the pictures Killa had shown me.

"John." Simply said but I cringed. Turning away from the window I faced a rather tall gaunt but rather distinguished gray haired man. His face held deep blue oval eyes, a noble nose and sticking out of his hair were thin pointed ears, the only feature that the Laositian Highbloods shared with their Ligithians. I knew my own ears had a slight curve as did Rays but I wore my hair so it covered them. The man had a warm smile but it was wasted on me. He held out his long fingered hand but I ignored it. I looked down at my own hands, they were similar. I clenched them, damn my Highblood connection.

"Chief Brown of the Crab Nebula," I introduced myself frowning deeply at him. "What is it you wanted to see me for? I'm a very busy man."

"No doubt!" He turned away, walking over to a cabinet where one of his slaves handed him a tall iced drink. "I gathered you didn't want any nourishment. I'm sure my folks offered you some."

"Your slaves did indeed offer me refreshments but I'm in a hurry as I've said." I was bordering on rudeness, something I rarely do to government officials. I deal with a lot of them at the dome and I've found sarcasm is wasted on them. Usually I keep my temper in check, usually.

"You look very much like your mother. Who does your brother take after?" He smiled again, sipping his drink."

I ignored him. "Is there something you wanted to discuss with me?" He wasn't going to bait me.

"I brought up my daughter to always be polite. Did she forget to impart this to you? Although I must admit Jacque, my son, was always on my case and he did influence you at a fairly early age. He was a very difficult child!"

I just gaped at him. Was he telling me, he was my grandfather? "Are we..."

"Related?" he finished for me. "Yes, I'm your grandfather. Jacque, Uncle Jack to you, was my youngest, your mother, Helen was my oldest. Of course, I never really knew your father, Dr. James Masters, but I did occasionally meet with your mom, she was terribly proud of her family. Her death was a terrible blow to me. It made me realize to stay away from you."

"You never met with mother!" I was furious, how dare he tell lies of her, "She wouldn't have anything to do with you! She hated you!"

"Ah, her cover story but I would meet her on Moss or at other conventions, if we could do it quietly."

"Stop lying! I know the truth. She would have told us if that was true! Jack really hated you, he never even told us you existed but he had nothing nice to say about Laositians. You're cruel bastards."

I could tell his Ligithians were upset. They all came out into the main room, ready to protect their master! Their eyes were deep purple and their ears were twitching. His few Laositian aides also came rushing out to see what the matter was.

"Please, all of you go back to what you were doing. There is nothing wrong." The command in the ambassador's voice was clear and everyone obeyed. I could see the Ligithians were still upset. If he was right, they knew I was of the same blood. It would confuse them. They would obey me as long as it did not conflict with my grandfather. I was sure now he was a relative as I could see it in the eyes of his slaves. They followed my movements intently. I was someone they should be concerned with. Damn! I knew I had Laositian blood but it was something else to be confronted with it.

"How is Killa?" He said as he sat down on his plush couch nonchalantly crossing his legs.

I just stared at him. I could feel my blood pressure rising, the back of my neck becoming tighter. I quickly reached into my pocket retrieving a blue pill and popping it in my mouth.

"Ah your methozine for your seizures," His intent blue eyes were focused on me. It was at that moment I realized the familiarity with my mother. She'd look just like that at me, especially when she was concerned. I cringed. I didn't want this man to be my mother's father, I wanted just to hate him but I found myself drawn to him.

"How do you know…"

He held up his hand, "There is very little I don't know. I have my resources and I've tried to keep up on you and your brother. Although it was from a distance, since I couldn't take the chance of giving you away. I know he is married and just had a baby boy. Jim, I believe they call him."

"You have no right," I pointed my finger at him, "no right whatsoever. Keep out of our lives. If Ray, Killa, Julie or Jim are hurt, I'll kill you myself. Do I make myself clear?" My temper was flaring and I was losing control but I didn't care. My family's safety net was melting away and there seemed nothing I could do about it.

He was off the couch and standing in front of me. "Do not take that tone with me, young man," he exploded. "I have risked much to protect you all. Don't lecture me!" His voice boomed and his eyes flared. I guess now I know where my temper came from. But he wasn't dealing with one of his slaves or his aides. I took a step toward him, pointing my finger at his chest.

"I'll lecture you anytime I feel like it. You keep far away or you'll regret it. If I find out that you have anything to do with sabotaging this conference I'll bring the weight of sector law crashing down on you. You aren't home. This is my jurisdiction and don't forget it! If I find out you had anything to do with the bombing of the ferry, you'll not have enough slaves to protect you!"

He wasn't use to anyone challenging him. He opened his mouth but nothing came out, confusion shown in every muscle on his face. I turned getting to the door before one of his slaves could. I jerked the door opened, stepping into the hallway then I slammed it shut with a loud boom.

I noticed two of Lont Pol's police peek around the corner at the end of the hallway. I felt relief that her security measures were working. I nodded at them, they retreated.

I got into the elevator. I went to push the lobby button but pressed the sixth floor button instead, getting off at our room's level. I walked down the hall arriving at our suite of rooms. There was a police officer sitting in front of our door. He stood, nodding to me, knocked on the door, and another officer peeked out, then opened it for me. Inside two more officers were sitting watching the news. Killa was sitting by the window, looking out. She immediately knew something was wrong. Her eyes flashed dark purple, she stood up coming over to me. "Skipper?"

"We need to talk. Let's go down to the coffee shop." Three of the officers followed us down and sat nearby our table. We had found one in the back corner, most of the tables were empty as the arriving guests were still checking in. I ordered a cup of java for me and black tea for Killa. She hadn't said a word all the way to the restaurant. She sat quietly, her eyes focused on me. They were still dark purple.

"I just had a visit with my grandfather." I looked at her, seeing her eyes darken, her white hair became wispy, almost electrifying, showing her twitching ears.

"Alphonso Medicinis is here?" She almost whispered it, cracking with emotion.

"Yes, he's Ligithia's ambassador." I said, noticing she shook her head, she knew.

"He's made some outrageous lies." I grabbed onto my cup of java, trying to steady my hand. I noticed Killa look away. "What do you think he told me?" I know my voice was harsh but I had a feeling my old nursemaid knew more than she'd been telling me.

"Don't badger her," I looked up to see Hill standing by the table.

"Go away!" I informed my lieutenant but of course she ignored me, sitting next to Killa, taking her hand. "You're not wanted." I iterated.

"I called her," Killa almost whispered it, "I did not know where you were, I knew you were upset, I…." her eyes teared up, her hands were shaking. I didn't know what to say, how to handle her, she'd always been so rock steady.

"Killa, would you like me to stay?" Hill still had a hold of her hand. Unbelievably, Killa nodded yes. Hill looked defiantly at me. "Can't you see, she's scared?"

"Killa, are you afraid of Ambassador Medicinis?" I asked but to my surprise she shook her head no.

"It is not he that scares me but his enemies." She looked at me. "His enemies are powerful. He should not be talking to you."

"Do you know anything about him?" Hill asked but kept going, obviously assuming I didn't. After all, she *was* from Orion sector. The lieutenant explained what she knew, "He's from one of the oldest most powerful families on Ligithia. He is also considered a moderate. Treats his slaves well and has been preparing the Laositians for the day a cure will be found. It has not made him many friends. Don't misunderstand, he doesn't want a cure, he just thinks it inevitable."

Hill had obviously done her homework. "Then you don't think he's trying to sabotage the convention or planted the bomb on the ferry?"

It was Killa that answered me, "No, it is not he."

"Killa, did my mother see him after she escaped Ligithia?" I asked her but she looked away. I tried again, "Killa please, I need to know!"

"Yes." My old nursemaid seemed to shrink down into the chair. Hill angrily stared at me. "I'm not mad Killa, I just need to know."

"She saw him a few times. You don't understand Skip, he was her father. He helped us get away." I was shocked, I didn't think I was hearing right. I just stared at her. "I could not tell you Skipper, I promised your mother. She was always afraid for you, always." Killa wrung her hands.

Hill glared at me. What did she expect me to say, to do? My whole past life was coming apart in pieces starting with my grandfather.

My cellbutton rang in my ear, it was Lont Pol. "Chief, the Consulate Assembly's Governor General is here, he's heading toward the Hotel. Could you please make sure all goes well."

"Governor Pinote?" I confirmed. He was the most powerful man in our Humanoid Universe. He was our top representative to the Federation Assembly. "I'm on it," I informed my nervous Superintendent. "Killa, head back with the police officers to the room, I'll be there as soon as I can." I hugged her, "Don't worry, everything will work out."

Hill stood up, "I'll go with her." I watched as she led Killa to the elevator. My old nursemaid had grown fond of Hill, maybe because they were both from the Orion sector. As sparsely populated as the Crab was, Orion was even more so. Orion had only six planets. Hill was from the planet Orbo, the capital of the sector; it is the government hub like Fulton Station was for the Crab. Of course, Killa was from the slave planet Ligithia which although in the Orion Sector was half a day jump away from Orbo, on the very outskirts of Orion. Still, they shared a common sector bond.

Besides Ray and I, and now Julie and the baby, Killa had no close ties. Despite my efforts to get my apartment superintendent to make friends in my apartment complex, she had still kept her distance. Perhaps her heighten sensitivity to people's feelings kept her isolated. Killa had once told me she smelled "good blood" in Hill. Whatever, I was glad they got along.

Speaking of Orion, I remembered Governor Pinote was from Orbo but I imagined he spent little time there. Most of his time was spent at the Federation Assembly in the huge Timexis Nebula Space Station, where most of the known Universe species gathered several times a year to govern. If not there then he was probably in Harte, Sol Sector, where our Humanoid Assembly gathered.

I saw Dr. Hibnet fluttering around the lobby. He was barking orders to the hotel's personnel making sure they were ready for the Governor. He didn't have to wait long as Governor's Pinote's entourage came rushing into the lobby, taking all the air out with them. His body guards were extremely professional, all dressed in light brown suits, they scanned the lobby. The head security guy looked at me and nodded. I was obviously known.

The Governor entered, walking with him were four young men who looked very much like him. "Those are his sons." Lara had positioned herself next to me. I noticed she was wearing her specialized suit coat that disguised her long ranged gun in her right arm. She wore her badge hooked to her pocket. One of the body guards gave her a nod. My lieutenant, Lara Null, was also known.

She was scanning the lobby, her sniper instincts on high alert. "He has, I believe, six children." Typical Orion, large families were promoted there since they needed to populate the sector. I remembered Hill telling me she came from a large family.

He was dressed in an expensive gray striped suit, so were his sons. They radiated that they were diplomats right down to their wing tipped shoes. His thick bush of hair was totally gray but it looked good on him. The Governor General was a large man and was probably considered handsome, as were his sons. All four sons were over six feet and looked fit and trim.

I focused on the sons. Each carried a suitcase, and were totally centered on their father. They all had auburn highlights and of course the fair skin that went with it. Even from this distance they looked intelligent, their light green eyes took everything in when not looking at their father.

After them came several aides, all dressed like the ambassador but not quite getting his distinguished look. They looked haggard and overworked. Of course Dr. Hibnet put himself front and center, greeting Pinote, almost bowing.

"Do his sons always accompany him?" I asked Lara.

"He usually has one or more with him. I've heard he also has a daughter that comes with him, lost one of his daughters tragically a few years ago and that was followed by the death of his wife shortly after that. The Pinote family is big in politics. His father was Governor before him, might call it a Dynasty."

I watched as the group loaded into the elevators with Hibnet fawning over the Governor with a constant barrage of compliments. I'm sure Pinote was used to it but it annoyed the hell out of me. I was glad when the lobby lay open and quiet reigned.

Lont Pol was issuing orders. "Most of the guests will be here by late afternoon. There is a multitude of cocktail parties in the suites tonight. Tomorrow brings all the conference meetings with Dr. Hibnet and the other board members giving tours of the different Rings. Then tomorrow night is the formal dinner in the main ballroom." I nodded. All my detectives would be mingling in their formal attire. It would be a couple of long days. We'd have to be on high alert for anything out of the ordinary.

All afternoon into evening a variety of guests registered. I saw our sector Dome representatives, famous athletes and cinema stars. My head hurt trying to cover the convention hall and the hotel. I was very glad when the activities slowed down and I sat with my detectives in the lounge nursing a glass of cognac. It was past midnight and deserted as all the guests were either retired for the night or at one of the private suite parties.

"Where have you been Hill?" I asked. I hadn't seen her since I'd left her at the cafe.

"I've been in the monitoring room, helping to cover the surveillance of several of the venues." Her eyes looked tired, she even looked a little disheveled. It was so unlike my prim and proper lieutenant.

"I'm worried about Killa, she needs to get out of the room." I told her. My old nursemaid had been stuck in our room with the police escort since she had arrived.

"She's coming with me tomorrow morning to go shopping for something to wear to the formal dinner. I don't have anything to wear since they never found my suitcase. I've been borrowing clothes. I've had no time to get anything. I'm borrowing from everyone."

"You're welcomed to anything of mine." I laughed, getting a smile out of her.

"Yeah, maybe a pair of socks," she quipped. "I'm desperate. Even my underwear is sagging."

Well, I wasn't going there and I didn't have to as Lont Pol came striding in, "We have a big problem. I mean BIG problem."

Chapter Nine

From the look on my Superintendent's face I gathered I wasn't going to like what I was about to hear and I was right! She sat down, her face was lined with worry. "We've lost our Jump lines, the Bassodians are dragging a sphere through."

"Shit. Damn those reptiles!" Fred Stoshingburg said what everyone was thinking.

"Well, at least most the guests are here. If it had happened yesterday, it would have been disastrous," Hill commented. That was my rookie, always looking for the positive.

"How long before they are out of the sector?" Lara asked.

"That's just the problem," Lans Ororo had walked in. The normally impeccably dressed man looked a mess; his tie was askew, his hair disheveled, his eyes were bloodshot. "They are coming here. They'll be parked not far from Moss. They'll be sending someone to the space station. I've been in touch with Dr.Hibnet's office, it is chaos in there, the good doctor is in a panic. I think he forgot to tell us about the planet they're dragging. He only told us about the serum they needed. We could have been better prepared for this."

"What!" I think we all shouted it at once. I swore under my breath!

Ororo collapsed into a chair. "The damn sphere engineers need a type of anti-biotic. Hibnet's office has Ring Seven making it now. Evidently some of the Bassodian's crew are sick. They get space sickness every once in a while, they are prone to it. It is a reptilian thing."

"Well, it's nice to know those lizards have some weaknesses." Fred slouched down in his seat. "There goes my watching the futbol game tomorrow."

"Cripes Fred, is it always about you!" Lara interjected. "Some of us have families back home that we can't get in touch with. Think of all the patients here, how many of them have people worried about them."

Fred looked contrite. Lara could do that to him.

"It's worse than that," came from the doorway as Dan Bolker walked in, "we have to reschedule procedures because the patients can't get here!" He came over sitting next to Lont. I saw him squeeze her hand under the table. He looked at Pol's liaison, "Lans, we need to coordinate with you on this."

Lans Aroro looked all done in, "Yes, I know. I've been working on it. Hibnet's office has already contacted each of the Ring's department heads and as soon as the communication lines are up we'll contact the patients to make new appointments. You know we'll lose some of them, we always do. "

"Can't you get the Bassodians to help us out?" Elly asked.

"If you learn one thing about the Bassodians, they have no sense of our needs, nor do they care. You have to handle them with caution, or they'll really screw things up," Hill commented surprising me that she'd know enough about them but then my rookie was always full of surprises.

Dr. Bolker spoke up, "They'll send a tug boat here that will dock on Ring One while their mother ship stays not far with the sphere behind it. They stay just far away from us to keep their gravitational pull from influencing us."

Lont Pol explained further, "Ring One is set up for non-human species. The Bassodians have a section with lower gravity and the dock fits their smaller tugs."

"Why not meet them? Get them the hell out of here!" I asked my Superintendent.

It was her boyfriend that answered, "It is rare that the lizards let anyone near their precious ship with its precious cargo. They'd blast us right out of existence," Bolker snorted, "and think nothing of it either. Their space ships have enough power to pulverize even this space station. Hauling that sphere takes a lot of energy. That's why they commandeer all our Jump lines."

"Humpf, damn lizards," Fred grumbled and got nods from around the table.

We all headed back to our rooms, tomorrow would prove to be even more difficult. I couldn't help but think that Hibnet now had a captured audience. No one could leave the space station, there'd be no Jumps from the Ferry Satellite Station. The guests couldn't even call home. How long would the Jumps be down? I'm sure no one was going to be in a good mood tomorrow.

The police were still at our suite of rooms, I sent them home until morning, which wasn't that far off. Killa had already gone to bed but I heard her talk to Hill when my rookie went into their shared bedroom. Marcus was sound asleep by the time I entered. As soon as my head hit the pillow I was out, but dark dreams with huge lizards filled my night and I woke up several times from the nightmares. I was glad when the light filtered in and I had to get up. By the time I showered and dressed it was well past dawn.

Killa and Hill had already left to go shopping. I gathered the police escort had gone with them. All my detectives had their assigned places. We'd all meet back in the suite late afternoon to get ready for the formal reception. After my cup of java I headed for the convention hall. The police command center was busy, their monitors showed the guests were up and about. The tours had begun and the meetings were in full swing.

Grumblings of being "stranded" could be heard in the hallways. "Those damn Bassodians," was a common complaint. I also heard large complaints about the futbol game not being Jumped. Fred had plenty of complaining company.

Other than that, everything went smoothly. Dr. Hibnet and his board of directors were everywhere, calming complaints, making sure everyone was comfortable. I heard one of the doctors surmise that at least their schedules were lighter due to the conference and the lack of patients being able to be transported.

At noon, I visited the control center. Hill was there monitoring the hotel screens. "Did you find anything to wear?"

"Yep, all set. It did Killa good to get out. She's back at the hotel." My lieutenant didn't take her eyes off the screens.

"How's it going?" I asked her, leaning over to look into the monitors. "You'll go blind; make sure you take a break every hour. Don't want you with red eyes tonight, doesn't go well with formal attire."

"You know, I almost think I should skip the formal dinner. I should stay with Killa instead."

"What and miss all the excitement? That doesn't sound like you." I half laughed, "You're not getting out of it that easily Hill. If I have to dress up in a monkey suit, you can join me and suffer along with all the rest of us." Given my newest rookie's busy-body tendency, I was more than a little surprised. "We need you, the more we can watch the crowd the better."

She nodded still not looking up from the screen. "I can watch it from here," she ventured.

Now I was concerned. "Not feeling well or do you think you're not ready for prime time?"

That got a sharp response, "I'm fine! Don't try and goad me, Chief. I'll be there!"

"Great!" I cheerfully told her, getting a scowl, first time she'd looked away from the screen. "You do look tired Hill."

"I'm fine, I told you!" she scowled even deeper. "I'll see you later today at the room."

I walked over to Lont Pol, who was issuing orders for the day. She was adding some of her people to the tours Hibnet's staff was giving the guests. "Make sure they only go where they are allowed. I want everyone within sight of monitors."

"You seem to have all the bases covered," I told her. "Dr. Hibnet seems to be cooperating at least."

"I still don't trust him," she expounded. "He's not telling us something. He was off sector a few weeks ago. No one knows where he Jumped. I have someone tracking down where he went but with communications down I'll have to wait. My contact was supposed to be here today. It could explain what the good doctor has been working on, why he's so nervous."

"It could be as simple as he was meeting someone for a romantic rendezvous. The man's a notorious womanizer." I told her about my interrupting him and his secretary.

She shook her head, "What a hypocrite, he's so strict with all the rest of us. He had the nerve to lecture me on my relationship with Dan."

I just shook my head. I wondered if he'd been like that when he knew my parents. He had been one of their best friends. He had been like an uncle to Ray and I. He helped with my recovery, making sure I had the best the station could offer.

"The Governor's sons are taking one of the tours. Why don't you sit in, make sure all goes well?" She looked at me. "I was going to go but I need my gown adjusted…"

I held up my hand, "I'll go, don't worry. I can play diplomat if I must."

She chuckled, "Now that might be worth going along just to see. They are leaving from the train depot in twenty minutes."

I grabbed my suit jacket and headed out, checking in first with all my detectives via cell. Fred and Marcus were checking the entry ports, closing most of them. Elly was with Pol's security equipment specialist, Evie Melca, doing one last sweep of the convention center for any type of incendiary device. Lara was with Pat Telexis, Pol's weapon's specialist, setting up tonight's checkpoints for the swat team. Hill was supervising the monitors. I headed toward Eupie1's train station.

I sat in the back. The General's sons were two rows up from me. I didn't recognize anyone else. One of Hibnet's aides was standing out front facing us. "I'd like to welcome you to M.O.S.S. He held a sign with the letters. It stands for Medical Operating Space Station. Most just call it Moss. These trains run constantly between the Rings. Our medical staff goes to work in them and come home on them."

The train started moving. We came out to the clear outer part of Ring Five. The gasps for the first timers were so typical. The train was so smooth with huge windows on either side. Fresh air flowed into the cabin, relaxing like a warm summer breeze. I sat back and just enjoyed the stars.

The aide hurried on, holding on to the center post to keep his balance. "I've left a brochure with a map of the station. It has all the data about the size and the makeup of the rings. As probably you all know, the center core," he pointed to the black cylinder that could be seen as we emerged above the city on our way to level six. He continued, "The lower part of the center is made up of atonimum. It is the heaviest particle known in the universe. The core was built by our friends the Bassodians and placed in a specific orbit that the space station was then built upon."

Most of the train's occupants snickered. The Bassodians were not real popular right now. I heard one of the sons say, "If they weren't such pompous lizards, I'd slap them on their scaly green backs and thank them." He got laughs from his other siblings.

"I can't understand how dad can stand them," said another son, getting nods from everyone in agreement.

Hibnet's aide continued, "As the brochure says, humans and only humans built the actual nine rings. So we can be very proud of that accomplishment. When our engineers were done, we had built the most sophisticated hospital in the cosmos. Even other species look to our research for the many treatments we perform and the medicines we have discovered."

He sat down. We traveled to level six which was the Emergency Room and the location of other wards for total recovery and rehabilitation. It also housed pediatrics with a state of the art maternity section. The lobbies lay open to the trains and some mocked up surgery rooms that came into view were interesting. I knew this tube very well. Then up to seven and eight rings that were used as research labs. We didn't see much as the labs were closed off from view.

We reached level nine. The regular administrative offices were housed on this ring. We got glimpses of offices when we stopped at their train station. We were served pastries and drinks. I grabbed a cup of java and some type of tart. I noticed the sons only grabbed water and nothing else. One of them looked back at me and waved. "Aren't you Chief Brown?" he yelled back.

"Yup, that's me," I said between bites of my tart. "And who are you all, besides being the General Governor's sons?"

What looked like the oldest introduced everyone, "I'm Matt, this is Ben, Lars and Colin."

They all looked like their father. "Well, I'm Skip Brown, glad to meet you."

"I see you on Crab's news. Don't envy your job." I believe it was Ben that spoken.

Matt explained, "It's his sector to cover." Realizing I didn't understand, he went further, "Dad assigns us all a sector to keep tract of. Ben's is your Crab sector."

"Well, Ben, remember the only time I get on the telescreen news is when a bad crime has been committed, so don't judge the sector by me."

"No, I don't, it is those damn Dome politicians that piss me off." He contorted his face in a grimaced frown."

"Ben!" the other three yelled at him, "Dad would kill you."

"Don't worry, I won't tell him." I liked the sons.

The train started up again. "We will be heading down to Ring Four, our burn center is located within that ring. It'll take a few minutes to get there so relax and enjoy the ride. We are taking the out route, so you'll all get a good view."

Everyone was quiet as the train slowly traveled downward and the open space around the station surrounded us. It was a gorgeous display, soothing.

Again we saw the lobbies and mocked up operating rooms, this time with intricate robots. The guide expounded further, "This ring is set for lower gravity as it helps the burn victims heal. We are known for our advanced burn healing techniques. We have the best specialists."

We traveled down to level three, the neurology center. I knew of their wondrous works, I was a walking example. We finished on level two which served the residents of the space station. Here were all the medical services, such as optometrists, dentists, general practitioners that were used by the residents. We got off here. He led us to the tram which brought us to the center cylinder and we took the elevator back to Level Five which housed the cities of Eupie1 and Eupie2. I left them there as they all got on a buscart that was giving them a tour of the cities. The sons all came over and shook my hand and said they hoped to see me at the conference.

It was getting to be late afternoon. I headed back to the room. I showered and dressed, quickly struggling with the damn monkey suit. Most of my detectives were doing the same; in their rooms getting dressed. When I came out Killa was helping Lara with her long black hair. My old nursemaid was brushing the silky shiny locks that hung down to my detective's slim waist. Her hair was absolutely gorgeous. Lara looked gorgeous. She was wearing a sleek black long gown, cut up the sides to show her long well shaped legs. The gown had long dangling sleeves which I knew on the right side held her long stun gun. Out of sight but easy to raise and shoot.

"Hi Chief, how was the tour?" Lara turned her big gray steel eyes to me. As gorgeous as my top detective was, her ruthlessness lay in those eyes. She was a seasoned soldier and not to be taken lightly.

"I got to meet the Governor's four sons. They are smart but approachable," I told her. Marcus and Fred came out. Poor Fred looked uncomfortable in his tuxedo, nothing quite fit right. The jacket arms were too short, his cummerbund was half on and his bowtie askew.

Lara shook her head, "Come here, big guy, let's get you straightened out." She fixed him as best she could, but he still looked totally out of his league.

Elly and Hill came out together. My brain just didn't register my rookie detective. She wore a long emerald gown that shimmered. Judy Hill radiated elegance and sophistication. My mind could not make the transition from the woman I knew to this beautiful creation. Her hair was half braided with green ribbons entwining down to her waist. I hadn't noticed how green her eyes were, they were enhanced by long emerald earrings. I must have been gaping because Elly said, "Chief?"

Elly was by my side. She was dressed in a fancy pant suit outfit that really did look nice. "Don't you look great," I told her, seeing her blush. Still my eyes went back to Hill.

She must have seen my confusion because she smiled, lighting up her face, including those deep green eyes, then said, "You look great too, got dressed all by yourself?" and laughed.

Damn the woman!

Chapter Ten

"Let's go folks." I told them, "Guests start arriving in a little over an hour. If anything is going to happen, it will probably be tonight. Look sharp. Let's get into position. There will be press there tonight, stay clear of them. Let me handle them."

"Yeah, sure Chief. Whata ya gonna do, throw rocks at them?" Fred quipped, getting everyone to laugh but me.

"You know Fred, foot patrol can be very hot and sweaty on Fulton," I told him. The big guy just grunted and ignored me.

Lara went over and put her arm through his, "You know Fred, do you think you could keep out of trouble tonight?"

"I doubt it," said Elly taking his other arm. "I really doubt it."

He just snorted at her. The two women looked tiny next to him.

Judy Hill walked between Marcus and me. She had waved goodbye to Killa, "See you later tonight. If you need, buzz me."

"She can buzz me too!" I motioned to my little Ligithian superintendent, "Anything you need just let the guards get it for you."

I saw her frown, her ears twitching, "Don't worry about me. Get going!" She reminded me of when she'd send me off to school. "Good luck tonight."

Lont Pol met us at the reception table handing each of my people a name tag that just said "security". For me, I got "Chief Skip Brown, Fulton Station"; lovely, no anonymity for me.

We all scattered to our respective duties. I noticed Hill was in a conversation with Lont and then she took off to the control center probably checking on the computer monitors. Waiters were rushing around bringing hors d'oeuvres out to the side tables. The champagne fountain was all set up. The band was setting up on the far stage in-between the two immense elegant staircases. Round tables, each sitting ten, were set up with white linen tablecloths with fancy flatware and stem glasses. Flower arrangements were everywhere including on the dining tables.

The huge chandelier was dimmed and the dance floor softly highlighted. When the band started up they sounded like they came from Fulton, slow and bland. I checked in with Lont and the rest, all were fine. I noticed Pol's people everywhere. I also noticed the Governor's security attachment checking everything out. They nodded to me, I guess they hadn't found anything amiss.

The guests started arriving. I noticed Governor Pinote mingling with the crowd. Of course, he attracted a lot of attention, everyone wanted to talk to him. I saw that several of our Dome legislators were vying for his ear. His sons seemed rather good at deflecting their persistent attention, keeping each to just a few minutes of the Governor's time.

Several of the Fulton government representatives came over to me. Judge Karine Button sauntered over. I had helped her with her corruption inquiry into the Senate Speaker's finances. Afterwards we'd become friendly and despite it cooling off, she'd stayed my friend.

"Hi Skip," she radiated power as her position as chairman of the Crab Sector Parley. Federal Sector Judges command respect. She is about ten years older than me. She is brilliant and although not beautiful, still was attractive just on her forceful personality and intellect. "Never saw you here before, it worries me a little that you'd be here. I've been looking for you since I heard you were on Moss, you're a busy man."

"You should have just left me a message." I was surprised she hadn't.

"I didn't want it obvious that I wanted to speak with you." She linked her arm in mine, "I don't want it known what I'm going to tell you."

I smiled down at her folding her arm in mine as if we were just being friendly. "I'm here because Dr. Hibnet asked the consulate for extra security. Borger asked me to come and supervise the security, although my superintendent, Lont Pol, is more than capable. You know the good doctor, likes to be in charge."

"Yes, he knows how to kiss ass." She smiled at me, making me blush, "You could learn a thing or two from Hibnet."

"You wouldn't want a Chief of Police kissing ass," I responded, taking her by the hand and leading her onto the dance floor. "Too many kiss-asses on Fulton as it is."

"True. That's what attracted me to you. You're one person who never brown nosed me." She laughed. "Way too many do." The judge squeezed my arm affectionately. "I hear rumors of financial problems here on the station, although Dr. Hibnet denies it. I was wondering if that was why you were here." She said it softly, looking around that no one was listening.

"No, but that info is interesting, I'll have to look into it." I bent down whispering in her ear. "Hibnet is nervous about something."

"Yes, it might behoove you to see what's going on. The space station is too important."

"Agreed," I pointed out, "I'll keep my eyes opened."

The hall was filling up, almost all the tables were full. There must have been over a thousand guests. I saw Hill, she was talking to Lara. The two were in some deep discussion. They seemed to get along well.

"What are you two so focused on?" I asked.

"I was just telling her that with the sector Jumps closed down, it might discourage anyone from causing mischief, as we have a captive audience here. They'll have no easy escape."

"True but if someone is fanatical enough, it won't deter them," I countered getting nods from both.

"Come on Hill." I grabbed her arm and led her onto the dance floor. "Notice anything out of place? How are the monitors, all quiet everywhere?" Two questions at once as I drew her to me. She was pleasant to hold, slim waist and she smelled nice. "You smell better than you did on Nestor," I reminded her. On our last case she'd worn a perfume that smelled like fuel, it had been the latest fad among Nestor's racing fans.

"I'm surprised at you Chief, being from Nestor, you'd think you would like it." She snickered, "I was thinking of giving it to Killa." She knew that Ligithians have a weird sense of smell. They can smell someone's blood type but not the sweetness of a rose.

"Don't you dare! She'll wear it just to please you and drive me and the dogs crazy." I twirled her around, scanning the room for anything out of the ordinary. All seemed normal, the dome representatives were already hitting the booze. "Everything looks fine," I told her, looking down at her light green eyes that at times reflected gray. She really did look great, holding her was a real pleasure especially since she was a good dancer. I was about to tell her she should look like this all the time when her eyes darted to Lara.

Lara was looking up at the balcony above the band. Her arms flew up, immediately her long range rifle appeared and she aimed and fired. We were close enough to her to hear the swish of the gun's energy. I looked up but only saw something fall behind the baluster of the upper hallway.

I saw Lara immediately covered the gun again. "Someone was firing a gun from up there." I heard Lara's voice in my ear.

"I'm on my way up," I told her, "stay here, look for others." I headed up the large marble stairway taking two at a time. Hill had rushed up the other side. All my detectives were checking in, no one else reported any other shooter. "Keep your posts!" I told them. The crowd generally hadn't noticed anything; Lara had been so quick but I did get a look from the Governor's guard. Two of them were looking up at the balcony. Great, I didn't need them sticking their heads into this.

I reached the top of the stairs and rushed over to a small crumpled figure lying against the baluster. Hill was already there. I knew immediately that it was a Ligithian from the white stringy hair and the small pointed ears. Hill rolled him over. He was dressed all in white, like a medical orderly. On his right shoulder was a small burn mark where Lara had hit him.

"He's been stunned but he's coming around." She was checking his pulse. His eyes were opening and within his dark purple eyes I could see fear. He looked up at us. Hill said something to him in Ligithian. Her words sounded guttural with an urgency that even I picked up on. When did Hill learn the Ligithian's language, briefly crossed my mind?

She looked up at me, "He's going to commit suicide. I can't stop him!"

I kneeled next to him, "Stop, we can help you. Don't!" I yelled at him.

He looked at me, his eyes almost black purple, "Must" was all he said and then his mouth leaked white foam, he'd taken a pill that had probably already been in his mouth.

"Someone help us." Hill called out as Lont Pol had come running up. "Get some medics up here."

"They're on their way." Pol informed us.

The Ligithian was dead. His head lolled back against Hill's arm. She lowered him to the floor. She shook her head in disgust, "Damn!"

I saw red. I knew who was responsible. I headed down the stairways. I'd seen the Ligithian ambassador near the bottom of the stairs. I found him there, talking to a group. I grabbed his arm, dragging him away. I heard him gasp as I hauled him up the stairs.

"You are being rude!" he growled at me, the tone reminding me of myself.

"And you're a criminal and deserve it!" I growled back.

For an old man, he kept up with me, I swear I was huffing and puffing more than him on the top landing. Still I kept a tight grip on his arm, forcing him to where Hill was still bending over the body. Several Medics personnel were there also.

"What is this?" my grandfather demanded.

"It's your dead slave." I yelled at him, "Who was he shooting at?"

"Mine? He's not mine. I never saw him before, he'd be wearing my uniform which he's not!" he spat at me, his look told me he thought I was an imbecile.

"Hill, do they know what killed him?" I asked her, taking her by the arm helping her up.

"They think it was strychnine, a fast killing chemical." She said.

It wasn't Hill's answer, however, it was my grandfather who got my attention. "Judith?" his voice full of surprise, "Judith, is your father involved?" He was looking straight at my Lt. Hill.

"Do you know her?" I asked my grandfather, who looked at me with like I was an imbecile again.

"Of course I know her…" he started to say but Hill interrupted.

"Good evening Ambassador Alphonse, no my father is not involved." She held out her hand and shook the ambassador's offered hand, but he quickly kissed her hand which she withdrew rapidly.

"What the hell Hill, what is he talking about?" I yelled at her.

It was the ambassador that answered, "Please forgive him Lady Judith, I'm afraid my grandson has no manners."

I barked, "Lady? What the hell is going on here?"

At the same time, Hill said, "Grandson?"

A strange look came over the ambassador's face, "Don't you know to show respect to Governor's Pinote's daughter? "

"Daughter, Pinote." I stumbled over the words.

"Grandson?" Hill said again.

I grabbed my rookie's arms, making her face me. "Who are you?" I asked. My grandfather was having a fit.

"I might ask you that!" She shot back, "Grandfather?"

"Don't change the subject!" I ground the words past my clenched teeth.

As my grandfather was rapidly approaching us, she turned to him, "Please, do not concern yourself, Ambassador. Your grandson," she spat it out, "and I know each other. I don't live in Orion any longer, I don't work for my father, I work for the Chief here."

Ambassador Medicinis looked incredulously at her. Bowing slightly he said, "I honor you're request Lady Judith. I know when to retreat."

Lont Pol had come over as the medics were taking the body away. "Is everything alright, Chief?" she asked.

"Just hunky dory," I sarcastically replied. "I'm about to arrest the ambassador here for sending his slave to murder. I just have to get out of him who he was targeting."

"It wasn't him," Hill interjected. "Think about it Chief. If this was his slave it would have obeyed you. You have his blood."

"Ah, finally someone with brains!" The Ambassador quipped. "She's correct Skip, whether you like it or not you are tied to me."

Even though I knew they were right, I still pointed at him, "I don't know how you did it but you're involved in this and I'm going to prove it."

He laughed, "Go right ahead and waste your time." He turned and walked away.

I reached in and took one of my blue pills as I could feel the back of my neck tensing. Hill looked at me, concern in her face but she didn't say anything.

Two of Pinote's security men stepped up to us. I didn't know how long they'd been standing in the shadows listening. "What has happened here?" one of them asked, his tall muscular frame towered over us.

I had no intention of lying to them. As much as I disliked the Federation Agents, they were not to be trifled with. The Federation Assembly had no sense of humor. So I told them as little as I could, "We had an attempted assassination but we don't know who the Ligithian was targeting. I don't think it was the

Governor as he was over the far side not in sight of the gunman."

"Yes, we figured as much. We saw Ms. Null shoot." Another agent had come up, he had an air of authority about him. He looked at Hill, surprise suddenly filled his face, I'm sure his face didn't show surprise often. "Lady Pinote?"

"Yes, Raymond, it's me," she answered him obviously knowing who he is.

He seemed to be at a loss for words. Finally, "I think you should see your father." He suggested. "He's been very worried."

"Yes, I suppose so." Her voice dripped with reluctance.

"Allen, take care of this while I escort Ms. Pinote down." He nodded to me as he gently took Hill's arm.

I stepped in front of her. The agent looked shocked. He went to reach for me but she held up her arm stopping him. "I'm not done with you!" Anger dripped from my voice.

"Right, you probably aren't...." She looked at me. I didn't know what to say. I was angry but more confused and I hate to admit it, hurt. I had trusted her. I stepped out of the way as he led her down the stairs.

Lont was at my side, "You shouldn't judge her. Like the rest of us, she really just wants to be her own person."

"So you knew?" I snarled at her.

"Whoa, Chief. It wasn't my place to squeal on her. I'd met her before when she'd come here with her father. I knew of her connections, that's why I had her check the guest lists to see if she could pick out an irregularity."

"It's also why she kept a low profile staying in the computer room. She was afraid of bumping into someone who knew her." I thought of how she'd made herself scarce when Hibnet had come to Fulton. I'd bet he knew her. Damn. I felt hoodwinked. That's why so many people had asked it they knew her. Double damn.

Everyone was checking in, questioning what was going on. I explained the assassination attempt, although Lara had pretty much covered it with them. "Keep to your posts, keep an eye out especially for any Ligithians."

The Governor's body guard wanted a full report but I just gave him the rudiments of what happened. I put him off by telling him I'd contact him when the morgue on Ring Six had done it's autopsy. It seemed to satisfy him and he actually congratulated me on a job well done. *Yeah sure*.

I saw Hill from a distance talking with the Governor. His four sons were flocked around him, adamantly talking to their sister. Hill didn't look happy and shortly she was gone. I didn't see her for the rest of the night but then I was busy patrolling, checking in with Lont Pol. I kept a quiet eye on my grandfather, who completely ignored me. I didn't think I was his favorite person right now.

The rest of the evening went well. By midnight, most of the guests had had a good amount of champagne and were dancing rather animatedly. The band had picked it up. Dr. Hibnet looked happy, flitting from one table to the next. Despite my dark mood, I danced with several of the female guests from Fulton, being as charming as is possible for me. I found myself looking around for Hill. Why? I don't know. She had lied to me, deceived me, yet I wasn't as furious as I wanted to be.

By three in the morning, the festivities were winding down. Lont Pol had sent most of her people home. I heard tiredness in my detectives' voices. When the last of the guests were gone I told them to head back to their rooms, get some sleep for tomorrow. It was going to supposedly be the last day of the conference, but with the Jumps closed the guests could be stuck on the station. More headaches, damn Bassodians.

Lont Pol with her Dr. Dan following in her wake, said goodnight to me. I walked over to the hotel, heading back to the room. There was a police guard at the door, I told them to head home, I'd handle it from here. I opened the door and saw Killa and Hill in the small kitchenette table talking. All the bedroom doors were closed.

They had obviously been in a deep talk as they looked up startled to see me enter. Even by the small light that shown by the lamp on the wall, both Killa and Hill looked drawn and distraught. Killa looked at me and I could tell I wasn't her favorite person right now. I guess I was on everyone's shit list. I slumped down on the living room chair, exhaustion getting the better of me.

Hill was dressed in jeans and a t-shirt but her hair was still braided reminding me how she'd looked earlier. "I should be going," my rookie said, standing up to leave.

"Going back to daddy?" I couldn't help it, the hurt of her betrayal just flooded out. I regretted saying it but I wasn't going to take it back either.

"Skip!" Killa snapped at me, a rare occurrence.

"Did you know who she was?" I asked my old nursemaid and got a nod. So I was probably the only dupe.

"I was going to tell you." Judy looked over at me, "I was going to tell you when you got back to Fulton. I wasn't supposed to be here. I... I..."

"Don't bother, I don't care for any more lies." I snapped at her, getting a gasp from Killa.

"Lies?" Hill's face flushed red. "You, you tell me of lies! And who are you? Are you Skip Brown or John Masters?"

I stood up, "You know why I have to hide my identity. I am not doing it because I'm a spoiled princess."

"You, you…" she sputtered, "imbecile! How dare you judge me! Do you think you are the only one trying to live your own life? I'm spoiled? You have no idea, none of who I am!"

She walked to the door, turning back to Killa. "Thank you for who you are. It's an honor to be your friend." and left.

"You are acting like a fool, Skip." Killa pointed to me, "She's a good person, and you should not have talked to her like that."

"Do you have any idea what the Governor of the Federation Assembly could do if he found out we were hiding his daughter? You think I have budget problems now, he'd throw us on the goddamn street. As it is, I'm sure the Dome representatives are going to call for my head."

"When did you become afraid of those that try and control our lives? I was always proud of you being the champion of those that fight for what's right." She stood up, pointed her finger at me, "Take a look in the mirror, Skipper, at what is staring back at you?" Killa's eyes were almost black, her hair stood on end, and her ears were twitching rapidly.

She disappeared into her bedroom, leaving me alone, I felt really alone. I walked over to the large picture windows overlooking Epie1. Am I as fake as this city, I wondered? I took out a blue pill but put it back, I could handle this. All was quiet down below; I looked out over the shops and streets. If I didn't know better, I'd think I was on some planet that evolved around a regular sun. Life was a lot like this space station city. Not anything is what it seems. Hill came drifting into my thoughts. Damn that woman!

I slumped back on the chair. The next thing I knew I woke up as the light of the windows was filtering in. Dawn seemed to be peaking through. I hit my cellbutton, *05:30 federation time,* I clicked it shut. My head felt like it was stuffed with cotton balls. My body ached from sleeping in the chair.

Killa, despite the early hour, was in the Kitchenette, still in her nightdress. I doubted she had slept at all. When she saw I was awake the little Ligithian padded across the room, her slippers hardly making a dent in the carpeting and handed me a hot cup of steaming java. Yes!

"I'm sorry for getting upset with you, Killa," I told her between sips.

"It is forgiven," her eyes were back to her normal violet, "you're a good man, Skipper, you will do the right thing. I have faith in you."

I'm glad she had faith, I had none right at the moment. I had to find the Laositian who was responsible for the assassination attempt. Lont Pol had no other Ligithia guests registered other than the Ambassador Alphonso Medicini's. How had my grandfather done it? He was right, the dead Ligithian wasn't his. Something as strong as a killing would require that the Laositian master give the order that day. Since the Jumps were down, the Laositian was here! Was my grandfather hiding him? Too many questions, my head hurt.

"Killa, tell me about my grandfather." I saw her struggling. "It's alright, I need to know. I think he's involved in the assassination attempt last night."

"No," she simply said. "He is not a bad man, Skippy. Your mother loved him."

She didn't get any further as a knock on the door interrupted us. I had placed my gun on the table next to me, I grabbed it. "Get in the kitchen," I told my nursemaid. "Hide behind the counter."

I went to the door looking out the peep hole. It was Doctor Angi Ditterset. What the hell was she doing here so early? I pressed the intercom, "Yes, Doctor?"

"I need to talk to you," she said but seemed to hesitate a second and then added, "and I need to see Killa."

I was startled, how did she know about Killa? I just stared at the door, not sure what was going on.

"Please Chief Brown, I was the one that brought her here." She spoke right into the speaker by the door, quietly emphasizing each word as if hammering them into my brain.

I swung the door open and glared at her. "What do you mean, *brought her here!*"

"May I come in?" she asked. "Better to talk inside."

I stepped aside, letting her enter. The room was now flooded with light, it was coming on to six. She came in and went to the windows, "I always love it when the city comes alive. I live over in the med op section. It gets the dawn the quickest since we leave for work the earliest. We pass Epie2 workers heading to their night."

I was in no mood for small talk. "Explain what you meant by *you brought Killa here*." I stood near her, getting in her personal space. She actually backed up a few feet.

"I'm not proud of what I did, Chief, but I would do it again. I'm the one that sent your Captain Issam the message that Killa was needed here." She backed up even further.

"You did what!" I snarled, "You tried to kill her." I changed the word to "us!"

"No, no," she held up her hand, "I didn't plant the bomb on the ferry. I don't know who found out you were on the transit ferry. I thought I was careful."

"Obviously, you were not!" I barked, anger dripping with every word.

Killa came out of the kitchenette. "Would you care for a cup of java?" she asked the flustered doctor. "I can feel you are exhausted and ready to collapse. I believe your intentions were good. I remember what a good friend you were to Helen."

"She was a friend to my mother?" I was shocked as my former nursemaid, now my bondee, shook her head yes.

Ditterset looked at the small Ligithian, "Yes, thank you, a cup of java would be nice, cream and sugar please." I did notice that fatigue dripped off her. She smiled, "It amazes me their sense of smell and how it makes them almost psychic. The Ligithia slaves have acquired their sensitivity over time but then it is the key to the blood cure."

"What?" both Killa and I said at once.

"Yes, it was your mother that discovered that their sense of smell was the key to the bonding." She looked at us, satisfaction written all over her face, as if she had won some championship.

"You'd better explain yourself and fully," I told her in my no nonsense voice.

"They tried to burn me out." She told me, "They thought they'd destroyed my research records."

"You're talking about your lab being destroyed in the explosion?"

She nodded, her head taking out a cell tab from her coat pocket. "I have everything on this. Do you know they even destroyed my lawyer's safe where he kept my extra records? I'm being very careful, I haven't slept well in a long time. They aren't sure they have everything or I would probably end up dead like your parents."

"Start from the beginning. How did you know about my parents' research? According to Dr. Hibnet all their records were destroyed."

"I found them on Nestor." She smiled as our faces scrunched in surprise.

"Nestor? Where?" I followed her over to the small table, taking a chair next to her. Killa stood next to me, her hand on my shoulder.

"They were buried with your father. Your Uncle Jack put them there, in the mausoleum draw. He told me when I showed him your mother's letter to me asking me to continue their work if something happened to them.

"He never told me." I was shocked.

Killa was not, "Jack wouldn't tell you, Skip. He thought of little else then to protect us. If we'd known it would have been hard for you not to contact Dr. Ditterset.

"She's right. I tried to stay away from you as much as I could. It wasn't until your tissue samples were destroyed in the lab fire that I had to get you here."

"Does anyone know? Think carefully, how did they know you'd sent for Killa?" I stood up going to the window, looking down on the now busy city. I heard a door open, Lara walked out of her bedroom. Despite being in baggy pajamas with her hair a mess, she still looked gorgeous.

"You're up early," she mumbled, "didn't we just get back? You're still in you tux?" Killa handed her a cup of java, which she grabbed onto like a lifeline. Fred came stumbling out of Lara's bedroom, half awake, hair all in a tumble.

"What's going on?" he somehow got out of his need to shave face. "Didn't we just go to bed?" Reaching up, Killa hardly came to Fred's shoulders, she handed him a big cup of java. He looked at her, at first not comprehending, then gladly grabbed the mug.

Lara and Fred? I looked at Lara, surprise written all over my face. She just shrugged and I decided to ignore the whole situation. Now what would Hill say, entered my head. I angrily pushed it away. What did it matter what Hill said. My brain wouldn't listen to me, as the thought came again.

I turned my attention to Dr. Ditterset, "Well? Who knew?"

"No one. I didn't even tell Gale, who's been very helpful in getting me set up again. I didn't tell anyone!"

To my surprise it was Fred that spoke up, "If you sent any type of off station message, this place leaks like a sieve." He sat up in the chair, he hardly fit, "Trust me, this place can hold no secrets."

I knew he was right. Despite Lont Pol's efforts, Hibnet had created a nightmare of insecurity. There were no secrets on the space station.

"So what you are saying," Lara said what I was thinking, "it could have been anyone."

Marcus came out of his bedroom, dressed in his *ready to go to work* suit. He was usually the first up. He looked amazed at how many people were in the suite. "Am I late?" he asked. "Did I miss something?"

Elly, came out of her bedroom with a big fuzzy bathrobe and a towel wrapped around her head. "Shower ready for the next person," she announced looking squarely at Fred.

Fred groaned, Lara laughed and Killa handed out two more cups of java.

Knock! Who now?

Chapter Eleven

Everyone looked startled, automatically their hands went to their non-*existent back in the room guns.* Only Lara had hers. "Hold steady." I told them as I walked to the door, looking out the peek hole. My eye settled on Lont Pol and behind her three officers.

"It's alright." I said as I opened the door. "It's only our guards," although I did wonder why Lont was with them. "Good morning, wish I could say I'm glad to see you, but I'm afraid you aren't here to wish me a happy day."

"Why Chief, never knew you had a sense of humor," Pol quipped. "Do you ever have a *good* day?"

"Don't push it Lont, still angry at you." I waved her in.

"Like I said, ain't in my job description to tell you personal info on your detectives. Everyone has something." Her eyes held amusement, enjoying my discomfort.

"This about Hill?" Lara asked, "We can't all pick our relatives." I saw Marcus and Fred nod in agreement. Only Elly looked confused.

"What - did you all know but me?" I said exasperated.

"Crap, Chief," Fred told me between eating a stale donut left from yesterday and downing his java, "Hill didn't make anything of it, why should we care!"

"Why should you care? Her father could have all our jobs. He's probably close to being the most influential politician in the Human sectors?"

"We aren't worried," Lara Null smiled, "we have a ferocious Chief, known for his temper. It would be good to see you go head to head with the Consulate Federation Assembly Governor General."

"You're so funny Null," I sarcastically said as I turned to Pol. "I need to have Fred check the ports again looking for any possible Laositian Highblood that might have slipped in. Lara and Elly need to go over the gun registry, if there is one, of the gun used by the dead Ligithian. Marcus needs to go over the autopsy of the gunman and check for any identifiable evidence. Marcus, look for any motive - if you find who he belongs to. We need to know who he was targeting."

They all nodded. Pol put her two cents in, "I have all my people checking the monitors looking for any sighting of the assassin. Also we still have to cover the last of the conference meetings today. I had the luncheon switched to three conference rooms instead of the ballroom. The smaller rooms will be easier for security reasons."

Great, as usual my police Superintendent had everything covered.

"Chief, I need Killa to spend time with me in my lab," Dr. Ditterset pleaded.

"No, it isn't safe." I emphatically pointed a finger at her, it is not a good idea!

"Skip," my old nursemaid shook my arm, getting me to look down at her. "I have to do this. If she is right and I hold the key to the cure then I have to do it!" Her eyes were dark purple, her ears were actually twitching so fast it was ruffling her hair. I was not going to win this battle.

It was Dr. Ditterset who spoke up, "Please, Mr. Brown, what would Helen tell you?"

It wasn't fair, she knew my mother would risk everything, even our lives to fix the slave problem. "Fine, I will go with you."

It was hardly out of my mouth when Lont Pol said, "No, I'm afraid you can't."

"And why..." I knew I wasn't going to like this.

"You have a meeting with the Bassodians." Her eyebrows went up as if apologizing before my temper kicked in.

For a moment I was too shocked to say anything. "They can wait!" I spat out, I had no desire to see the lizards close up.

The room exploded with everyone yelling at once.

"Are you crazy?" Lull yelled, "You don't say no to the rulers of our universe!"

Killa frantically cried, "No, they'll kill you."

Marcus was, "They will just force you to go, better to go willingly."

Fred just said, "Damn lizards, better you than me."

Dr. Ditterset said the most responsible thing, "Can't Dr. Hibnet intercede?'

Lont Pol just shook her head, "I doubt it. Hotda Hoffstedt is here. She's the Human Federation Interspecies Ambassador. She travels often with the Governor General.

"Tell her to go herself!" I shouted at Lont. I'd had enough of diplomats and politicians screwing up my life.

"You can tell her yourself." Pol nodded to look behind me.

There stood in the doorway or should I say *blocked* the doorway, the biggest woman I had ever seen. Now when I say big I don't mean fat. She was a female Fred Stoshingburg. I guessed she towered over 6ft 7 inches tall. She had wide shoulders, muscled arms and a sturdy stance on her dark brown well-toned body. The only out of portioned part of her was a small sized head. She tried to compensate that with a bush of dark brown fuzzy hair that created a ball around her face. It was her crazy two colored eyes that made her formidably crazy looking. One eye was amber, one eye was green. Worse, they could look in two different directions.

"Good morning, Mr. Brown or do you prefer Chief Brown?" Her voice came out almost in clear clicks, each word crisp with just a slight hesitancy between each word. I just stared for a long moment. I had never heard an accent like hers, foreign yet I had no trouble understanding her. Where the hell did she hail from?

"I'm from the Sombero Sector. From Lorenzi, to be exact. Are you familiar with that planet?" she asked.

She had stepped into the room, I looked up at her, "Did you just read my mind?"

"Like most inhabitants from Lorenzi, I can vaguely read your thoughts. I rarely use my psychic talents outside of my home planet but I'm afraid you were rather forceful in your projection."

Wonderful, now what the hell, she probably could tell my brain was a mish-match of crap.

I saw her smile, "I'm not going to read your thoughts. Please be at easy about that."

I decided the best way to handle her would be open honesty, "I haven't the time to meet with the Bassodians, nor have I any interest in meeting them. Send someone else."

"I'm afraid we don't have that option, Mr. Brown. They do not ask, I hate to say they just order - but in reality they just assume they will be obeyed." She had her amber eye on me but her green eye was looking at the room.

I could feel my anger rising, she stepped back reacting to it. It was Fred that broke the tension, "Pompous green reptiles! You show'um, Chief!" I looked over noticing he'd eaten almost the whole box of donuts.

Lara noticed too. "For god's sake Fred, you're gonna be sick."

The look on Hoffstedt's face, I didn't need to read her thoughts, she thought us a bunch of imbecilic idiots. Perhaps she was right.

"Excuse us, Ambassador Hoffstedt." I told her, "We are a tired bunch of overworked cops. You can call me Skip, if you'd like. We are in the middle of a case involving an assassination attempt, a bombing incident on a ferry and a lab being blown up. We are knee deep in conspiracy threats. So when I say, *I haven't the time for a meeting with the Bassodians,* I'm not being difficult but realistic."

She seemed to relax, nodding she understood. "I can assure you, Skip and please call me Hotda. I wish I could be more accommodating but I can't. They are a difficult species to deal with but they also control the Federation Assembly. Do you have any idea why they want to see you?"

"None. We don't have any mutual friends," I told her.

"Well, let me put it in perspective for you. Their tug is docked on Ring One. That "tug" is as big as a Federation Cruiser. Awaiting this tug's return is their "Mother Ship" which is only 500,000 milaspecs from the hospital. Their ship could blow up this entire space station."

"They wouldn't dare!" Elly shot across the room. "This is a hospital with 25,000 people on it."

"Probably, maybe not." Hotda looked around the room both eyes roaming, "However they are a strange non-feeling species. At least not with feelings we can associate often with. Do you want to take the chance of angering them?"

She had made her point. "Fine, let me take a shower and get dressed. Where do I meet you?"

"I'm afraid we have to go now." She sharply clicked her words, emphasizing their importance, her eyes actually looked in opposite directions. "You're getting a ride on that tug in less than an hour and I need to get you ready." The ambassador brought both her eyes around to focus on me. She stood with her hands on her hips as if daring me to disagree with her. She'd probably pick me up and carry me to that tug. The woman looked powerful enough!

"Wonderful." I looked down at my wrinkled tuxedo. "I'm going to make a great impression."

"I don't think they will notice. Shall we go?" She went over to the door, underlining her impatience to get going. I could tell the ambassador was not use to any type of disagreement. I suppose when you are that size, you can afford to be demanding.

"Okay, one second, please." I went over to Dr. Ditterset, "Can you wait until I get back?"

She almost whispered so only I could hear, "No, Chief Brown, I'm really running out of time. I've kept those that killed your parents at bay only because they are not sure I haven't got a backup of my research. If they get too scared they'll kill me too."

I turned to Killa who was almost hyperventilating. Her eyes were dark purple, her skin pale, her ears twitching. "Go with Dr. Ditterset. Lont please make sure the guards go with them. No one is to get into the lab unless authorized." I saw Pol nod.

"Skip, please do not do this!" my old nursemaid said clinging to my arm.

"Killa, think of mom and dad. You do what you need to do, I need to do what I need to do."

I had gotten through to the little Ligithian. Her eyes lightened, her ears settled down but a tear fell from her eye. I reached into my pocket slipping a blue pill on my tongue. "I'll be back before you know it."

"*Chief Brown!*" the ambassador was getting impatient, clicking her words out sharply.

Lont Pol walked me out the door, "I got a special police escort, it'll get you to the crossover quickly."

"You all have assignments. Good luck today." I nodded to my detectives.

As I started to leave, I heard from behind me, "Please be careful Chief." It came from Lara.

"Goddamn slimy bastards," came from Fred.

We went down to the Hotel's entrance; sure enough there was a police vehicle. The ambassador talked the entire way. "I have to warn you that you'll need to watch your sense of humor."

"Well, I've been told I have none, so I guess you don't have to worry," I told her.

"Good, because the Bassodians haven't any either." I could tell she was excited, her voice was clicking every word. "Everything is literal with them. Our common language has over a million words with double meanings and slang expressions. The Bassy language has only 200,000 words. They are plain spoken and don't often translate us very well. We keep trying to update their translator modules but it doesn't do any good. So keep it simple."

"How long is this going to take?" I asked as her eyes swung back to me.

"They have instructed me to pick you up on their mother ship, the ITTHIUS at 15:00 hours. I have commandeered Dr. Hibnet's medical shuttle ship."

"You're not coming with me?"

"No. They did not request I be present." I could tell it irked her to be left out. Her two colored eyes went up with her bushy eyebrows. "Obviously there is something about **you** they need." The words came out in clear clicks.

Great, I was on my own with the lizards. I silently walked next to the large woman. I'm sure I should have lots of questions but my mind was almost numb. I was tired, the late night getting to me.

"Don't worry Skip, I'll not let you face them alone." Now what was the giant woman getting at? "The Bassodians do not understand our existence as a sexual species. They reproduce themselves. In other words, they are asexual." She stopped, both eyes focused once more on me alone. Her large hands again went to her hips as if she were talking to an ignorant child.

She pointed one of her fingers at my chest. "They are both male/female and thus do not understand the concept of a family as such. They raise their young in a community type atmosphere. So they get very confused and think when someone human is married that the two people are in concept one."

"Well, too bad I don't have a wife," I laughed. I could just see my ex-wife worrying about what she'd wear to visit a bunch of reptilian giants. Her first question would be *what's the 'in' fashion?* "Sorry, I'm divorced." I told her.

"Not today. I'm a known quantity so I've found you a *wife*. I'm sending a female diplomat with you who knows the Bassodians. She'll help you survive this with as little *faux pas* possible." God help me if she was sending another Lorenzi woman. The thought of another ambassador type of female with me made me reach for another blue pill.

"I can manage. Truly! There is no need to put someone else in jeopardy," I told her as we rode the tram down the crossover to the elevators. Hotda pressed the button for Ring 1 and down we went.

When we got out she remarked, "We must keep to the corridor as all these doors," she pointed to the various marked doors as we passed them, "are for the different species." They have different controlled atmospheres. Ring One is the slowest rotating ring, allows them to take sections and control the area.

I noticed several marked doors. The first one was labeled Avian Labs. So, those were the birdlike Assanians, I'd seen one of them at a lecture at the Dome - very mild mannered bird-like individuals, very intellectual. Through a translator you almost forgot they were lecturing from a swinging perch. Then came one labeled Serpentes, ugh those were the snakepeople or Bisselians who lived on the far side of the cosmos. I'd only seen pictures of them. The third door was labeled Reptilian lab or better known as Bassodians. It was to this door that the ambassador led me.

We entered a small room. It had benches on either side. "Please sit," she briskly instructed me then spoke into her cellbutton. "We are here."

A few moments later two lab assistants dressed in white lab jackets came waltzing in.

"Has the serum been delivered?" Hotda in her stark clip voice demanded of a lab technician.

"Yes, the doctor delivered the vials earlier," the medic told her.

The other lab coat came over to me. "Okay, Chief Brown, we got your medical records. Everything we are giving you has been approved by Dr. Bolker." They handed me a cup with two pills in it.

"Okay, tell me what I'm taking." I looked at the pills skeptically.

"The white one is Corozithia, it helps you handle the lower oxygen atmosphere. The pink pill is a Broniaide, relaxation pill, so you don't have to worry about having a seizure."

"I have a blue pill for that." I told them, taking them out of my pocket.

"This is a little bit stronger, as this will be an intense situation. Don't worry, it won't make you incoherent or sleepy. It just strongly inhibits the chemical combination from stirring up your epilepsy. You can't take them too often, but once will not kill you."

"Great." As if my brain needed any more pills. I swallowed both. I went to get up but the lab assistant pushed me back down.

"Wait." He instructed me and a good thing he did because my head swam. The room turned upside down, then settled down to normal. He took out a flashlight and shined it in my eyes. "Follow the light." He told me. When I did he said, "You're set to go. It always takes a few seconds for the body to adjust. The dose is good for a twenty-four hour duration."

I got up, taking a few steps. I felt a little light headed. "This is a normal reaction. Once you get in the right atmosphere you'll be fine. Your intake of oxygen is high right now." The other assistant told me. "You need to put on these gravity boots and we have a coat that you'll need until you get to the mother ship."

I felt like a snowman. On Fulton, where it never goes below ninety, I didn't ever wear any type of jacket. I waddled a few steps. I felt like I weighed five hundred pounds.

I heard the ambassador chuckle, "You'll appreciate Fulton now."

"No, it'll never get that bad." I responded.

An inside door opened and another snowman entered. "Oh, glad you're already here, I'd like you to meet Chief Brown…"

Before she could get any further, the snowman lowered her hood and Lieutenant Hill said, "I know the Chief, Hotda."

"What are you doing here?" I yelled at her.

"She's going with you." The Ambassador said, surprise dripping from her clippy voice.

"No, she's not!" I growled.

"The Governor General thought it would be a good idea, he's sending her. Believe me, Chief Brown, his Honorship does not want an international incident. Please think of all the people on this space ship!" Her voice carried panic, her eyes swinging wildly.

"She's right, be responsible Chief." Hill pointed her finger at me. "Are you going to chance it because you're a stubborn selfish vindictive prick?"

I heard the Ambassador's intake of breath. Perhaps she'd heard I had a bad temper. What would this crazy person do next? I could feel the large woman shaking her head at Hill. Her amber eye was on Hill, the green one on me.

"Stop, she's right," I told Hotda. "Let her come, she's been a thorn in my side for so long, I won't even notice her! Let's get this over with!" I headed toward the door Hill had just come in from.

As I opened the door, I heard Ambassador Hoffsted with clip sounding words tell Hill, "My dear, your father would want me to warn you to think twice about this. This is a very unstable situation. He would not blame you if you did not go."

"Don't worry Hotda, I'm in good hands," Hill told the giant as she followed me through the door. I regretted now yelling at her. Damn the woman!

As the door closed another door in front of us opened. The air felt cooler, and as we progressed down the hallway my light -headedness left, I didn't feel heavy but could feel the gravitational boots keep us to the floor. The Bassodians not only used more oxygen but had less gravity on their planets, after all they were huge.

I looked in on one of the hospital rooms. The beds were gigantic and specially shaped. "They have tails." Hill reminded me.

We kept going down the long hallway, passing lounges with enormous chairs, again shaped to accommodate their huge bodies which included their good sized tails. The only room that looked half normal was the galley, although I noticed jars labeled "rodents" and "crisp bugs".

We finally came to the end of the hallway. It opened on a stairway's upper landing. Below was their dock and in the dock was what they had told me they called a "tug". It was a gigantic ship. The front of the tug stuck in the dock's opening. It was bright red and obviously made of a sturdy metal. It lacked any type of stylish exterior. With its jagged lines and plain exterior, it looked more like one of our floating rusty garbage trucks.

Several humans, dressed like us were flocking around the ship. They waved to us as we clomped our way down the stairs. One of the snowmen met us at the bottom of the landing. "He's waiting for you." I wondered how he knew it was a male, considering they were asexual.

I was soon to find out as the front part of the ship lowered with a clang, bang, scrape. At the top of the ramp there stood a very large Bassodian. At least he looked humongous to me, he could have been a midget to them, and he was a "he" to me too. A raspy, "Come up" came through our interpreter modules, even in its crudeness his voice dripped with impatience.

We hurried up, our boots causing us to stumble as we tried to run. When I got to the top I was huffing and puffing (of course Hill was perfectly fine) and out of breath. "Are you Skip Brown?" croaked over our modules.

"Yes," we both answered him.

Hill half smiled at me, "We are one, remember?"

"We are here…" but I didn't get very far as the Bassodian had already turned his back on us and had returned to the interior of the tug.

"He's goddamn rude." I said to Hill as we rushed after him. The ramp was already closing.

"They don't know the word rude, they are just naturally it," Hill assured me. "Don't take any notice of it!"

The interior was as rustic as the outside of the ship. It was larger in the back as the front was used for docking. The ceilings were so high they were out of sight. Only a few windows graced the inside, letting in a small amount of light. Hill dragged me over to the side where long benches lined the wall. We sat and she reached over inflating my seat with a button. Immediately warmth came into my extremities.

"It gets cold, they keep these heated pads for species that require more warmth. The Bassodians don't require heat as such, they are not cold blooded but close enough to it. From the far side, a wide set of stairs seemed to lead up to a control panel. I could barely see the controls and what looked like a cockpit window. Coming down the stairs was the huge lizard, his tail dragging behind him. He clumped over to us.

"Skip Brown?" He didn't wait for me to answer but lowered his face down to mine. I had taken my hood off as the warmth from the seat was enough. His eyes came level with mine. "Captain Xssos is awaiting you." He actually smiled. To my surprise, his breath was warm, his teeth quite yellow and his tongue pointed but the uplifted lips left no doubt that he was smiling. "Skip Brown," he repeated, "it is a pleasure to meet you!"

I heard Hill's intake of breath. I wasn't sure how to respond but there was no need as his hand or paw or whatever patted my head and then slapped my arm. I felt like I was some kind of pet.

He turned and left, clomping up the stairs again. "Hill?" I ventured, after all she was the expert.

"I… I have no idea." She stumbled over her words. "None what so ever."

"Great, so much for my expert!" I growled.

"You know, you're one of a kind." She sneered at me. "I risk coming with you and you do nothing but whine."

"You?" I looked at her. "The Governor, your father, didn't send you did he? He doesn't even know you're here. You lied to the Ambassador." I looked at her seeing that I had guessed right by the guilty look on her face.

"So? He doesn't need to know." She sounded like a petulant child explaining further, "our family has been a diplomatic dynasty for as long as there has been an Assembly. It is expected that everyone in the Pinote family enters the diplomatic arena. All my four brothers are steeped in the intrigues of galactic affairs, doing the bidding of my father. My oldest sister Danielle defied my father. She ran away and made some bad choices. My father will not even talk of her, it's as if she never existed to him." She sat silently staring out the window to her right. "He wouldn't even seek justice for her death. He expects total obedience from his children."

I could see her looking out the window, intensely engrossed in her thoughts. "The answers aren't out there," I told her. "You can only find them in yourself. Decisions on what you want in life, no matter what happens, are still left up to you. When I was blind for a year, it left me questioning everything that was left to me. When I got my eyesight back, life looked a lot different than what it had before. But I knew, even in the darkness, that it was still MY life."

"Why Chief, that has to be the most introspective thing you've ever said." She laughed, "Sounds strange coming from you. You are always so practical like my father, I suppose."

"Good god Hill, I'm not that old!" I actually gasped. "So I look that old?"

"Of course not, I meant in your manner. So sure of yourself, so demanding that others give their all but the difference is that you let people make their own mistakes, choose their own pathways. My father feels he needs to not just guide us but directly steer us. My brothers don't mind but I do!"

"You should have told me!" I forcefully said. "I don't like being blindsided. I don't think I need tell you that your father wields a lot of power. Think of the havoc it could cause the department. A lot of people could be affected."

"I should have said something but I couldn't, I needed you to be unbiased in the assignments you gave me." She looked out of the window again perhaps avoiding my accusing look. "I'm sorry," she softly whispered.

I was going to deny that I would have been biased even though I knew I wouldn't have been but the tug started moving - we were undocking. The creaking and straining of the metal ship was horrendous. All talk was impossible. We both grabbed onto the straps that lined the walls as the ship actually swayed. The lights went out and for a few moments we were in total darkness. I felt Hill grab onto my arm. I was glad for the pink pill that the medics had given me as my brain remained calm, my neck not tensing. A dull almost purple light suddenly filled the interior. A welcomed relief, despite the eerie shadows the low level light caused.

We actually felt the ship accelerate. The groaning of the metal slightly increased then became a low constant rumble. It became colder. I was thankful for the heated seat and putting up my coat's hood helped. I noticed Hill had done the same.

Since talking was impossible we sat in silence as the ship reverberated forward. It wasn't long before we felt the deceleration. Grabbing tightly to the handholds, I stood up, looking out the window. As the tug swung around the mother ship came into view. There were some strange markings on the ship's metal hull and below them the name ITTHIUS in glaring white letters. The ship was gigantic, I could only see perhaps a third of it. Like the small ship the mother ship was ugly in its stark naked jagged lines. It had a red glare, like its baby tug, that reminded me of the rust protection I'd seen on the huge tankers that I'd seen on Fulton's oceans.

The tug had completely turned around and was backing into an open dock. The loud cranking and moaning began again. It grated on our ears, both of us wincing almost in pain. It abruptly stopped with one deafening clang. The smaller ship shuddered as it settled in and came to a complete stop.

The Bassodian tug pilot came hoofing loudly down the back stairs. He crossed to the back pushing something that caused the ramp to lower. Light flooded in as did all the noise from the dock workers. We could hear loud speakers spewing out instructions. Our Bassodian clumped down the ramp. He didn't even look back at us.

"Friendly Chap. Rather rude." I told Hill.

"They don't know what friendly means and rude is a natural state for them. Understand something Chief, they don't think like us. They keep everything simple and to the point, feeling that any unnecessary action is a waste of time. The pilot knew we had to follow him, so why pay attention to us. It's the way their civilization works."

"Boy, this is going to be a lot of fun." I followed her down the ramp. There were lots of lizards everywhere, all in what looked like a type of green striped uniform with their tails swishing out the back. Large black boots covered their feet. The reptilian dock workers were very intimidating just by their size. They all were over seven feet tall and wide enough to make two of Hill. Notice I didn't say two of me!

One of the reptiles pointed to follow him. I think he was our original pilot. He was standing on a platform. When we got onto it, the floor started rising. Hill grabbed onto me as it took us to a landing several stories up. "Come, Captain waiting." Our guide told us through our translator cells.

We went through a sliding door down a long corridor. The further we went into the ship the more modern and more accommodating it became. The walls became a smooth blue exterior, then we passed several lounges with furniture large enough and shaped for their lizard bodies. Every piece of furniture had an open lower part for their tails. It was eerie. Every Bassodian we passed stared at us. We obviously were an aberration, humans on board!

We came to a blank wall. Suddenly a panel opened and an actual elevator, quite large mind you, appeared. When we got in the lizard spoke and our translator whispered "eight" in our ear. So there were at least eight floors on this ship.

Our guide hadn't said one word to us. I wondered if "conversation" was absent from their vocabulary. When the doors opened he didn't move. Hill grabbed my arm and led me out. The doors closed.

"Good god, Hill. Not even a *goodbye*." I looked around, there was another uniformed Bassodian waiting for us. His uniform had an array of symbols. Somehow I got the impression that this one was a ship's officer.

The large lizard mouth croaked out and then we heard in our translators, "Follow me."

"Wow, a talker!" I whispered to Hill, putting my hand over my trans module so that he wouldn't hear.

"Chief!" she looked wide eyed at me, but she smiled.

We followed our officer to two wide glass doors that slid opened and entered what I presumed to be the bridge of the ship. It was breathtaking. Large data screens floated throughout the cabin. Lizards were everywhere in floating rotating reptile chairs checking screens which had everything from sector maps to data printouts. What really blew my mind to the point where I could only stare in wonder was that all around the bridge, on every wall, was a race car. That's right - a race car! A large-scale miniature model of our humanoid circuit cars. It looked like every car that had ever won a championship. There amongst them was my "Blue Thunder" car.

"I see you are admiring my collection," a huge highly decorated uniformed Bassodian addressed me. "I have every one of your racing cars."

I stood there with my mouth opened, speechless. Silence, I guess it was catching....

Chapter Twelve

I presumed that my non-response was considered normal as he took no notice of my amazement other than to remark, "You like, yes it should be so."

I noticed the whole bridge was looking at me. It was Hill that spoke, standing behind me as inconspicuous as she could make herself. "It is an honor to be noticed by you, Captain."

It must have been the right answer because he smiled. I wished he wouldn't smile; it was a frightening sight, all those huge yellow teeth and the red flickering pointed tongue. He patted me on the head, three times, like the pilot had done. Unlike on the tug, this time I had the light to notice his big, almost claw-like hands. "We are very interested in the mechanics of your engines. Primitive, yet highly efficient. Our ship is often in your sectors. We watch your races with amusement."

He walked over to my car, pushing something, the car lowered itself down. He walked over carrying the model, putting it down on the floor in front of me. I was guessing that it was an 8:1 scaled model. I couldn't help it; I bent down and touched it lovingly, feeling the tapered front.

"No make that front anymore?" he pointed out, "most efficient for air flow."

"It was too dangerous, it cut another car in half."
I told him.

"Yes, aware of accident." His voice sounded
irritated in my translate module, "Foolish humans, better
to have air flow."

I wasn't going to argue with him, as Hill was
pressing her hand in my ribs, warning me to shut up and
not respond. I took her advice. I was even more amazed
when he lifted the front hood, my complete engine had
been copied down to the minutest detail. Again, I stood
in complete silence, awed beyond speech. I wondered if
all these cars actually worked but I didn't want to offend
them by asking.

He croaked some orders, which didn't come
over our modules, at one of the other lizards, who
promptly came over and put the car back. He then stood
behind me and bellowed which came loudly over our
translator modules, "Here is Skip Brown. Most famous
human racer, *Trainee of the Year."*

I was going to correct him to "rookie" but Hill
was digging hard in my ribs. I doubt they would have
heard me anyway as the floor erupted in loud noises that
sounded like a combination of yowling and barking.
Whatever, it was Hill that told me to smile, so I did.

"Come." The Captain instructed me and we did
just that, following him and his large swaying tail off the
bridge. We returned through the glass doors, past the
elevators to another set of glass doors. We entered a
rather dark room. It took a moment for my eyes to
adjust. As my eyes adjusted, I began noticing flickering
lights. We kept close to the Captain as he went over to a
side wall and seemed to touch something that resembled
a panel. Suddenly, the room came alive around seats
each facing a hologram depiction of a race track.

"That's Nestor's Strom Super Track," I told Hill.
She just nodded, my lieutenant had been there with me
on Nestor. Each seat looked like the interior of a race car

but in proportions to Bassodian bodies including a place for a tail.

The Captain sat in the end seat, motioning me to stand next to him. As I stepped next to him a 360 virtual world surround us. He motioned for me to sit on what looked like a box that I guessed had just been put there. Although I couldn't see Hill, I guessed she was just the other side of the illusionary screen.

I was fascinated. The hologram made it feel like I was on Strom's two mile track. It even smelled like I was sitting in a race car. "You teach." He started up the engine. I had noticed before that the other seats in the room were filled by ten of his crew members. They had built a car racing simulator, the best I'd ever seen.

The roar of the other ten car engines starting was so like the real thing that I grabbed my chest as I felt the pressure of the rumble. My heart sped up, good thing for that pink pill as my brain seemed to be working normally, no sense of an episode coming on. My adrenaline overflowed as he followed the pace car around the track. I noticed he was in eighth position. I looked past him noticing the seventh place car. The Bassodian driving the bright yellow car looked over at me and growled, showing his teeth. I flinched! Good god, I guess the enthusiasm for racing is universal!

The pace car exited and the race began. The Bassodians may be great engineers, top scientists and all, but they are lousy race car drivers. I cringed as he ground the gears; his car was setup too tight including his shocks, tire pressure. All wrong. I could just feel the car struggling. It hurt my racing sensitivity.

Although the other racer drivers, I say that loosely, were beating him, they weren't much better. Some went too high, some too low and absolutely no wind dragging. It was like they were scrambling with only speed being the factor. When the four lap race was over, the Captain finished in next to last place. Now I realized why he had started in eighth.

His big square lizard head swung over to meet my eyes. I guess I wasn't too successful in hiding my contempt as his tongue flickered in and out; a discernable frown graced his face. "What wrong!" he demanded.

"Everything!" I told him, getting an elbow hit from Hill who was on the other side of the screen but could still hear everything. I didn't care. I knew driving, they didn't! "Okay, let us start from the beginning. Pull up the car's specs."

He grunted as he pushed some buttons and the car's setup came on screen. "What I do wrong?" he half growled it, his big paw shaking near my face.

"Well, for one thing let's tighten the shocks - this is a two mile track, let's get some air out of the tires for gripping these corners and for god's sake you've got the fuel too rich. I leaned over pushing some of the other buttons. "Since you're only racing four laps, you don't need to watch the fuel gage but remember on longer races to check the fuel and tire wear!"

He shook his head that he understood. "What else?"

"You are using your brakes too much, shift down instead, it gives you better control."

"Let us give this a try." I pointed my finger at his nose, "AND listen to me!"

I heard him growl and snort but he didn't argue with me. He yelled over to his other racers, or I should say his loud grunts got returned grunts and the engines started up. The pace car left and the race began. "Shift down! Shift down, get behind that car!" I yelled continuously at him. He still ended up in sixth place.

Twice more didn't do much. "Okay, enough!" I'm not known for my patience. Hill was frantically poking me, telling me to calm down. It didn't do any good. "Let's switch places." I told him. "Come on, sit here." I patted the big box he had gotten me. He looked at me like he was ready to kill me, his teeth were showing in a snarl. "Do you want to win or not?" I sternly told him. He nodded his scaly head. "Get up then."

He shut down the system and got up. I walked around the back of the car with Hill busting my chops, "Chief, you can't talk to them like that!"

"Shit, I can't. He wants to win, he'll put up with me," I told her. I heard her groan, she knew me, I wasn't going to change.

I got into the driver position. The seat was gigantic. My legs wouldn't reach the pedals. "Hill, take off your gravity boots and come in here!"

"I don't…" she stammered.

"Just get in here! And give me your jacket, disconnect your translator module." I yelled.

She dumped her boots and grabbed me as the sudden weight lost made her disoriented. I took her jacket, and guided her to sit between my legs, keeping her head from bumping into the steering wheel. I stuffed our two jackets behind me, I could now easily reach the controls and shifter. Hill was jabbering on about us causing a cosmic interspecies incident.

"Listen!" I yelled at her making sure my translator unit was off, "If we don't do this right, the Captain will kill me. He's losing face with his crew, so shut up and listen." She made one last groan and shut up. I explained what she needed to do, "I will put pressure on your right leg and you press the gas pedal. The other leg will be to press for the brake. I don't use the brake a lot. Go easy pressing that one and for god's sake don't press both pedals at the same time!"

I turned to the Captain putting my module back on. "Tell them to let us make one turn around the track." I heard the captain bark loudly and silence as they shut down the other engines. "Okay, here we go Hill. I pressed on her right leg lightly and I slowly, albeit rather unsteadily, we pulled out of pit row.

I have to give Hill credit, by the second turn she had it down pat. I increased the speed as the car screeched around the third turn. This may have been a virtual car but it ran like a real one. My heart thumped in excitement. I raced down the final stretch and then headed into pit row. It was a little hairy getting into my sixth place parking place. I just missed hitting the car in front of me but Hill put the brake on hard and we stopped inches from the car.

The other engines started up. We followed the pace car, coming up two by two. I looked at the temperature of the track, it was warmer than usual. I got my tires warmed up by jiggling the car back and forth. I kept a running dialogue explaining to the captain exactly how I was driving. I could feel his hot breath as his face was near mine watching.

The pace car left the track, we roared ahead. My biggest problem was keeping the other cars from sliding into me. I down shifted coming behind a bright yellow car. I heard the Captain huff in shock. I explained I was riding his tail wind. Then I zoomed past him, whipping by him into the straightaway, passing the front two and headed towards the lead car. The third turn loomed ahead. I took it low, skidding as I down shifted, no brake, and passed him.

The track lay opened and empty. Away I shot. I heard the Captain give a high hoot but I ignored him as I raced around. I repeated my performance as I lapped the other cars and on the third lap took the white flag and then the checkered flag. I told Hill to brake hard and I did a 360 on the inner field, whooping as I did it. The Captain reached over patting me again three times on the head.

"Do again!" he demanded.

So we did it again, with the same results. The feeling was so good. It had been a long time since I had raced. I took a minute to enjoy the rumbling of the engine under me; at least it felt like the real thing.

"Okay, your turn." I pointed at the Captain. I could have kept at it forever but that wouldn't help the Bassodian. "Let us switch." He shut the system down and got up from his box that I swear creaked in relief.

I helped Hill get her boots on and we were glad to get our coats back on, there was a definite chill in the room, damn coldblooded lizards. I lumbered over to sit on my box as the system went up. The Captain started his engine and the roar of the others filled the room.

His first try was better, he ended up in second. I kept yelling instructions at him, one time I actually reached over and shifted, once I hit him on the shoulder telling him to "hit it". The second time he actually bumped the car in front of him trying to wind drag but he saved it and spun around, passing beautifully. On the third time he came in first.

"ARK, ARK, ARK..." bellowed out of his mouth, the room erupted in loud barking noises as the other Bassodian racers congratulated him. I had to admit he was a fast learner. We spent the rest of the day going over the rest of the 12 circuit tracks. He had a hard time with the Vesti quarter mile track. It took him awhile to get the constant turning but he got it. He started to win every race.

Hill told me it was time to go as our cellbuttons announced it was almost 15:00. The space station would be coming to get us. When I told the captain, he nodded shutting off the machines. I got up to go when he suddenly said, "You," he pointed his green clawed thick fingered hand at me, "you, now you race me."

"I don't think...." I started to say.

Hill grabbed my arm, "You can't refuse. It will be a big insult."

"Fine," I said as the racer in the next car vacated. "Come on Hill, take your boots off and give me your jacket."

I got us settled, she now knew the drill. She covered her translate module, "You can't win Chief, he'll lose face with his crew." The urgency in her voice was almost to panic level.

"I always race to win." I told her. "Just watch your foot brake."

"Chief…" She started to say but I cut her off.

"Don't worry, trust me." I patted her shoulder, "I know what I'm doing."

We started. I was driving a bright yellow beauty. It felt beautiful. I had set up the car to run a little loose. He had picked the Nestor track and the temperature on the track was a little hot. The two of us followed the pace car. When it left the track, the Captain roared ahead. I drifted behind him until my tires were warm and hugging the pavement. I whipped around him using his drag and headed out on the straight away. I let him catch up to me around turn two and he zipped around me. I let him take the lead for the next two laps. On the white flag lap, I passed him low as we took turn three side by side. I carefully kept my nose even with his. I saw him look at me as we sped down the last straightaway. I had him and he knew it. Just before the checkered flag, I let up, letting him win by a nose.

The room erupted in volumes of barks and roars and stomping. I saw the Captain get out of his car and raise his arms in victory. I helped Hill out and into her boots. "I know it was hard but you did the right thing," she whispered to me.

"It wasn't that hard," I told her, "he knows I beat him, that's all that matters."

"Come show you." He said as he got out of his simulator. "Me show." We followed him back to the bridge. I couldn't help but take one last look at my "blue thunder" car. Hill took hold of my arm.

"Look," she simply said pointing over to a corner where the captain had gone. There was a large hologram of a planet floating, it took a whole corner of the bridge.

"Planet we haul," the captain's voice came over my translator module. Then he pressed a button and the entire front wall became a window, then he pressed another button and a beam as bright as a sun lit up the planet they had in tow. We were both flabbergasted as we could see it quite clearly. They were dragging it behind them. I looked over at the hologram, an exact duplicate. I walked over seeing the screen lit below it. Hill stood next to me. It was mostly written in Brassy but we both saw something we recognized. We didn't dare even seem like we had seen it, turning back to the windows quickly.

"I thank you for honoring me." Hill spoke up behind me. The Bassodian Captain smiled.

"Go home now," he said.

We followed the Captain as he led us to the elevators. "You go. Dock One." He seemed to be at a loss for words, shuffling his massive scaled feet, an almost human gesture. "Me know." The words came over our modules, almost a whisper. He patted me three times on my head, and then shockingly he held out his hand. I stood for a few seconds, realizing he was trying to shake my hand. I reached out grabbing on to his massive paw and shook it. Then he walked away.

Hill followed me into the elevator, for once she seemed at a loss for words. She was silent the whole way down to floor one. We walked to the platform that lowered us to where we could see *M.O.S.S. MEDICAL* written on the side of a space liner. It looked sleek and modern and out of place in the jagged looking rust colored dock. It also looked extremely small compared to the huge docking area; while in fact the ship was big enough to hold a medical team and several patients.

Hotda Hoffsted was standing at the foot of the stairs leading into the space ship. In her gravity boots and big jacket she looked almost bear-like. The woman was large. Still the Bassodian standing next to her made her seem small. She waved to us.

"I was getting worried. They wouldn't tell me a thing." Her words chirped out loudly with each word being crisp and pointedly annoyed. She focused on the dock crew that was mulling around the port. "Good god they are pompous. So relieved to see you are alright." Nothing like calling the kettle black! At least both eyes were on us.

"No problem," I told her, as I nodded towards the Bassodian.

He came over and touched me three times on the head. I heard Ambassador Hoffsted draw a deep breath. She looked stunned. Hill grabbed onto her arm and led her up the stairs but the surprised woman kept looking back at me as if I was some odd creature. Her green eye watched the Bassodian but her amber eye looked straight at me. Then they switched and then switched back. I just followed behind.

Inside was indeed spacious. We took off our now heavy boots and coats. I sat in one of the cushioned white leather seats, sinking down, letting the tension roll off me. I hadn't realized how tense I was. Those pink pills worked really well. I suddenly felt light headed, the extra oxygen in my body having an effect.

The ambassador took up two seats. When she stood her fuzzy hair touched the craft's ceiling. She had to go down middle isle sideways.

"Here, take one of these." Hotda handed me a huge pill with a bottle of juice. I gulped it down; I hadn't realized how thirsty I was, how dry my mouth and throat had become. It took only a few minutes for my body to right itself.

I looked up to see the Ambassador staring opened-eyed at me - both of them. Her big bushy eyebrows slanted upwards. "You are strange, Mr. Brown," she cautiously said. "How did you get the status of *honored being*?"

"I have no idea what you are talking about." I almost snapped it, her tone was one of total surprise at me being anything to warrant recognition. Hill, knowing my tone, put her hand on my shoulder.

"I'm sure you didn't mean it to come across that he is unworthy of such an honor," my lieutenant frowned, as only Hill can frown, at the large woman. Evidently Hill knew what *honored being* meant."

"Someone enlighten me." When neither of them said anything, I growled "NOW!" in my best cop voice.

Hill said, "*Honored being* means you are someone due a lot of respect. Every specie has an *honored being*. Humans show it often in the handshake. I am guessing but the Bassodians must show it by tapping the head three times." She looked over to Hotda for confirmation and the ambassador nodded.

"The Bassodians only honor themselves, very few warrant recognition. What is it about you that caused this?" Again, I didn't like her tone. I wanted to punch both her roving eyes out.

"Really Chief Brown, not even the Consulate Ambassador Governor General is afforded that honor." The large woman bent over, both her eyes scrutinizing me as if I was some aberration.

She sounded so surprised I wanted to stick my tongue out at her. Childish as it seemed, I didn't but I knew envy when I saw it. *Why Brown and not me?* It was so obvious.

"They just find me irresistible, it's my outstanding personality." I quipped.

"Ambassador, please sit and buckle your seat, we've been cleared for takeoff." Our pilot, who was a gorgeous brunette, loudly yelled back. "I want to get out of here! We're already late. The Bassodians are anxious to Jump."

I saw the big woman take her seat in front of me. Hotda took up two seats. I could hear the chair groan. Hill slid beside me. "A little temperamental aren't you?"

"She got under my skin," I told my rookie. "I don't get along with politicians and diplomats. What are we going to do about what we know about that planet?"

"We're going to tell my father," she said it matter-of-factly yet cautiously perhaps thinking about my relationship with diplomats. "He's the only one who can do something about it. We can't let the Ligithians start a new slave planet."

"Yeah," I almost whispered it as I didn't want the Amazon woman in front of me to hear it. "I couldn't read the exact Bassodian words but the word "Ligithia" stood right out."

The Moss space ship exited the dock. "Is there anything from Lont Pol," I yelled to the ambassador. I was hoping to get news of Killa.

"She said to tell you all is under control. When the Bassodians are gone you'll be able to contact her. We can go ship to ship once their influence is behind us. We'll be at the space station in less than an hour."

I relaxed into the deep cushions on the seat. Closing my eyes, I realized how tired I was, the adrenalin was leaving me with an exhausted body. Suddenly, the whole ship shook.

"We're under fire!" the pilot yelled. "Hold on!" She banked sharply; I could feel the "g's" pushing me sideways. I heard Hotda whimper as her big body absorbed the impact.

"Are we hit?" I yelled up the cabin, the pilot was frantically pushing buttons.

"They only scraped us but they are right on our tail!" the pilot almost screamed it. I saw the Bassodian mothership come into view, she was heading right toward it!

"What's she doing?" I asked Hill but got no answer as my lieutenant had gone across the ship to look out the other window.

Suddenly the windows went darkly blank, no more stars shown. We were under the Bassodian's big ship. "They won't dare to shoot us here, if they hit the mother ship, those damn lizards will pulverize them."

"Let's get in touch with the Bassodians, they'll help us." I told the pilot.

"I already tried." The pilot answered me, "They aren't responding. They don't interfere in human conflicts."

"Guess my *honored being* status doesn't mean so much does it?" I sarcastically pointed out to the large woman, who was pacing the isle between the seats, her head almost hitting the ceiling. "Who could be shooting at us, we're a hospital ship!"

"It's a small cruiser, I have it on my radar, and it's circling the ship waiting for us to come out from under. We have to go sometime. We can only out run it for a short stretch, especially if I time it when it's on the opposite side of where we are. We don't have any weapons, we're a hospital ship for god's sake." The pilot sounded exasperated, "We don't have any options."

"We have to get out soon, the Bassodians are about to Jump. We'll never survive being caught in a Jump," Hill pointed out. "What if we run just before they Jump, the other ship will be caught in their field."

"I have no way of knowing when they are going to deploy the Jump. We'd need to run just before they engage their final drives. We are going to have to make a run for it."

"Wait!" Hill yelled at her. "We do have a way of knowing when they're going to Jump. Chief, you are sensitive to the Jump. You should be able to tell!"

"You mean, when I throw up, you'll know." I looked sternly at Hill, "Not really reliable."

"Got a better idea?" Hill stood putting her hands on her hips. "The second you feel nauseous tell us!"

"Fine. But make sure the enemy ship is on the opposite side. How far away do we have to get to be out of range?" I asked.

Hill already had her tab out; I should have known she was on top of it. "We have to get a half a parsec away. Can we do it?"

"We can try." The pilot didn't sound too sure of herself. "At least it's something."

We all settled down, but everyone was watching me except the pilot, who was fidgeting with the ship's controls explaining she was giving it the most power she could for a quick dash. "Everyone strap in this could be a real stressful bumpy ride."

"Sit down Hotda," Hill sternly told the ambassador. "I'll watch him, I know the signs!"

I felt the seat in front of me absorb Hoffsted's weight and heard her irritated huff as she did what Hill told her to do.

It hit me hard, the feeling of nauseous, perhaps being so close to such a huge transporting body has that effect. I must have turned a pale shade as my head went for the bag my rookie was holding close to my face. "NOW!" she screamed.

I heard the pilot exclaiming, "They are almost on the other side." Then moments later the ship lurched and accelerated. I was flung back into the seat hard, I was still holding the bag to my face. Thank goodness I hadn't eaten much because it was all in the bag now. We rocked back and forth, good thing for the straps as we would have bounced to the ceiling. I could feel the ship straining.

"Come on baby," I heard the pilot croak out, "Come on."

Then it was like standing still. Almost too quiet. I was afraid to ask, "Did we ditch them?"

"They are off my radar, as is the Bassodian ship. We made it!" The pilot raised her hands in triumph. Good for her, I felt like shit. The spatial sickness had been really brutal, it would take a while for me to recuperate. My stomach felt like it had been turned inside out.

"Here, drink this tea." Hill put a mug in front of me but I pushed it away. "Really, Chief, it will help, it's a special blend. Come on, don't be a baby!"

The look I gave her would have killed a horse but not Hill. She was gonna stand there until I took it, waving the friggin thing in front of my face. I grabbed it and gulped it down. Of course, it burned my throat and she ended up slapping my back as I had a coughing fit.

The strange thing was once it landed in my stomach, I did feel better but I wasn't going to let her gloat. So I kept silent. "Can we contact the station?" I growled.

"The Jumps are coming back up but it took all my power to escape in time, so I have a weak signal. I can't spare the energy, I just sent a message that we are returning. We are limping back home."

"Great!" I exclaimed. "How long before we get there?"

"It'll be close to two hours but at least we're getting there."

I settled back in the chair and was falling asleep when I heard Hotda Hoffsted chastising my Lieutenant, "Judith, you lied to me. Your father is furious. He was furious at me."

"He shouldn't have blamed you. You had no way of knowing." Hill was actually contrite, amazing, "I knew he wouldn't have let me go and I wasn't about to let the Chief go it alone. "

So that was why the Ambassador Hoffsted was so huffy. The Governor had put some of the blame for his daughter's deceit on the large woman. I smiled as I drifted into sleep, I had a feeling I was going to need my wits about me when we went to Judy's father. Still, it didn't keep me awake. I was just drifting off when the thought that perhaps my lieutenant had put a sleeping draught in my tea entered my brain. Damn woman.

Whatever it was, I slept like a baby. It took Hill several tries to get me awake. "Chief, we are only a few minutes away. Time to resurface."

I opened one eye. My dreams had been deep and to be frank entertaining, as I sped around the Nestor track. I won every time. It was the first time I'd dreamt of racing without waking up in a cold sweat from reliving my crash. I would have kept sleeping. "Strap in, our landing pulses were damaged by the attack. The landing crew is going to air-float us into the dock, but it won't be a smooth landing."

I could hear the pilot talking to the flight dock operator. I hadn't realized before that we had sustained some damage. The underbelly of our ship had evidently gotten a direct hit. The ship banked to head to Ring Six, which worried me because it contained the ER dock. Were they expecting us to get hurt? Great, just great!

I looked out the window; I could see the black burnt scrapes along the side of our ship but worst I could see black soot stripes coming up from the bottom. The dock's tower was giving the pilot advice-

"Come in from zone 4 Moss II. How bad are your brakes?"

"I don't know," the pilot said, "I'm at half power. My instruments may be faulty."

"*We got full lift power near the dock's floor so come in high and stall.*"

"Got it," she sounded nervous.

"*We have emergency personnel standing by, good luck.*"

"I'm going to need it." She told them. "Oxygen is running low, so get to us quickly."

"*Got it, we're ready.*"

Shit, I tightened my seat belt and grabbed one of the oxygen masks that had fallen from the ceiling, not that it would do much good if we ran out. Hill already had her mask on and was helping Hotda get hers over the massive hairdo that the ambassador sported. When Hill had taken her seat I asked, "Did you get hold of Lont Pol, I'm worried about Killa?"

"The pilot finally did and Pol had enough time to tell her all was well."

Good, at least if something happened to me I knew Killa was alright. Hill looked over at me and took my hand, guessing what I was thinking. She squeezed my hand, "It will be Okay." Yeah, sure, glad she thought so!

We felt the ship make one last turn, the lights of the dock were now in sight. They were especially bright as the cabin went dark.

"Okay, folks, here we go, hang on tight," the pilot sounding very professional yet with an edge to her voice.

We slowed down to a crawl. As we entered the dock the reverse engine squealed, the back pressure of the thrusters pushed us back in our seat. The brakes clunked when the pilot applied. Then the whole ship lunged to a stop, pushing us hard into the seat ahead of us. I heard the Ambassador hit the small wall in front of her seat with a thud.

Then the ship dropped hard. It took the breath right out of me. I heard Hill gasp and then there was silence. Judy was already out of her seat. The light coming in from the window silhouetted her making her way to the pilot.

"The pilot's unconscious." She explained. "I think she hit her head on the dash."

I unbuckled the safety harness. Hotda was out cold, her nose was bleeding. The plane was slowly being lowered on the heavy air cushion they had created. The craft's air was stuffy and getting worse. "We need to open the door." I told Hill.

My lieutenant was checking the dash. She started pushing buttons but the door wasn't opening. I tried to force it open but it wasn't budging. I heard Hill swear as she kept pushing buttons. The air was almost gone. I was gulping. I saw Hill pass out, falling over the pilot. I heard people on the other side of the door but I couldn't even yell out. Then I joined Hill, passing out on the floor.

Chapter Thirteen

When my eyes opened, it took a few moments to focus. I had an oxygen mask over my face and a man was leaning over me. "How long have I been out?" I asked.

"Only about thirty seconds," the medic replied as he was taking my pulse. "We had to wait until the dock's door closed and the room pressurized. You seem fine."

I nodded, looking around for Hill who wasn't far away. She had an oxygen mask covering most of her face, her eyes were wide open, looking directly at me. "You okay Chief?" she managed to mutter, the mask making it difficult to hold any kind of conversation. Hill was helping the medic hold up the pilot. The woman aviator was bleeding from her forehead. I gathered she'd hit her head hard on the dashboard.

I saw them working on the ambassador. One of the medics was clasping an oxygen mask close to her face while another was trying to stop her nose bleed. It took another two to hold her down. She looked a mess but was conscious as her mouth was going a mile a minute, "Let me up! I need to report to the Governor General. I'm fine. Get your hands off me!"

What I wouldn't have given for some mouth tape. A medic gave her a shot. No more arguing as she slumped down, sedated into silence. It took five of them to get her on a stretcher. They loaded both the ambassador and the pilot into an oversized cart-type vehicle and whisked them toward the ER.

To my surprise, Dr. Dan Bolker came running across the dock. Hill and I were standing at the foot of the mangled ship's stairway. "I came as soon as I heard," he excitedly informed us between gasps of breaths.

"I'm fine," I explained. "I was out a few moments when we ran out of oxygen but they were already at the door."

"Let me take a look at you. I insist!" he said, pulling us into a room right off the dock. He checked me over; peering into my eyes with a pocket flashlight, taking my pulse, and making me follow his fingers. I did fine. I saw the relief in his eyes. He quickly checked Hill and she passed fine. "You are lucky. They said the ship hit the deck hard." Then he spoke into his cellbutton, giving Lont Pol an update. Seconds later my own cellbutton came on.

"Chief, I hear you are alright. What happened? The hospital ship came under attack?" My Moss superintendent's stressed out voice came over my cell, concern was still in her tone despite having talked to Dr. Dan.

"Hill is here, we are both fine. Tell you all about it later. How are things here? Did you hear from Issam? How is Killa?"

"Killa is in Dr. Ditterset's lab. I have three cops outside their door. I haven't gotten hold of Issam yet, can't get a communication line. Things are slowly progressing here. The Jump lines are coming back, being restored. Our conference guests are leaving as soon as they can make departure plans. Communications are jammed. Of course with so few lines all coming from Hibnet's office, most will have to wait until they can get to the satellite ferry station. Hibnet has got to open up some more lines!"

"He won't, save your breath," my anger rising to the top. "I plan to have some long talks with the Dome representatives about Moss' outdated lines of communication."

Hill tapped my shoulder, "Be careful Chief, we are not on a secure line, he could be listening."

"I hope he is. I won't be going behind his back." I threw up my arms, "What else can we do, he's too much of a control freak." I saw Hill wince at my honesty over an insecure line. I was so mad, I didn't care.

"When will I see you?" Pol asked over the cell. "Dr. Hibnet is calling every few minutes asking if I'd heard from you." Even as she said it the doctor's name was softly repeated in my other ear. He was trying to get hold of me. I ignored it.

"Tell him we have to report to the Governor General. That will shut him up, he won't try to out-muscle Pinote, and then I will see you back at the police station," I quickly informed my police superintendent. "I'll contact my people now, let's get everything wrapped up."

After Pol hung up, I called all my detectives. They all sounded like they were ready to go home. Hell, I was ready to go home.

We were on Ring 6's large docks. From what Dr. Dan Bolker told me it contained the best supplied docks for emergency landings. It also housed the emergency rooms. Normally our ship would have docked near the Administrative Offices on Ring 9, easy access to Hibnet's office.

I was just grateful we had made it. I followed Hill as we crossed by tram over the center passageway to the elevators on the black cylinder. I felt the weariness settling in. Hill pulled me along to the elevator. We went down to Tube Level 5, Eupiel Center, then coming out at the train terminal. A police vehicle was waiting for us and sped us to the hotel.

It was evident that the exodus of the conference guests had begun. Limo trolley carts were loading up passengers with their luggage. I recognized most, including our futbol star and his entourage and some of the Dome representatives. Hill knew where she was going, we hurried through the lobby to the back elevators that led up to the more exclusive suites. Her father was sure to have the best one.

She hadn't said much on the trip over but on the elevator I got an earful. "Listen, my father can be rather forceful. He is used to being in charge. I swear it's in the Pinote dominating genes, so don't try to out wrangle him, it'll just make for a unproductive conversation."

"I'll be diplomatic," I countered but from the look on her face I could tell she thought that quite impossible. Oh well, I'd try.

We got off on the top floor. The carpet was thick, the walls richly tapestried, it smelled *opulent*. "He has the whole floor," she informed me. Why was I not surprised? Government at its best! Hill side-glanced me getting my reaction. I guess my frown told her what I was thinking. "He normally doesn't go in for luxuriousness, this was Hibnet's doing," she was trying to placate me, naturally defending her father.

There were security people all along the corridor. They just nodded to us, well really nodded toward the governor's daughter. I got quickly scrutinized, then recognized, and then ignored. A door at the middle of the corridor had two bulky guys. They greeted Hill but made us stand as they did a rapid scan of our bodies. I had left my gun in the first docking station when I had started the journey to the Bassodian ship. The attendants had assured me that I'd have it back when I next saw Lont Pol. Hill, however, was carrying one inside her jacket. She handed it to the guard; a small finger Taser.

"Thank you, Lady Pinote." He half bowed.

"What the hell. Did you have that when we were on the Bassodian ship?"

"Yes, it's mostly undetectable," she informed me as my rookie walked into the suite, leaving me with my mouth opened.

I was so mad, I didn't even take in our surroundings. "Are you crazy? You could have gotten us killed!" I pointed my finger at her, "Talk about breaking regulations, I should write you up for that, for being *stupid*!"

"Oh and look who's talking about following regulations!" Now her finger was pointed at me.

"Ahem," came from somewhere, bringing me back to the here and now. One of her brothers, half smiling, trying to hide it with his hand, was standing next to us. "Judy, Dad is waiting for you."

We followed him through what looked like a reception area into a type of conference room. A large table lay in the middle with several couches and chairs spread along the outside walls. We took a seat at the table. Looking around, the room was set up with video screens and several cell outlets.

The door opposite the one we had come through opened up. I recognized the Governor General. He seemed to suck all the oxygen out of the room. Up close he was even more impressive; tall, peppered with gray, deep set serious eyes, dressed impeccably in a tailor-made suit. I noticed how large his hands were. If I didn't know who he was I'd guess by his hands to be a carpenter. They were rough and calloused.

"Good day Chief Brown," his intense green eyes scrutinizing me. It felt like he was X-raying me. "I'm anxious to hear about your encounter with our Bassodian friends. You must excuse me for just a second as I need to urgently talk with my daughter." He opened the door wider nodding for Hill towards it, standing aside as she went through.

It wasn't long before I could hear raised voices. I couldn't tell what was being said but I got the jest of loads of anger from each voice. Her four brothers who had followed us in and had taken seats on the couches against the far wall, perked up. One of them went to the door, as he opened it I heard, "Don't be an ass, you are coming home!" the Governor General's voice booming with ire. The son went in and closed the door and the voices quieted.

A few minutes later, Hill flushed and her face still holding anger, came out with the Governor following close behind. His face was composed, a true diplomatic demeanor probably from years of practicing.

"My daughter tells me you have discovered something of *ultimate importance* on your visit to the Bassodian's freighter." He was verging on the edge of sarcasm as if there was probably nothing this "Chief of Police" could tell him. I have dealt with the Dome politicians for so long that I took no offense. He had probably come across plenty of people trying to impress him and he was guessing I was just another one.

"Yes, sir," I replied. Hill seemed to relax a little, glad I wasn't going to make an angry ass of myself. Oh, how she underestimates me! "I do believe there is something you should be made aware of."

He had taken a seat opposite me. He looked at me and then his daughter. "I am surprised that the Bassodians asked for you to visit their ship, it's not like them to show any interest in anything we do."

"Dad, he's a former race car driver, they wanted to meet him. They follow the races." Hill was trying to explain to a non-fan. I could tell by his look of incredulity that it wasn't something on his radar screen.

I held up my hand, shutting Hill off. "Let me explain. The planet engineering crews that haul the spheres and have our sectors on their routes must get bored traversing throughout humanoid worlds. They are mechanical scientists and what fascinates them is our highly efficient gasline racing cars. Studying the in and outs of our racing gives them something to do. The racing circuit does not race hovers, the cars are combustion engines, highly tuned and take a degree of engineering that fascinates the intellect of the Bassodians. The Captain saw my name on the lists of people attending the conference and took the opportunity to quiz me on the workings of our cars."

"Dad it was fascinating. They have miniature models of the all the famous race cars, and then created a virtual race track simulator."

"I gather you were of some notoriety, Mr. Brown or they would not have shown an interest in you?" So, the Governor was paying attention.

Before I could answer Hill rapidly spoke up, "He was Rookie of the Year and won two championships and an unheard of thirty one races." I have to admit I probably blushed, her enthusiasm spilled over.

"Please Judith, let the Chief talk for himself," her father rather sternly told her. "Why are you not a racer now?" He cocked his head as if my answer was important to him.

"I wanted to go into Law Enforcement." I told him rather too forcefully; it was none of his business that I was an epileptic, a flawed humanoid. I felt my anger rising at being grilled.

It was one of the sons that spoke up. "He had a bad accident, father. He can't race anymore."

"Oh, my apologies Chief Brown, I did not mean to intrude, believe me. I just find it fascinating that the Bassodians are so interested in you."

I may have responded with something bordering on insubordination but the door flew open and Ambassador Hotda Hoffsted burst in. She was a sight. The large woman looked like she'd been in a tornado.

Her orange-red hair flew out in all directions, giving her a fiery crazed look. She had a cape semi-wrapped around her, underneath a hospital Johnnie could be seen. Her feet held infirmary slippers, the large flip flops made a loud sucking sound when she walked. Her eyes fluctuated from one person to the other, each pointing in opposite directions.

For the first time, Governor General Pinote seemed rattled. His eyes were wide as he took in the Amazon woman. "Ambassador Hoffsted?" he stuttered.

"I came as soon as I could Sir," she yelled, "they tried to imprison me!"

"I was under the impression you were in the Emergency Room." He looked over at one of his sons for confirmation.

"Yes, she is supposed to be in Ward D in ER on Ring 6, his oldest son Matt confirmed, "she obviously has escaped." He was trying not to smile but it was a lost cause. Ambassador Hoffsted turned around exposing her naked backside. She finally flopped down on one of the couches. Ben, the youngest scrambled out of her way as her butt came close to him.

"Hotda, you've been hurt." Hill tried to placate the angry hysterical woman. "You need to go back."

"Don't you lie to me again!" Hotda was having none of it. Then half coming to her senses she looked at the Governor, "I'm sorry, she did lie to me."

"It's alright Ambassador." He stood up going over and pushing her back down onto the couch as she was getting up. At the same he motioned to his son but Matt was already on his cell, I presumed calling the ER.

"Sir," Hotda urgently pulled on his sleeve, "they patted him three times on the head, they consider him an *Honored Being*." The Ambassador almost spit it out, as if it was so unconceivable that she had trouble saying it. I wished for some duct tape, anything to shut her up!

Pinote looked at me. I saw a little bit of respectable awe in his eyes. "Truly Chief, I am amazed."

"Dad, he taught the Captain to drive, and then when he raced him, he let the Captain win so he could save face with his crew. It is why we saw the planet and where it is going! He wanted to thank the Chief." Hill had stood up in her excitement, pointing her finger at me.

"Calm down, Judith." He motioned for her to sit, which she totally ignored. Meanwhile, Pinote was also trying to calm Ambassador Hoffsted, who did not want to stay sitting on the couch.

"Sir, I think you should listen to what Judy has to say." Colin, one of his sons spoke up as he got up from his seat. He had a tab in his hand. "You need to look at these images."

"What is it?" the Governor's voice made it clear it had better be important.

"I have Judy's pictures. It shows what she's been trying to tell you. I had the photographs blown up and it gives a clear picture of where this planet is being dragged to."

"Photos?" It was my turn to stand up. "What pictures?" I glared at Hill. "Did you take pictures?" I half yelled at her, "Do you have a death wish?"

"The camera was well hidden," she responded, facing me with that hard determined look of hers, as if challenging my intelligence.

I pointed my finger at her, "You're getting written up!" I was so mad.

"You just try!" she yelled back. "You're lucky I was there."

"I didn't ask you to come. I didn't want you there!" I countered, forgetting how indeed I was glad she had been there. Damn woman!

"And if I wasn't there to get between your legs, how would you have coped?" I wanted to swipe that sly look right off her face.

"What!" Pinote barked over. "What are you saying? Legs? Which also brings us to why you disobeyed me? I denied you permission to go on that ship!" Her father had his hands clenched at his side, obviously extremely angry. The oxygen went out of the room, a thunder cloud hung over the chamber. The diplomat was not someone anyone could ignore. Even the crazy Hotda cringed into her couch seat.

"Father…" Hill tried to interrupt but one look and she shut up. It was her brother Colin that saved her from further harsh words as he put the tab folder in front of his father and opened it up. A holographic screen flipped open in front of the Governor General.

"As you can see the words are mostly in Bassodian but the word Ligithia is quite easily recognizable." Colin was pointing to several areas of the screen.

"Ligithia?" the Governor repeated the word and almost choked on it.

"Yep, right there." His son pointed to the word. I was leaning over the table trying to get a look at the screen. Sure enough it was a picture of the monitor that was under the planet's holographic monitor.

"I need an engineer, preferably one that understands planetary engineering. Considering this is a space station, there should be some qualified person." Hill's father looked over at his other sons, "Ben, go find one and be quick about it. It will help if he understands Bassodian."

He wasn't done, turning to his other son, "Lar, get Ambassador Medicinis here pronto. Do not tell him what it's about, this mustn't leave this room."

"I'd put him in chains," I commented. "He's probably responsible for much of the trouble on the space station and I'm sure he has his hands on this."

"I doubt that." Pinote remarked looking at me strangely. "How do you know the Ligithian Ambassador? Why is he in Crab Nebula's Chief of Police crosshairs? It's not like Orion is in your jurisdiction."

"He's his grandfather." Hill let it roll right out of her mouth. If looks could kill my glare would have done her in. She wasn't even apologetic, "Chief, I know you don't like it known, but he needs to know. He'll find out anyway, better it is out in the open."

"Grandson? There has to be a tall tale behind this one. This day is full of surprises. I don't have the time for it now but I'll need to know about it. Meanwhile, let it be known Alphonso Medicinis is one of my oldest friends. He had been an undercover agent for me for many years and is under my protection."

"Undercover agent?" I could hardly get the words out, "He's a slaver!" I was beginning to worry what I'd gotten myself into, was the Governor a traitor?

"He's been cooperating with me, as did his daughter, Helen, to bring his planet away from slavery. He's been working with the Highblood Laositians to accept the inevitable end to that horrible practice. He's a loyal Federation agent."

I was flabbergasted. "You knew my mother?"

"If your mother was Helen Masters, then *yes*. I did know her. I didn't, however, know that you had survived. We believed the whole family had been killed. Alphonso did not even tell me. You are a bundle of surprises Chief."

It was at that moment the ER personnel showed up. Hotda tried to get up but they were too quick for her. A shot in the arm and she was out cold. They wheeled her away as Ben came back dragging a very confused man with him. The bulky type man was dressed more like a farmer with yellow overalls, a hard hat hung on his arm with thick gloves peeking out of his hat. Seeing the Governor General sent sweat running down his brow.

"This is Osso Timerlic, he's chief operating engineer here," Ben explained.

"Do you know planetary engineering?" Pinote asked him.

"Well, I did my internship on a Bassodian frigate as I needed to understand the engineering behind the Space Station's structural web. Learned as much as those pompous lizards would teach me."

Pinote shoved the tab screen his way. Osso sat at one of the chairs peering closely at it. "This is a standard planetary profile. Regulation mass of 5.9 times 10 to the 24th power. Radius looks like 3.9k miles. Circumference is 24,900…"

"I don't care about that." Pinote interrupted. "Can you tell me where it is going? Where the hell were those Bassodians dragging that sphere?"

"Well let me see…" the engineer put on some bright yellow lensed glasses.

"What are you doing?" Conlin asked him before anyone else did.

"These blueprints are always in three dimensional readings. The Bassodians have special lens in their eyes. They naturally see three dimensional, we need these glasses. Let's see. It is being dragged to coordinates 59,36,58,33…" He stopped, taking out a tabloid that was in his back pocket. It was a long cellbutton, I'd seen them used by scientists who used them for complicated calculations. He fiddled with it, entering data, when he finished he said, "It's ending outside the Federation boundaries. I believe somewhere close to the Orion Sector's main Jump. It's not chartered space."

"It is now," I ventured. "I would bet the planet is being placed outside of the Federation where there are no "slaver" rules but within an easy Jump to Ligithia."

"Yes, Chief, I believe you have hit it right on the head." Pinote sounded tired but even more a disgust permeated from the man. He turned to the engineer, "Can you tell when it's being delivered?"

"Well, the outskirts of Orion is at least a two day regular Jump. It'll take a good week or more to get it into position." He stood up, realizing he'd given them all the information required. He was about to leave when Hill asked him one last question.

"How much do you figure these Bassodians were paid to do this?"

Sarcasm dripped from his voice, "More than you can imagine, lady. It's not just the dragging into position, someone has to pay their engineers to set the planet up. I can tell you this, that this here planet is full of methanilum to mine. Look at the sphere's makeup, especially the outer core." He pointed to the picture but it was wasted on us. "I'm only guessing but I'd bet the Intergalactic Xil Energy Company had a hand it. They sure have the money."

As he was leaving, Ben was entering with Alphonso Medicinis in tow. My grandfather looked surprised when he saw me, half grinning but with a leery look in his eyes.

"What is this about Thern?" He sat next to the Governor; he looked old and worn next to the strong virulent diplomat. "How are you, my dear?" giving Hill the nod.

"We have a document, gotten by Chief Brown and my daughter, which shows a new planet being dropped just outside of the Federation claimed space and most likely in a new nearby Ligithia Jump line." Pinote put the screen in front of Medicinis. "As you see, this was obtained on the Bassodian ship, clearly Ligithia has ordered it."

"Impossible." My grandfather almost shouted it. "Do you have any idea how much an engineering like this costs? Only the Federation has that type of resource and it must be approved by the Council."

"Ah, not quite true my friend." Pinote went further, "It is a planet with a supply of methanilum to mine. I'm guessing the Xil company with rebel Laositian Highbloods have done this."

"We cannot allow this. We will be stuck with the slavery problem forever!" The Ligithia Ambassador was pale, his hand was shaking. "We must stop this! Those damn Bassodian only care about the damn money."

"Don't worry, Alphonso, my sons are already in contact with President Hxitxs. He will put an end to this or at least call a temporary halt to the delivery. It will give us time to present our case to the entire assembly."

"Why would the President of the entire Federation, who is a Bassodian by the way, stop something that is totally human?" I asked, sarcasm dripped off my tongue. "Come on General, they aren't going to stop their own engineers from delivering!"

They will, or I'll pull permission to travel throughout our sectors." Pinote stood, going over to a map showing the humanoid sectors. "It would be very inconvenient for them to have to go all the way around us, and most importantly, it would cost them a lot!"

Suddenly things started adding up. "The Bassodians came to the space station not for space sickness serum but to get paid." The Governor first looked questioningly at me, and then nodded his agreement. I went further, "I would bet Hibnet, who was off sector a month ago picked up the money. Lont Pol learned he was in Sol, the headquarters of Xil company.

He didn't go to a lover rendezvous as everyone suspected, he went to get the money."

I got up pacing the room. I hit my cell to connect with Fred Stoshingburg. "Listen Fred, head down to the Bassodian docking station on Ring One. Find out, I don't care if you have to strong arm them, who brought the Serum down this morning to give to the Bassodians. Hurry, I'll be waiting for the answer."

"It'll take just a few minutes, I'm on Ring two right above them," he assured me.

Hill was pacing the other end of the room. "It's beginning to all fit together but why did Hibnet want you here?" she said. Her father watched her, for once listening to what she had to say. She answered her own question, "He was also concerned about Dr. Ditterset's slavery serum that is almost ready. If the serum came out too soon, then the new planet would be moot. They'd never get the planet up and running before the antidote could be administered. He wasn't trying to protect you and Killa, *someone* had him trying to prevent the serum from being developed. He had to know about Dr. Ditterset being close to discovering the cure. Find that person and you find the key to the lab fire, the bomb on the ferry and the attempted murder at the ball. I think that Ligithian was trying to kill *you*, Chief."

My cell hummed in my ear, it was Fred. "Hey it was Dr. Gale Lawry, your girlfriend." He must have heard my growl because he quickly added, "Only kidding. Want me to find her?"

"No, I'll find her!" and cream her ass I thought. I told the Governor who it was but the name meant nothing to him but Hill let out an "Ah-ha!" Her remark was not appreciated. I felt like a fool. Perhaps I was jumping to conclusions; perhaps she was an innocently ignorant stool pigeon and was just being used. Somehow my gut told me that it was not the case.

My cellbutton buzzed softly in my ear informing me Superintendent Pol was trying to get hold of me. I touched the cell, "Yeah." My ear was full of a lot of static. I could hardly hear the call. "Pol is that you?" I almost shouted in my cell.

"Hibnet's office. Shot," I think she said.

"How bad is it?" I tried to keep my voice calm as to not alert the Governor General of my shock.

"Dead." Was the only word that came across. Then the cell went completely silent, not even static.

"On my way," I tried to quietly say, hoping Lont Pol had heard but doubting she had as the cell was completely silent. Despite trying to act calm, Hill picked up on it. I saw in her eyes, she knew something was wrong. "Excuse me, I have urgent police business to attend to. If you need me call the station's police number, they'll know how to get in touch with me." I didn't wait for a reply but headed out of the room, crossing to the outer door and into the corridor. I was so deep in thought that I didn't notice Hill was with me until I got into the hotel's elevator.

"What's wrong?" she asked.

"I believe Pol called me from Hibent's office." I found the words had trouble emerging from my mouth. "I have a bad feeling about this, is your cellbutton active?"

Hill fumbled with her cell, actually taking it off her collar. "It won't work."

"Pol didn't say much, like you said the lines aren't totally secure," I couldn't keep the anxiety out of my voice. "Let's just get there. Even with the little I got, Pol sounded shook up."

We weaved our way through the hotel lobby. A lot of the conference attendees were leaving but many were confused as their cellbuttons weren't working. It was causing a frenzy bordering on becoming a panic situation. I heard one woman complaining loudly to the desk clerks, "This damn station has more communication glitches. Are the ferries working?" The clerk looked totally confused, seemingly unable to answer the woman.

The taxis were all commandeered. Thank goodness our police vehicle was waiting for us just outside of the Herriden's entrance. It put on its flashing lights and got us to the crossover quickly. We took the elevator to the very top of the central core and were met by a police guard who nodded us down the corridor.

The outer office was chaotic. Some of the receptionists were crying, others were just standing around stunned. Marshie, Hibnet's personal secretary, was over in one corner sobbing. Lont Pol was trying to talk to her while barking orders at the crime lab personnel. Lont had a look of relief upon seeing me.

It was to Hill, however, that she explained her problem. "Marshie was the only one in the office, all the others were out running errands. She's so hysterical, I'm not getting anything out of her." Then she turned to me, "I need Marcus here to see what he can get out of Hibnet's data banks. Whoever shot him, also played with his communication system. Cells are not working! I want Marcus to see if he can restore the system. I want him here before a member of the Board comes and stops me from going through his files!"

It hit me that Pol hadn't realized I didn't hear her completely. Hibnet was dead, shot?

I pressed Marcus' number. Got nothing, my cell was dead as a doornail. Hill was over by the receptionist trying to calm her. The secretary was sobbing loudly and muttering, "He's dead, he's dead," over and over.

I walked into Hibnet's office. He lay slumped over his desk. Lont Pol was with me. "He was shot at close range, his whole chest is burned from the laser being so close. Whoever did it was angry. The gun was set to kill, not stun and it was a long duration hit."

The crime photographer was snapping shots. When she turned him over for frontals, I saw what Pol was explaining - his whole front shirt was burned away, and most of his chest with it. Whoa, this was true hatred. The smell of burnt flesh was overwhelming. I headed back to the main reception area.

Marshie had a cup of tea in her hand. Hill was sitting next to her with her arm around the secretary's shoulder. The tears were still flowing but the woman seemed to be getting herself under control.

My ears picked up as she was beginning to talk to my detective, her words were just slightly slurred. "She just came into the office and shot him!" Marshie grabbed onto Hill's arm, "She just shot him and his computer cabinet and then walked out."

"Who?" Hill softly asked, trying not to get the woman into hysterics again.

"Dr. Lawry," the woman half sobbed it, grabbing onto Hill's arm so hard I saw my lieutenant wince from the pain.

I was stunned. What the hell was going on with Lawry? Hill looked up at me to see how I was reacting. I must have looked like hell because Hill stood up taking hold of me. "Chief, do you need a pill?"

I reached into my pocket and took one of the blue pills, swallowing it dry. What a fool I had been. Was I totally blinded to the woman's treachery?

Then both of us said together, "Killa!"

Chapter Fourteen

Pol was just coming out of Hibnet's office. "It was Lawry," I excitedly told her. "Killa, we are worried about Killa!" I was almost shouting, my nerves ready to explode. I never should have left her.

"Don't worry. I have three armed guards protecting her at Ditterset's lab on Ring Eight" Lont tried to calm me but my mind was racing with visions of a dead Killa.

Hill was already heading to the door. Thank goodness Marcus was heading in. "Help Pol," I told him, "someone sabotaged the communications software. When you can - get the others here."

He nodded, "Your cell - I couldn't hear you but I saw where you were."

I didn't wait for anything else, I rushed after Hill, catching up with her as she was pushing the elevator button. I could see in her eyes an almost uncontrollable fear hung just below the surface. "If she harms her, I'll kill her!"

"You'll have to wait in line!" I said as the doors closed and we went down two tubes. We came out at the crossover, taking the tram through to the Ring 8. We turned left running down the corridor, one lab after another passed. We guessed by the passing labs, we had several to go. A cart passed us and stopped.

"Need a ride?" a man in a white lab coat yelled over. We jumped on, getting off at the entrance to Dr. Angi Ditterset lab before he could even brake. We raced down the entranceway coming upon the big glass doors. Two carts both were marked *Doctor* on the back were parked at the entrance to the lab. A sprawled out police officer in front of the doors brought us up short.

Hill bent down, feeling his neck. "He's still breathing, thank goodness," she loudly sighed as she turned him over. On the top of his chest there was a small discolored mark on his uniform where he'd been shot. "He was tasered. I'd say he was taken by surprise, his gun is still in his holster."

I nodded, stepping up to the door, it slid silently open revealing another cop spread-eagled across the entranceway. Hill felt his neck, "Another one alive but this one had started taking his gun out. He probably saw the first one go down but hesitated, I'm guessing because it was Dr. Lawry." Since my gun was still down in the docking area on Level One, I took his firearm.

The reception area was empty. I went over to the welcome desk, peering over to see a woman in a lab coat that read **Mary, Nurse, Level Two** lying prone on the floor. I jumped the desk and felt her wrist. I breathed a sigh of relief when I felt a strong pulse. "Out cold, shot just like the other two." Hill was over by the lab door, another cop lay unconscious by the wall. He'd been shot and had slid down the wall. He must have been in the lab and gotten surprised as his gun still lay in his holster.

I crossed over to the lab door marked "Experimental BioChemical Lab". I punched the "open" button, nothing happened. I pounded on the door, rammed my body against it. Nothing!

"It's a solid explosion door," Hill commented, looking around furtively. She went over to the receptionist desk leaning over the counter. She must have found some buttons, for the door across the way opened, then the glass doors opened as she punched another button. Then I heard the click of the lab door.

"It's opening," I told Hill, who quickly joined me, her gun preceding her in. We hugged the left wall leading into the lab. It wasn't far when I saw Killa and Ditterset standing in front of a long lab table. Hill rushed forward but didn't get far past the corridor wall as a gun went to her head.

"Put your guns down, both of you." Gale Lawry threatened as she held her small gun to Hill's head. I saw her press the handle, Hill groaned and dropped her gun. I slid mine to where the murderous doctor could see it. "Good. Now go join your slave, Chief." She actually snickered as I crossed to the middle of the lab. "Behave yourself or your lieutenant will have mush for a brain." She slightly pressed her gun handle causing Hill to cry out.

"Alright, leave her alone. Let's switch, it's me you want." I held out my palms in surrender.

"Nice try Chief," she laughed, "I don't trust you to save yourself but you'll not want someone else to suffer." She was right, damn it. "Now tell your slave she is not to harm me, she is not to shoot me."

When I hesitated, Hill got another taz. I quickly spoke up, "Killa, you are not to harm Dr. Gale in any way. Do not shoot her or touch her. Do you understand?"

Killa seemed to struggle with it but finally saying, "Yes, Skip I understand."

"Good little Legi." Lawry kept her gun to Hill's head. "Now when I tell you, you will go get the guns and put them on the side table. Do you understand?"

I looked at the doctor. Despite everything, I still looked at her with awe, my attraction was just as strong. Killa must have seen it in my face.

"She is *poison*, she's a conniving bitch," Killa spat out. When she saw I didn't understand, she blurted out, "She's taboo. She uses the Hillow plant to attract men. I can smell it in her blood. It is illegal."

I saw Hill's eyes widen, she obviously knew what my old nursemaid was talking about. "It is an odorless tasteless plant that somehow when eaten on a regular basis attracts men." For her outburst she felt Lawry gun, this time a loud scream emitted from my rookie.

"Leave her alone." I yelled, getting an evil smile from the gun woman.

"Then behave yourself." She grimaced at Killa. "You should know, you puke," she hissed in Killa's direction. "You squealed on my mother, didn't you?"

"Yes, she was an evil woman," Killa said. "Your mother tried to seduce Dr. Masters. I told your father, Dr. Hibnet, and he sent her packing back to Ligithia in disgrace." The disgust and anger spun out of Killa, her eyes were dark purple, her hair flew haphazardly around her oval face, her small pointed ears twitched back and forth.

"Your father?" I asked, totally confused, but for the first time looking at the doctor and seeing through the façade. She wasn't even pretty! I guess knowing about the attraction negates it. I felt like a total fool.

"Dr. Hibnet is her father." Killa told me. "They lived on Moss when your parents were here."

"*Was* my father," Dr. Gale sneered, "*was*!" She repeated. "I wish I could kill him again! He sent my mother back and she spent ten years in jail. His precious space station was more important than us. Until I showed up last year he hadn't even bothered with me. Then he was all affectionate, tried to tell me how much I meant to him. Bullshit! I'm glad I killed him."

"So you are the one who set the bomb on the ferry?" I couldn't believe what a chump I'd been. "You must have help, who tried to kill us on the spaceship?"

"I have others helping me, other loyal Highbloods that want our independence from the Federation. Once Dr. Ditterset has handed over her research I'm out of here and back to the safety of Ligithia." She turned to Angi and held out her hand.

"I don't…" Ditterset started to say but stopped as Hill moaned as she got another taz

"Don't play with me Angi," the doctor frowned at the researcher. "I know nothing has been sent off station, I've been monitoring Hibnet's communication files. If I guess right you have a tab in your pocket. I've already searched your home on Nestor and your apartment here. Once I get the tab I'll destroy this lab. So hand it over!" She went to pull the trigger on Hill.

"Stop, please. Angi give it to her!" I pleaded. "You gave the Bassodians the money for the new planet, didn't you?" I was trying to get her mind off of hurting Hill.

Dr. Lawry looked shocked. "Those damn Bassodians! How did you find out?" Her anger dripped from her words. "Never mind, it's too late to stop it. Chief, get that tab now." Hill moaned as the laser gun gave her another zap. "How's it feel, lieutenant, getting zapped by you own gun? I enjoyed going through your luggage, by the way. So careless of you to leave it behind."

"Ditterset, give it to me," I said, walking over to her.

"Wait," Gale Lawry said, "Ligi, get the guns and put them on the table over there, out of reach of the Chief, just in case."

Killa seemed to hesitate, "NOW!" Lawry yelled taking the gun off of Hill and pointing the gun at my nursemaid. Then she shifted the gun towards me. Hill just slid to the ground, her eyes rolling backward.

Killa went over to the guns, bending down to get one. She quickly stood and fired. She hit Gale Lawry square in the chest and kept shooting. "I'm free you damn murderer, I'm free to kill you."

"Stop, Killa, enough!" I said as the Lawry collapsed on the ground, Killa kept shooting her. "Stop, we need info, don't kill her."

I heard the gun drop and I ran over to Hill. She was convulsing. Killa and Dr. Ditterset were kneeling on the other side.

"Help me!" Angi was grabbing onto Hill. "Hold her down while I get something to calm her. Put something under her tongue."

I unfortunately knew the drill, my own epileptic seizures were similar. I hadn't anything handy so I placed my fingers under her tongue pressing upwards until she couldn't bite her tongue. She bit down hard, I winced but kept them secure. Killa was holding her feet down. Dr. Ditterset rushed over with a shot canister and pressed it against Hill's arm. Judy went limp.

My fingers were bloody when I took them out of Hill's mouth. I wrapped them in a cloth while my other hand went to my cellphone. Damn nothing! Marcus must not have gotten the communications up.

The doctor was working on Lawry. "She's in a bad way." I saw her go to her cellbutton and shake her head. "We need the medics."

Suddenly my cellbutton buzzed, relief filled me as I answered Lont Pol's call. "We need medics here. Hill's been shot in the head and Lawry has been shot in the chest!"

"Right, medics are being called," Pol informed me. "Communications are up! You can thank Marcus for that. A team is on their way to secure that crime scene." She buzzed off.

I checked quickly with Marcus. He not only had fixed Hibnet's computer files, he had all my detectives working on the Hibnet crime scene. "Is Hill badly hurt?" he asked.

"Yeah," was all I could get out, my voice choking with emotion. I didn't say anything else as the medics had arrived and began immediately to work on both shooting victims. I was relieved to see Dr. Bolker come running in. He was in street clothes, Pol must have called him.

They had Hill on a gurney. Dr. Dan felt her pulse. He looked at the side of the head where Lawry's gun had been placed. I could see the hair was burnt leaving raw skin.

"Angi, do you have a portable skull analysis bonnet?" he looked around the lab but it was Ditterset that found it and brought it over.

"It's not programmed to heal. I use it for research."

"Just give it to me. He played with the controls on the side and put it on Hill's head. It softly hummed. Hill started moving her fingers, her eyes opened and closed. Her mouth opened and closed and her legs moved. "Let's get her down to the ER," Bolker told the medics. They had already moved Lawry. The taboo doctor was hurt bad, big burn marks covered her whole chest. Before they had arrived I had felt her pulse though and it had been strong.

Lara and Elly walked in. Lara had a few words with Dr. Bolker, and then turned to me. "He's got a good handle on it. Judy couldn't be in better hands. I nodded, I knew he was the best, he'd been my primary doctor for over a year after my accident.

Pol's assistant, Lorna Lune, came in with several police and Toby Graciea, who headed the regular police force. They yellow taped the office, marking it as a crime scene and off limits. "We have to be careful," Lorna informed me, "not to touch anything until the crime lab guys get here. They are still down at Hibnet's office, although I think the recorder guy was done taking pictures.

"My people know the drill," I informed her. I turned my attention, however, to Killa and Angi Ditterset. "You cured her," I said to the lab researcher, "you finished what my parents started."

"Yes. We finished the treatment before Gale came charging in here. It obviously took hold because Killa defied your order and shot her."

I looked over at my former blood bond. Killa was so excited, she was bursting with energy. Her eyes were dark purple, the darkest I'd ever seen them, her hair almost sizzled as the white locks stood straight in the air. "My people are going to be free, Skip. Your mom and dad would be so glad! It feels strange not to have the feeling of obligation hanging on to everything I do."

I went over and hugged her. She clung to me and then started crying. "I hope Judy is alright, please let her not pay the price of my freedom!" Then it hit me, Gale Lawry had expected to get away, was planning to escape to Ligithia. How?

I called Stoshingburg. The big guy answered on the first buzz. "What's up Chief?"

"Fred, I think Lawry was going to make a getaway after she killed us and blew up the Ditterset lab."

"Craps!" Fred muttered.

"Where is the ship docked? You and Marcus have been all over this station, where would they have a ship the size of Hibnet's Jetliner docked?"

"I know where it is!" Fred exclaimed. I saw it when you sent me down to Ring One's dock to see who had paid the Bassodians. When I went to speak to the dock workers to confirm it was Lawry, there was a cruiser where usually the Bassodian tubs dock. I thought it strange but I was in a hurry."

"Get Pol to help you send some police down there. Have the dock workers shut the bay off, they are not to let anyone leave!"

"Got it!" Fred clicked off but I was still worried.

Turning to Lara I told her what I just told Fred but added, "I'm worried she might just have some explosives somewhere. She hated this space station. I want to make sure she didn't plant some explosives somewhere to do damage."

Elly, who was scanning the lab for any type of explosive had heard us. "Lawry would place it where it would do the most damage. Let me get hold of Evie. She might have an inkling, being their security specialist."

Lara went even further, "We need to retrace her steps, find out where she's been. Her cell may help along with that identification badge. I'm guessing she didn't try to disguise her whereabouts, why would she? She thought she'd be getting away."

It was a good idea. I called Pol who was calling in extra cops for the searches.

"I'm going down to the ER," Killa informed me. "I want to check on Judy."

"Call me if there are any developments," I told her, watching as she hurried out of the lab. Dr. Ditterset came over.

"She was the key to it all," the doctor explained. "The problem of the Ligithian slave cure was twofold. First you have to change the synapse of the brain, which takes several days by the way, and then you disconnect the addiction of the smell of the masters. Of course, I'm putting it in layman's terms."

She still was way over my medical knowledge but I got the idea. "They had prepared Killa for the second treatment."

"Yes, somewhat correct. Killa only needed to be injected with the final treatment and her sense of smell would have been disconnected from reacting to the smell of your blood." She had tried to make it sound so simple but of course it wasn't. "All these years, Killa was right in front of me," Ditterset lamented.

Lont Pol entered, going over to Lorna first and getting a report, then she came over to me. "The Ligithian ship has been secured. They almost made it out as the doors were closing but we got them. They actually damaged the dock's gateway. They tried to ram their way out. There were several Ligithians aboard as well as several Laositian Highbloods. We learned that they had two ships, you destroyed one of them at the Bassodian's ship."

My cell button buzzed. It was Lara, "You better get up to Hibnet's office. We found his daughter's booby trap. She was going to blow up the whole top of the center cylinder. We're trying to figure out how to defuse it."

"On my way." My heart was pounding as I hurried to the top executive offices. Lara, Elly and Evie were in Hibnet's office. They were over by his outer wall. Everyone else had evacuated the area.

"Her cell trace showed she spent a lot of time in Hibnet's office this morning. Her father was making sure everyone was departing for home, so Lawry had it all to herself. She set the bomb up with a remote."

She saw the alarm in my face, "Don't worry Chief, I already had them look for it in ER, we have it, the remote was in her pocket. But look at this."

Lara opened a cabinet just under his skyview window. The whole cabinet looked like it was packed with electronic flashing lights. "This is full of lidieum. It can blow this room to smithereens. I guess it was to be her last statement on her father."

"Can you defuse it?" I knew my voice was cracking but I could picture what an explosion on the top cylinder could do. It scared the hell out of me. If it blew up, would it destabilize the whole station? I had no idea.

"I have to think the station's builders set some safety in its structure. No one seems to know! I'm playing it as safe as I can. We're taking the entire cabinet console out and loading it on a ship and exploding it far from here."

It took the rest of the day to slowly get it to the dock on Ring 9. There was a dock that was right below the Executive Offices, being there for the convenience of the board members.

It was a nearby dock for only the board members to use, giving them easy access to their jets. I commandeered two of them. Mili Embers, a top executive of the station had come up but left as soon as the danger was explained. She had issued orders for Rings 7, 8 and 9 to be evacuated.

Lara helped load the bomb into a ship that looked very similar to the one we had come back from the Bassodian freighter in. They had removed all the seats so the cabinet fit snuggly inside behind the pilot.

From an observation deck I watched the ship leave with another following it to bring them home. After getting the first ship into position, the crew would transfer to the second ship and get the hell out of the way while it blew up. I wished Lara and Elly good luck. To my surprise, Fred climbed in with them. His only comment, "She's not going alone", his tone leaving no room for discussion.

Several hours later they were on their way back. I hadn't realized how tense my nerves were until I got the call. I was finally free to head down to Ring 6 to check on Hill. Killa had been keeping me abreast of her condition. They had a newly developed high-tech brain boot on her and she hadn't regained consciousness yet.

The Emergency Room had bright hallways and dimmed rooms to the sides. The intense corridor lights hurt my pounding headache. I had been popping my blue pills, so I had no danger of a seizure, but I felt like shit. I saw Killa sitting on a cushioned chair in the hallway. She looked tiny, she looked worried.

"Chief Brown," a nurse was at my shoulder. "Ms. Hill is doing as well as can be expected. No visitors yet."

I knew I could pull rank but I let it go. I walked over to Killa, she seemed somewhat calm; her eyes were light purple and her hair and ears were quiet.

"Nurse says she's doing okay," I told my old nursemaid. I slouched in the chair next to her. The room in front of us had a large window, they hadn't closed the drapes. Hill lay prone on hospital bed. I could make out the large helmet that lay on her head. The monitors on either side of the bed were flashing. My lieutenant looked small, the sheets almost swallowing her up.

"The doctors have her in an induced coma." Killa grabbed my hand squeezing my much larger fingers with her small ones. "She will be alright, she has to be." A sob came out of the small woman, it made her whole body shake. Her hair started to fuzz, her delicate ears began twitching. She sat up straighter getting herself under control again.

"I need to know about my parents' relationship with Dr. Hibnet. Did you know Gale Lawry was his daughter?"

"I knew he had a daughter, that was many years ago. I never got close enough to that woman to realize who she really was or that she was using Hillow." My former bondee sat up even straighter, her hands grabbing onto the chair's arms as if anticipating my next question.

"Why did you hate him?" I took her hand, "He was our family's best friend, I remember him spending a lot of time with us."

"Perhaps he was once." Her Ligithian eyes flashed.

"Easy Killa, he's dead, let it go." I tried to calm her.

She drew in a breath, "Yes," a big sigh followed by, "I believe he was responsible for your parent's deaths."

I was stunned into silence just staring at her. Killa turned to face me, "His wife tried to seduce your father. I followed him and I caught them at a little café near the ferry station. I knew right away that she was *taboo*, her blood smelled of Hillow. That damn plant grows only on Ligithia. Of course, once your father knew, the addiction was broken but the damage was done."

"How did mom take it?" I couldn't help asking, did I really want to know?

"Better than you'd expect because she was from Ligithia. She knew of Hillow but she was hurt and extremely mad. She marched up to Dr. Hibnet's office and complained about his wife. Korba was her name from the Vante Highblood family. At first, that pompous man didn't believe her but the evidence was there. If I hadn't been a *damn ligi,* as the good doctor called me, she would have gotten away with it.

"Why did Korba do it?" I asked but knew the answer. "She wanted to stop the research on the blood bond, didn't she? That is why she married Hibnet to begin with."

Killa just nodded. "She got sent home with her little girl in tow. Hibnet was so angry he had her prosecuted and she spent time in a Highblood prison."

"Why do you say he killed mom and dad?" I waited patiently; she didn't want to tell me. "Killa, I need to know!"

"He blamed your father for the affair," she huffed out. "I think he let the Highbloods know when your parents were leaving. He visited our house the day before they departed. He drugged you so you'd be sick and we'd stay behind. I smelled it in your blood the day they died."

"Oh, my god," was all I could say. I sat back stunned. "Why didn't you turn him in?"

"A Ligi's word against his?" Killa said, "He kept you safe, getting us to Nestor. I dared not make any charges. Jack felt the same way, what could we do? I just hated him!"

I put my arm around my little old nursemaid, letting her cry on my shoulder. She had carried this burden for a long time.

We jumped up as a moan came from the opposite room. We rushed in, a nurse following right behind us. "Please stay outside." I showed her my badge. She'd have to get a doctor to kick me out. "Fine, but stay out of the way!" she softly snapped at me. Luckily, she ignored small Killa.

As the nurse was checking the monitors, Hill moaned again. I took her hand, like Killa's it was small, I could encompass her whole hand in mine. It seemed to quiet her. "Good," the nurse pronounced. She's calming down, don't let go. I've sent for Dr. Bolker, she should be in a deep sleep."

She didn't know Hill, like we do. If Hill wanted to wake up, she would. As if reading my mind Judy's eyes fluttered open. She tried to move her head but the helmet wouldn't let her. "Lay still Hill," I told her. "You've been hurt, stop fighting it."

Her mouth moved, a small croak, then, "Skip?" followed by "Chief?"

I bent over her, "I'm here." I told her, my eyes watering up.

I thought I saw her smile. "I love you," I think she said, but it was so soft. I didn't know what to do but Killa came over, "*Jiidi* Judy, *jiidi*." She told her to sleep in Ligithian, and then added "We love you too." My nursemaid touched her arm, concentrating, whispering *jiidi, jiidi* slightly. Judy seemed to settle back into the bed, her eyes once again closed."

"Good," the nurse breathed easier, "she's back to sleeping."

There was a commotion in the hallway, through the large window I saw the Governor General with his sons. I heard, "Where is she?" He turned into the room, his face was furious. His sons were cowering behind him, their faces alarmed. He saw me and abruptly stopped, causing his four sons to plow into him. "Why wasn't I called!"

The poor nurse had her mouth opened but nothing came out. I looked up, I was used to dealing with angry, irrational people. "They wouldn't know you were her father. It's not in her records."

"But you knew," he pointed his finger at me. "You knew!"

Part of me felt kinda guilty, but part of me also was angry at this domineering father, so use to having his way that Judy had run away from him. My temper forged forward, "I just got here, I've been a little busy. I hate to admit it but you were the last person on my mind."

"Why you, why you…" He was furious. "Get out, get out of my daughter's room, now!"

The nurse found her tongue, "Please keep your voice down." When it comes to their patents, nurses are very protective and this one was no different. "He is the police, you can't kick him out."

"Like hell I can't." The ambassador went over to the other side of the bed, "He's responsible for this. It's his fault she's here." Tears actually rolled down his face as he took his daughter's hand. The sons, obviously, not use to seeing their father like this, tried to assure him but he waved them away. "If I lose her, I'll kill you." His angry eyes looked at me.

I was use to this kind of behavior, it happened all the time in an investigation. The relatives of victims have no one they can focus on, so the police are blamed. Still, it hurt and some of me blamed me too.

Dr. Bolker came strolling in. "Whoa, too many people. Some of you out!" he pointed to the sons who immediately left, taking chairs right outside.

"He needs to go, get him out of here!" Pinote exploded.

"Excuse me Ambassador General, but you have no authority here. Killa, I'm told she responds to you and Skip?"

Killa, who had been hiding behind me, just nodded. I told him, "Lieutenant Hill opened her eyes and talked to us for just a second."

"Amazing," Bolker said as he adjusted her brain contraption. "She needs to sleep more."

"Will she recover completely?" her father asked.

"Don't know but her progress is quite remarkable. He looked over at me, "You've been through a lot Skip. You need to get some rest." His eyes told me what he didn't want to say in front of the Ambassador General, that I was risking an episode.

"Yeah, you are right." I dropped Judy's hand, her father glared at me. As I stepped out, his sons flooded back into the room - all except Matt, the oldest.

"He's just tired," trying to excuse his father's behavior. "The problem comes that he and Judy are too much alike."

I nodded my thanks to him as he followed his brothers. "The father's a jerk!" It exploded out of my mouth, fatigue clouding my judgment.

"No, Skip," Killa responded, "he's a worried father. He's let his diplomatic shield down, I don't suppose many people see that side of him."

I couldn't respond as my grandfather, Highblood Alphonso Medicinis strolled out of the elevator down the hall. Another diplomat I didn't want to see. My mother never told me much about him, not even that he was the long time ambassador to Ligithia. I gave him my worst scowl but it didn't do any good as he was heading in our direction anyway.

To my surprise Killa jumped up, crossing to him and giving him a big hug. He hugged her back. "How are you my dear? It has been a long time."

"It is good to see you, Alphonso." She grabbed his arm bringing him to our chairs. I gave her a scathing look but again, I must be losing my touch, she ignored me.

"He looks like his mother." Killa told my grandfather.

"Yes, indeed," he answered her, affection dripping in his tone. "You've done a good job with him, although he has his uncle's temper and can be very rude at times."

Killa laughed.

"How is Judith?" he asked me. "I was still with her father when word came in. This will not be easy on him."

"Oh for crying out loud," I exploded, "it isn't easy on anyone, especially Hill. I don't think we need to coddle the Assembly Governor, he certainly didn't show any to his two daughters!"

"He already lost his wife and oldest daughter. Don't think he didn't care. He has to keep up appearances, a lot rests in his hands," he exploded back at me. "Has being a policeman numbed your humanity?" His face was like an ugly thunderstorm.

I don't think I got my temper from my uncle, more likely my grandfather. I didn't tell him that I was surrounded by government politicians - most of them pompous asses. It has hardened me to be compassionate to them. I decided instead to change the subject, "Did you get the planet stopped?"

"I believe so," he snapped at me. "You can thank the Assembly Governor, if you can find it in your heart!"

I just shook my head. "Killa, I have lots to do. My people need to get home." I stood up, expecting her to come with me but she had other plans.

"I want to talk to your grandfather." Her eyes became darker, "He needs to know of the slavery cure."

I saw the Ligithian Ambassador grab her arms. "What! Has Ditterset done it?"

So he knew, "How do you know Dr. Ditterset?" I asked.

"How do you think she's gotten her funding? Hibnet wasn't going to fund her," he sharply put to me. "I also need a report on how he was killed before I go home." He didn't have a trace of sympathy in his voice. Yes, I guess my grandfather and I are more alike than we'd like to admit.

"I'll make sure Lont Pol gets you the report." I turned my back on him and headed towards the elevator but I could hear him and Killa excitingly discussing her freedom. I could see the Pinote family in with Hill. Her father still held her hand. Perhaps I was too hardened, perhaps.

Chapter Fifteen

I headed toward the Herriden Convention Center. I took the train down one level and ended up walking most of the way to the hotel. I let the City of Eupie1 soak into my senses. On the other side, Eupie2 must be just waking up to a new day. As an eleven year old boy I had enjoyed living here. Despite it being on a space station, it had felt like a normal childhood, a normal family life. A year later at age twelve I was on Nestor living without my parents and living with a race crazy bachelor Uncle. Yet I had fond memories of both lives.

The city was busy, it being early evening. Many were returning from their hospital shifts. Families were out strolling the streets, the parks were busy with kids playing. The street and shop lights were beginning to come on. Everything was spotless. As a kid I hadn't yet experienced real "city" life, so I had taken for granted the lack of crime, the cleanness of the environment. It was all a closely controlled setting yet it had completely escaped my knowledge of it being anything unusual. My mother never had to worry about where I was because Ray and I had to carry identification cards just to get around. She knew exactly where we were.

My stomach growled, I couldn't remember when I'd last eaten so I stopped in a deli on one of the side streets. Given that I'd be on a Jump soon, I had a light salad. The shopkeeper made it perfectly. My Chief identification came up on his screen and it was paid for automatically. Lond Pol had turned our own ID buttons back on. "Thank you for eating with us, Mr. Brown." I sat next to two doctors, who were discussing a patient's care. Even in the City the hospital life was not far away. My parents loved it, would I have liked it too? I'd never know. My present life was anything but clean and organized. Crime saturated my existence. I took one last look as I headed into the hotel. No regrets, it is what it is.

Back at the rooms everyone was packing. They all asked about Hill. I had checked with Killa and Hill was semi-conscious. Dr. Bolker had taken off the brain helmet and she was now just being sedated.

Killa also informed me that she was with my grandfather and not to worry. They had much to discuss with Dr. Ditterset about setting up a program to bring about the release of the treatments to the Ligithians. She sounded so excited. I knew it wouldn't be that easy to switch over a society but let her bask in the thought of freeing her family. If Hill had been right about my grandfather working with the Laositian Highbloods on an eventual transition, perhaps it wouldn't be too bad.

The lobby was almost deserted as the conference guests had mostly gone. Our Jump was set for tomorrow afternoon. It gave me plenty of time to wrap the investigation up. Lont Pol would do most of it. It was her job and I wasn't going to stick my nose into it unless she needed me. Lara, Fred, Elly and Marcus went down to dinner but I couldn't eat anymore as the Jump would take its toll. I swallowed two disorient pills and sat by the large windows looking out at the City drinking a cup of java.

I decided to go see how Hill was doing. "I love you," rang in my head. I just wanted to see her so I left the hotel and headed down to the ER. It was quiet, the overhead corridor lights had been dimmed. I walked down to the chairs and looked into the room but the drapes had been closed. I crossed to the door and the room was empty.

"Can I help you?" The night nurse asked.

"Where has Judith Hill been taken?" They must have moved her to another ward.

"She was released to her father," I was informed, along with a contingency of nurses and doctors. Her father had pulled strings. I returned to the hotel but went straight up to the top floor. I didn't even get off the elevator as two security men stopped me.

"Sorry, Chief Brown," they informed me, "no one is allowed on this floor." It was said professionally but it was said with a gentle force that left no exceptions.

I went down to our rooms, gloom hugging close to me. I could force the issue but to what end? Her father was too powerful to buck. I'd lose.

I packed my bags. I put in for a call for Issam. It took an hour just to get a data line. Perhaps with Hibnet gone the station would catch up and modernize their communication lines. So I explained everything via text. I'd give him more info when I got home. I took a shower. Killa came home before the others did. She went to the kitchenette and made me a cup of java. She knew me so well!

"How'd it go?" I asked her. I'd watched her all my life. Ligithians are high strung. They easily feel other's emotions. Some say they are psychic, although Killa never admitted that to me. She seemed for the first time at peace with herself, easily smiling, no dark purple eyes. Was it the treatment or the freedom?

"Alphonso is preparing the Ligithian Highblood government for the release of the Laositians. It will not be easy. As he explained to me it will take many years for our society to adjust." She looked at me for my reaction.

"I can understand that. Everyone's role will change and there will be those that fight it." She was so small, her legs didn't touch the ground as she sat drinking her own cup of java. Uncle Jack had gotten us all addicted.

"You know Jack married me to give me protections?" she half-asked it and went right on not waiting for me to answer, "Well, I'd like to go back with your grandfather. I'd like to help where I can."

I was stunned. "Are you sure?" was all I could manage to get out. Life without Killa seemed unreal but I had no right to tell her where she could go. Even when she was bonded to me I didn't have the right but then she didn't have a choice.

"Yes, I want to do this," was her only reply.

"I will miss you," I told her, "the dogs will miss you too."

A tear fell down her cheek but her eyes stayed light purple, "I will miss you and Hoover and Bear." She got up from the table, "I need to pack, we are leaving tomorrow at noon."

She started for her bedroom but stopped, "Your grandfather got word of Judy. She's with her father and is making good progress. She's actually sitting up and talking. Dr. Bolker is very pleased."

"Glad to hear it." I didn't tell her of my attempt to see Hill. When she closed her door, I slouched in my chair, holding on to my mug but not drinking. My emotions were all over the place. I went over to look out the windows. The city was shrouded in shadows, the lights had been dimmed. My life seemed to dim. No Killa, no Hill. I was happy for Killa but sad for myself. My old nursemaid had been with me since I'd gone to Fulton. I thought of my two dogs. They would miss her too.

Hill, I imagined, would be heading back with her father. I hated to admit it but I'd miss her. The dogs would miss her! I laughed at the thought of no more huge dog bones. No more pain in my ass. No more Hill. Why was I so sad? Damn woman.

The return of my four detectives saved me from wallowing in any more self-pity. They were all smiles. "How was dinner?" I asked.

"Great," Lara announced flopping down across from me. "Pol gave us a good recommendation on a great authentic Sol cuisine restaurant."

"I really liked the beef." Marcus took the seat on the couch next to me. "Tender as all hell and they cooked it in real oil. I'm not kidding!"

"I liked their pasta with meatballs," Elly announced. "Chief, it was made with real meat."

"Their fish dishes were real too." Marcus put his two cents in, "I truly enjoyed a dish they made with some kind of white fish meat. I didn't get the name."

"Cod, it was cod," Lara said. "Their salad was outstanding. They had little tomatoes, tiny ones. You had to see them."

"How about you Fred, what did you have?" I looked over at the big man spread across the rest of the couch. His immense shoes were taking up half the cocktail table.

"All of it. I tried everything!" Fred informed me, "Wait 'til you get the bill!"

Lara just "Umffed" and shook her head. "You big oaf. That stomach will catch up with you someday!"

"Hey," Fred looked at her, "I deserve it. This damn station has been playing havoc with my continence since we got here."

"Oh, you poor baby!" Lara shot across to him, "Suck it up!"

That brought laughter from everyone including myself. It would be good to get home. Then I remembered Killa and Hill and my heart ached. I filled them in on the latest Hill news.

"Gee, do you think she'll be back at work?" Elly always thinking practical.

"If she's smart, she won't." Fred moaned, "Who'd miss our dump."

"You're an asshole!" Lara half yelled at him. "I'm going to bed!" I saw Fred look over at her. "Alone!" she added. I said not a word.

The morning brought suitcases and last minute wrap ups. Pol had stopped by to say goodbye and thank us for all our help. She had her hands full with Millie Embers, who'd been appointed temporary head of the station. Like her predecessor, Dr. Hibnet, she was concerned that the Medical Space Station not suffer any loss of donors over the murder scandal. I couldn't imagine what kind of questions I'd get back on Fulton. I'd be hounded the minute we stepped out of the Jump Station. It was part of my job; take the good with the bad.

I walked Killa down to the lobby. Ambassador Medicinis and his entourage were gathered together. One of the Ligithians took her bags. "I will send for everything else," my former bondee told me. "Give the dogs a hug for me."

I could tell she was near crying, her eyes starting to darken. My grandfather came over and put his arm around her shoulders, "Don't worry, I'll take good care of her."

"No, she'll take good care of herself!" I interjected, getting a laugh out of him.

"Yes, I suppose she will," he answered, "but I'll be there to help her. Perhaps you'll visit."

"Perhaps I will," was all I could manage to get out. My throat was dry and constricted. I wanted to beg her not to go but of course, I didn't. I just hugged her. She left. I couldn't say more than that as my eyes were too clouded to watch her go.

As I was by the elevators, I noticed Governor General Assembly Ambassador Pinote's group was grouping on the other side of the lobby. His security people were fanned around him and his sons. Hill was by his side, she looked like a small doll compared to her father and brothers.

I could understand her feelings of being trapped by these domineering men. The Governor was bending down talking to her but she wasn't responding, only nodding her head. Oh, how I wanted to go over and talk to her and take her out of the shadow of these men.

She turned her head and saw me. She looked up, her eyes going wide. A smile started to form on her face. Pinote turned, seeing me. He frowned, grabbing onto her arm and started for the door. His security force closed in, shielding him from my view. I saw the limohovers at the door and then they were gone. Gone.

I pressed the elevator button heading back to gather my own suitcases. I popped a blue pill and another disorient pill. It was going to be a long trip home.

~~~~~~~~~~~~~~~~~~~~~~~~~~~~~~~~

The trip was the usual torture. While Fred ate his and my packets of pretzels and cookies, I spent the time throwing up in the lavs until I finally fell asleep, exhausted. Fred punched my arm, waking me when we got to Logan's moon and we transferred to the flight to Fulton.

On the final leg of our Jump, Lara made me sip on some type of strong tea. I must admit it did help and I didn't throw it up. Still, my head was pounding and I was glad when we arrived at Fulton.

We got into the main foyer and sure enough there were the reporters. "Chief Brown, Chief Brown hold up," they screamed, running up to me. I saw Lara pull Fred out of the way and glance back at me. I waved her on and stopped. The whole contingent of correspondents collided with each other. I hid my smile as I saw them pick themselves up and brush off their suits.

"What happened on Moss?" Cora Lensa screeched at me. I dealt with her before, her screeching manner matched her screeching personality. She was like a crow, picking away at her victims until she got a satisfactory answer.

I didn't give her one, "I'm having a press conference with Consulate Borger this afternoon. All your questions will be answered then, not any sooner, so don't push!"

"Ah, come on." It was Cora, "the public needs to know."

"And they'll find out this afternoon," I quipped and started walking toward the exit.

"We heard one of your police officers was hurt." It was Kin Mattie. He was a major anchor on our biggest telestation. I was surprised they'd sent him. It gave me a sense of how important this story must be here. "What's her name? How is she?"

I didn't want them investigating Judy. Her father would quash it the minute he became aware of it but still these guys could be brutal if they smelled the Governor's name associated with Hibnet's murder. "Sorry, you guys must have just missed her, she's fine. Just a minor injury." I pretended to look around as if searching for her. They almost got whiplash looking in every possible direction.

This seemed to deflate their reporting bubble, letting me slip away while they pondered this tidbit. They started to look around for anyone who looked like a wounded cop. I skipped down the stairs to the street looking for the car Issam had sent for me. Issam had come himself, waving from his car across the street. I ran and jumped in. He knew the drill and stepped on it.

"How's Lieutenant Hill?" he asked right off. "Lara tells me she was really hurt."

I filled him in adding, "I couldn't get near her the last day with her father nearby."

Issam shook his head, "Who would have thought she was HIS daughter? He's definitely not one to cross."

"Yeah, I suppose, but meeting him I could see why she wanted to be free of his influence. He sucks all the air out of anything near him. His sons don't seem so bad but they are completely devoted to him. No help for her from that end." It still stung she hadn't told me, but I at least could understand why she tried to leave the situation.

Issam filled me in on what had been going on while I was on Moss. Regular business; three detectives were on Mody investigating three murders, two were on Casey on three drug related shooting deaths. I was sure Fred would be on that as soon as he hit the office. Two detectives were investigating an art heist on Abbis. Several of my regular police officers were patrolling the Dome building as one of the senators had been robbed. Etc. etc.

"We have to do an afternoon press conference on the goings-on at the space station," I informed him, but Consulate Borger had already primed him for it. He dropped me off at the long-term parking. I picked up my Ant and then headed to the office.

The office was busy and my life on Fulton started again but this time without Killa, and Hill's cubicle was empty. It was still hot and I still sweated my shirts wet. Oh well.

~~~~~~~~~~~~~~~~~~~~~~~~~~

I was working on getting caught up on my files. It had taken two days to get Daisy to put them in my Queue and then I had to send them back several times as she had jumbled them all up with past files. She could drive me crazy. She waltzed in with her bright orange hair, her matching orange shoes with a purple outfit in-between. She could bring on a seizure. I found myself popping the blue pills every time she stepped in my office.

"Chief, what am I to do with Lieutenant Hill's files?" she threw two tabs on my desk that bounced off and fell on the floor. Her skirt was so short that when she bent over to retrieve them her flashing yellow striped underwear was in plain view. It was a not pretty sight, trust me.

"Oleg is covering for her. Give them to her!" I growled, popping another blue pill in my mouth. She whimpered and took the tabs back.

"I'm only trying to help," she sobbed, making me feel like shit, but only for a little bit. "After all, it has been three weeks!"

Issam stood in my doorway, watching her leave. "Good god, she's so skinny, the fans could easily blow her to the other side of the office."

She's so wacky she wouldn't even realize it," I countered getting a laugh out of Issam.

"Have you heard from Hill?" he asked me.

"No." I shuffled my coffee mug and tabs around the desk, looking down so my captain couldn't see how upset it made me to talk about it.

"We can't hold her desk forever," he remarked.

"Let it be!" I snapped looking up to see the surprised look on his face. I softened, "It's not like a new job posting would come up any time real soon. You know the paperwork involved."

"Yes, I do," he commented. "That's why I think we should proceed with it, we are already shorthanded."

I just nodded, "Pretty soon, let's give it a little more time."

Issam sat in the chair on the opposite side of my desk. "Do you need to see Lily?" he quietly asked, making sure his voice didn't carry outside my office.

"NO!" I angrily snapped. "I'm fine."

His slanted amber eyes looked concerned. "You've been popping those blue pills a lot. I think you really should see my wife.

I knew he was right, Lilly Issam was a tremendous therapist. She would see right through me and that was the problem. I didn't want her to *see right through me.* I'd rather believe all was well.

"How's it going at home?" Carl probed. "How are the dogs managing?"

"Fine," I lied. "Artchie is supervising the apartment building quite well with the help of old Mrs. March. She's filling in for him when he's at class, gives the old lady something to do. The dogs get along well with him. I help whenever I can. We're getting the hang of it."

"Glad to hear it." Carl stood up to go. "You know Lily and I are here for you. Wish you'd come to dinner."

"I promise, I will once I get used to doing all the rental books by myself. I'm getting the hang of it. Stop worrying about me. It's getting late, go home."

As he was leaving my office, I saw him stop. "Can I help you?" he said looking down the hallway towards the elevators.

"I'm looking for Chief Brown," a voice drifted into my office. A voice I recognized, standing up from my chair, heading towards the door but he had gotten to it before I could. Judy's father, Governor Pinote stood looking a little bewildered. "Is this your office?" He stepped cautiously in. I could tell he was not impressed. Hell, I wasn't impressed either.

"All mine." I countered, seeing the alarm on Carl Issam's face, he knew who was in my office. Everyone knew who Pinote was.

He seemed to have come alone, no security detail. Perhaps they were downstairs. He must have guessed what I was thinking. "I came alone," he said. "Trust me, it wasn't easy."

I'm not one for chit chat, "So, why did you come?"

He looked around, frowning at Issam who suddenly disappeared. Pinote could have that effect on people, he radiated power. "Have you seen Judith?" he looked down at his hands, he didn't want me to see his emotional state. I knew the drill. I had just played it with Issam.

"No, why? Have you lost her?" I snarled, angry that this big important man who could handle the known universe could not handle his relationship with his daughter.

Pinote looked up startled. He wasn't use to people talking back to him. When it came to me, he'd better get used to it. Politicians, big or little, didn't frighten me, didn't intimidate me. They had nothing on the mob families, now *they* knew how to intimidate.

"She wouldn't come back with me. I've been in Orion trying to settle that Ligithian mess. The Assembly is taking action against the rebel Highbloods who tried to set that planet. I believe we will find the Xil Co. is implicated. I suppose you know that the cure has been found for freeing the Ligithians? Ambassador Medicinis is leading the effort for unity."

I just nodded my head. I had heard rumors coming from off sector news. The Crab Sector, not being directly involved, had the article way back on our new tabs. Being one of the sparsely populated human sectors, we are somewhat ignored, so we ignore back. Oh well.

"You haven't heard from her for the entire three weeks?" I asked.

"Only untraceable notes saying she is fine." He started to get up, probably to pace but got himself under control and sat back down.

That was Hill, only she could make her notes untraceable to one of the most influential men in the cosmos. "Perhaps you should let her be?"

"I haven't asked for your opinion, Chief, only if you'd seen her!" he flashed back at me.

"Don't lecture me, you pompous ass. You of all people should know that you don't insult someone who you are asking help from. Where'd you get your diplomatic skills?"

I could see the anger flare up in his eyes as he glared at me. It was then that I realized how old he looked, his hair was grayer, his face had worry lines with his eyes looking tired. Taking pity on him, I offered some advice. "Look, we are butting heads for no reason. I haven't heard from Hill. Her desk is still loaded with her stuff, she hasn't come by. One thing I've learned about her is that she can take care of herself."

"Umf," he snorted, "she belongs with her family. Judith has been groomed to be a diplomat, it is what we do!" He put his head in his hands, "I worry about her."

"Yeah, I do to,." I admitted.

He looked up, his face losing its anger. "Why is she doing this?"

"She wants to be her own person." I held up my hand as he was going to argue with me. "She is a damn good detective. She came here with the intention of finding her sister's killers." I saw the pain in his face at the mention of his older daughter's death.

"It was a foolish notion, Danielle was responsible for her own death. She took drugs and it killed her." His voice choked with emotion.

"It's never that simple, Governor. You of all people should know that. Judy went to Skantie Row and got evidence on the Blithie family's drug operation. They got your older daughter addicted to drugs. They get many *daughters* addicted. Thanks to your daughter, the Blithies head honchos are serving prison sentences." It had almost gotten both of us killed but I didn't tell him that. "Then she helped me find who was responsible for the murders on Nestor which implicated an arms deal with the rebels."

He sat back, slouching in my expensive metal almost-falling-apart chair. "She'd be good at anything she attempted," he stated.

"Yes, but she needs to be good at what *she* wants to be good at," I stated. "Everyone misses her here. She's helped on some other crucial investigations. She's stubborn but that's what a good crime detective is. Believe me, those kind of crucial detectives are rare."

He broke down, "I've lost my oldest daughter, my wife - I can't lose Judith too." His hands went to his head again.

"But you will lose her if you don't let her follow her own path. She doesn't want the life you had planned for her. Let her find what she does want and you'll get your daughter back in your life, just not back in your work."

"I owe you an apology," he admitted. "I thought it was you that had convinced her to stay here. I realize now I was wrong."

"Oh believe me Governor, I can't convince Hill of anything! If anything she's the one on my ass."

We both laughed, perhaps realizing we'd both been fighting the same battle and both losing it.

He stood up, "If you do see her, please tell her I will leave her alone if she'll just communicate with me."

"I don't know if I'll see her but I will tell her your message." I stood up and shook his hand.

"I thought you'd have a modern facility being so close to your government center - what do they call it, the Dome?"

"Yeah, they spent all the money on that monstrosity and there was nothing left over for us!" I told him, "but we manage."

"God it's hot!" he stated the obvious.

"We don't even notice." I lied. After all it may be a dump but it was our dump. I walked him to the elevator, "Good luck with the Ligithians."

"I'm going to need it. Those goddamn Highbloods are hard to work with. They can be most uncooperative and stubborn." Then he must have remembered I was a Highblood. He smiled, I guess he realized I had those traits, just like my Grandfather. He punched the button and I saw him smile as the doors closed. Touché, Pinote.

I walked back to my office, "You can come out now Carl, he's gone."

My captain slunk out of a cubicle. "Be careful Skip, he's very powerful."

"Right now he's just a hurting father." I explained, "He's worried about Hill."

"I wonder where she is?" Carl looked over at her empty cube.

I just shook my head. She was probably still angry with me over getting angry at her for not telling me about her father. Shit, I should be angry with her, I thought.

"Get home Carl, your dinner is probably waiting." I wished my dinner was waiting. Maybe I'd stop at the fast food market on the way home. No, I'd had hamburgs several times already. I grabbed my suit coat and walked out with my head detective. I got in my Ant hover and headed home. It was over a hundred degrees and my poor little vehicle had trouble keeping the ac up high enough. "What, you taking lessons from my office?" I asked it while wiping sweat off my brow.

It was slightly cooler by my apartment building. Crow Bay often provided a slight breeze that although not cool, was still a relief. After parking in my underground slot, I took one quick wishing look at my turbocycle and headed into the lobby. Now that I didn't have Killa to help me with my rentals, I didn't have much time left to ride my bike. I looked longingly at the sleek fast vehicle and shook my head.

Artchie was behind the counter. He must have heard me as his wheelchair rose into standing position and he looked over at me. "Hi Chief." From behind the counter my two immense dogs came bounding out. I braced myself as their combined weight of 324 lbs slammed against me. I rubbed their ears.

"They are good company and I thought they could use a change of venue," he told me.

"I'm sure they appreciate it, Artchie. How's it going? Do you need me to cover tonight?"

"Nope, Mrs. March is coming down to watch the counter. I have class tonight. I'm still looking for more people to cover. I put an ad in the Gazette."

"Good. If you need me, I'll be upstairs." I headed for the elevator, both dogs bouncing around me reminding me it was their supper time. When we got in the elevator both pets sat obediently on either side. It was a strict rule that they were quiet and obedient in the elevator, or their tails would painfully whip me.

When we reached the fifth floor, they skipped out. They ran straight to the kitchen, sitting and woofing their anxious supper cries. "Okay, it's coming." I filled their two bowls. Only dry food for them, finicky stomachs dictated that's all they ate. I went through thirty pounds of dry food a week. It brought Hill to mind. She'd gotten them special bones from the vet. She had spoiled them. Stop thinking of her, I chastised myself. She was a royal pain in my ass, wasn't I glad she was gone?

I went to get myself something to eat. I'd been trying to lose weight. I opened the refrigerator, pre-made salads greeted me. I closed the door, I wasn't really hungry. "Come on guys, let's go upstairs. They bounded up the stairs to the roof, I slowly followed. It was cooler but still hot. They ran around the track I'd made for them. Good, maybe they'd tire themselves out and behave tonight. Maybe.

Going to the four foot perimeter wall, I leaned against the warm bricks. I could see downtown Fulton in the distant skyline. To my left was Crow Bay. Even in the twilight I could see the seagulls catching the winds. There were still a few small sailboats dotting the bay. The sun was just about down.

Where are you? entered my head as I looked to the horizon. *I love you,* she had said those words. Why did it bother me so much? I shook my head, trying to clear my thoughts.

"Come on guys." I yelled over to the dogs, who were drinking water from my cool hot tub. "Hey get out of there, you got your own water bowls." They bounded past me down the stairs. The air conditioned apartment felt good. Maybe I'd watch some programs and fall asleep early.

The buzzer rang. Shit, now what? Mrs. March was fine but she often couldn't handle much and she'd send the complaining tenant to me.

"Yeah." I tried to sound harsh, maybe I'd scare them and they'd go away.

"Chief?" Hill's voice seemed to float out of the intercom. I stood there stunned into silence. Before I could reply she said, "Can I come up?"

"Yes." I managed to get out, I hoped my voice wasn't shaking.

I heard the elevator start up.

How the dogs knew it was her, I don't know, but they started prancing around the front of the elevator, woofing to each other. Sometimes they were so human-like it hurt. The elevator doors opened and they lunged forward meeting Hill with tails wagging so fast you could hear the whipping sound. She was ready for them taking a defensive stance, gathering them in her arms. She hugged both of them, kneeling, getting tongue licks all over her face.

"Easy guys," I told them but their exuberance spilled over, I couldn't help but smile as she got the full greeting treatment. Only Killa and I ever get that.

"Here you two, got you something," she announced grabbing her bag. They knew the big bones that were coming, each snapping up their treat. They looked so funny with the big bones clamped in their mouths, their jowls puffing out. They pranced about, swinging the bones, and then flopped down to eat them. Good thing these are special treats that came from the vet, made especially for dogs with finicky stomachs.

Hill stood looking over toward me. "They can be rather overwhelming," she said. I could tell she felt awkward. As well she should, I thought.

Emotional anger swelled in me. The relief of seeing her flooded my brain. However, I had been so worried for three weeks that the release of pent up emotions came out in a furious rampage. "Where the hell have you been? Have you no idea how much worry you have generated? We've all been upset for weeks. Do you ever think of anyone else but yourself!" My voice was hoarse from yelling at her, weeks of nerves being taut spilled out.

"Nice to see you too, Chief," she said but her words came out as half sobs.

I took two steps and hugged her, drawing her close, as she sobbed into my shoulder. "You have no idea how worried we've been."

"We?" she managed to say into my shoulder.

"Yes, me included." I looked down, it was so unusual to see her cry. I didn't think her pride would ever let her cry or even show annoyance. I held her out. She had lost weight. She looked haggard and her eyes were dull. Even though she wore a baseball cap, I could see where the burned off hair was just barely coming back.

She noticed me looking. "I've tried to cut it short but I'd have to shave my head to make it match."

"It is fine," I lied. "Where have you been?"

She walked over to the large industrial type windows that graced most of my unfinished apartment left over from when it was a warehouse. Crow Bay was almost completely darkened but the white caps dotted the water, as usual the weather was stormy out in the inlet. It seemed to echo her thoughts, "I stayed on Moss with Dr. Bolker giving me more treatments. I needed them but it was more of a way to not go with my father."

"How are you feeling?" I was almost afraid to hear. I had popped a blue pill in my mouth when she had walked over to the windows. I didn't want her to have problems like mine. I could feel my nerves tense awaiting her explanation.

"The headaches are mostly gone." She turned to me. My face must have mirrored my concerns for she hurried on, "I don't have any permanent damage, it is just going to take time. I'm just on relaxation medicine, nothing more. Although, I hate my hair!" Her hand went to her hat, removing it. She now had short, short hair.

"It's cute," I told her, meaning it. The style mimicked her spunky independence. Of course the spot with no hair kind of ruined it. "Will it grow back?" I pointed to the spot.

"I guess." She didn't sound sure, "I've got cream I put on it every night. Maybe I'll start a new trend." She half laughed, turning back to the window. The Bay was hardly visible. The Fulton moon that they had put in orbit to give us tides was on the wane offering no shadows.

"Me and Stanley have been staying with friends this week," she said.

"Stanley?" I huffed, who the hell was Stanley, her boyfriend?

"She's my Amise cat. She's been staying with my friend Candiece. I didn't want to go back to my apartment so I'm staying with them."

"Stanley's a female cat?" I blurted out, "Kinda got that wrong Hill."

She laughed, "Yeah, she was already fixed and I guessed wrong."

"Lara has been checking on your apartment. Why didn't you go back there?"

"I knew once I went back there I would have to make some choices. I just couldn't face it yet. I'll go back tomorrow."

"So what choices have you made?" I wasn't sure I wanted to know.

"I may just go back to Orion and come to grips with my family." Her hands were clasped tightly. Her eyes switched to the Fulton City as if searching for answers there.

"Do you really want that? "

"I understand you are mad at me Chief. I don't blame you, I should have told you about my family. I thought it didn't matter. Fooled myself into thinking I could run away from it, that it was far enough not to touch me. I was obviously very wrong."

"I'm not mad Hill. I took it badly. I thought you trusted me." She was going to say something but I held up my hand. "In retrospect, I'd probably not have hired you. In that I would have been wrong. The department would have missed out on one hell of a detective."

"Thanks, Chief. I'll come by in a couple of days and pick everything up." Her voice choked. "I'd like to say goodbye to them." One tear fell down her cheek.

"So you've decided not to return?" I asked.

"Aren't you firing me?" she turned from the window, her face full of surprise.

"No."

"No?"

"No. Stop answering me with another question."

"I still have my job?" she looked wide eyed at me.

"There you did it again with the questions." I grinned, "If you want your job it's still there but for god's sake get a hold of your father!"

"My father?" There she went again with a question.

"He came to my office today," I told her but didn't get any further.

"He came to your office?" she stammered.

"For goodness sake Hill, stop with the questions, just listen," I gruffly sputtered out. "He came asking if I had seen you. After our initial sparing, he settled down and I rather like him. He said to tell you that he'd leave you alone to do as you please but just contact him to let him know you are fine!"

"Well!" Was the only word that came out.

"So, will I see you at your desk tomorrow?" Now it was my turn for questions.

"Yes," was all she said. I hoped I wasn't smiling too much.

"Issam and the rest will be glad to see you," I told her, getting a sideward glance from her with a big question mark on her face. "Yes, I'll be glad to see you too."

She laughed, a full out laugh. I smiled some more. My cellbutton softly rang in my ear; *text message from Killa Brown.* I took my tablet out of my pocket put up a screen pressing for double side read, so Hill could see it too.

I'm on Logan's moon, Jump arriving in Fulton late tonight, coming home. Killa.

Both of us stood there looking at the holographic message. Neither of us said a word then we both started yelling, bouncing around. I grabbed on to Hill and we danced around - we were so excited. The dogs began barking, dancing with us. I couldn't believe it, Killa was coming home!

"I knew it!" Hill yelled to be heard above the dogs. "I knew she'd come back!"

"Well I'm glad you knew it because I sure as hell didn't," I yelled back. "I thought she'd stay."

"No," Hill speculated, "she may be technically a Ligithian but she belongs here, like I do!" My lieutenant scratched the dogs ears, "I'm right, aren't I boys." The dogs gave her a big "*woof*"!

I looked up the Jump schedule, Killa would get here close to 23:00. "Hey, we have some time, have you had supper?"

"No." She looked at me, "I haven't been eating too well."

"Well, there's that new salad and soup downtown, we could…"

She interrupted me, "How about Cosmos Pizza on Lake Street? A large pizza and a beer sounds good to me."

"Sounds good to me too!" I agreed. We headed to the elevator, "Be good guys, Killa's coming home." They were sitting in front of the elevator as the doors closed as if they were awaiting her return.

Artchie was just returning to the front desk, relieving Mrs. March. "Hello, Lieutenant Hill. How are you, haven't seen you in a while."

"I'm good Artchie. How's it going?" she asked.

"We're managing, miss Killa." He told her. "I'll be here a couple more hours Chief, and then I close up."

"You'll want to wait for Killa. I told him, she's coming in on a late Jump. She's coming home!"

"Oh, thank goodness!" Artchie exploded then realized he might be hurting my feelings, "I mean, we did okay but it sure is nice to have her home!"

"I couldn't agree with you more," I said waving to him as I followed Hill out the door to the underground garage. The heat came roaring at us. "Come on we'll take my Ant."

She was over by my turbocycle looking fondly at it. I went over to my car's trunk retrieving two helmets. Killa's helmet would automatically adjust to her. I threw it to her. She looked wide eyed at it then pushed the button. Taking off her cap, putting the helmet on and pushing the button again made it fit perfectly. She was smiling from ear to ear. I climbed on, she swung on behind me.

She laughed loudly as I gunned the motor and headed out the underground garage to the road along the bay. I could feel her heart beating as she pressed against me as I increased the speed. It was a nice feeling...

Her father passed by us in his limo; his eyes went wide with surprise as he recognized us. *Shit*! But we kept going......

Thank you for taking time to read Murder on M.O.S.S., the second book in the Space Detective - A Skip Brown Adventure series.

If you enjoyed it, please consider telling your friends or posting a short review. Word of mouth is any author's best friend and is much appreciated.

Also by Pj Belanger:

THE HOUSES OF STOREM – AN EPIC FANTASY

Vol 1 - The Thunderstone

Vol 2 - The Treachery

Vol 3 - The Triad

COLLECTION OF SHORT STORIES

Sci-Fi a-la-mode

Soldier One - Warriors of Misfortune

THE SKIP BROWN DETECTIVE ADVENTURES

Racing on Nestor – Race to Death

Murder on MOSS – Medical Mayhem

Murder on Hilda – Slippery Slopes

See more information at

www.pjbelanger.com